Letters from Gerald

R. W. BUTLER

 FriesenPress

One Printers Way
Altona, MB R0G 0B0
Canada

www.friesenpress.com

Copyright © 2024 by R. W. Butler
First Edition — 2024

Letters from Gerald is a work of fiction. The names, characters, places, and activities are mostly imaginary or fictional. Any resemblance to real people, organizations, businesses, places, events and locales is coincidental with the exceptions described in the Authors' Notes and References.

ISBN
978-1-03-830546-6 (Hardcover)
978-1-03-830545-9 (Paperback)
978-1-03-830547-3 (eBook)

1. FICTION, HISTORICAL, 20TH CENTURY, POST-WORLD WAR II

Distributed to the trade by The Ingram Book Company

To Sharon

Table of Contents

Cast of Characters

Eleanor Hutchinson, protagonist, early twenties,
rents a cottage in Rabbit's Burrough, assistant
librarian at the British Library yearning for
a more adventurous life among birds

Marjorie Quimby, mathematician with a secret past,
landlady of Eleanor's at Rabbit's Burrough, motherly
to the point of being nosy, a bit of a village gossip

Miss Bradshaw, head librarian at the British Library,
Eleanor's boss, orderly, efficient but understanding

Jack MacLaughlin, village postman,
source of village gossip

Peter Saunders, land manager for the Royal Society for
the Protection of Birds, resides in Rabbit's Burrough,
neat, an expert birdwatcher, Patrick's partner

Patrick, Foreign Service Officer, friend
of Peter's, dashing, reserved

Anthony Ashford, father of Christopher, married
to Elizabeth, patriarch of the Ashford family

Elizabeth Ashford, sophisticated and approachable
mother of Christopher, married to Anthony

Christopher Ashford, son of Anthony and
Elizabeth, university student at Oxford,
volunteer guide at the British Museum

Dougal Spratt, married to Marjorie, heir to the Spratt
estate in Mularchy, Scotland, liberal, freespirited

Marjorie Spratt, married to Dougal, artsy, free-spirited

Bernard Spratt, son of Dougal and Marjorie, mildly
autistic, superb birdwatcher and musician

Mademoiselle Dupont, French friend of
the Spratts, resides in Normandy

Captain Furlough, English army
officer, friend of the Spratts

Gwyn Llewelyn, former librarian at the British
Library, retired, lives in remote Wales, bibliophile

Kalmia Rosenblum, resident in the Lake
District, family friend of Mrs. Quimby

Arnold Sneeze, watchmaker, quixotic
Mountain Rescue coordinator

CHAPTER 1:

A Letter from Gerald

In the Hertfordshire countryside north of London lay the small village of Rabbit's Burrough. The village consisted of St. Jerome's Anglican Church, Fox and Crow Pub, and a post office surrounded by a cluster of houses and cottages nestled in the arable land of southern England. Off the main road through Rabbit's Burrough ran Deacon's Lane leading to St Jerome's, along which, beneath a towering elm, nestled a thatched cottage where Eleanor Hutchinson was asleep. She was the only child of parents recently killed in the nightly bombings of wartime London. Living across Deacon's Lane was Eleanor's landlady Marjorie Quimby, who had lost her husband to natural causes just as the war had begun, and so the two women shared a common grief, albeit for different reasons.

Marjorie had taken pity on young Eleanor and offered her the cottage at nominal rent. Marjorie had had no children and taken on Eleanor as if she were Marjorie's own. Eleanor's perspective was quite different. Although Marjorie was very kind – perhaps overly so at times – Eleanor was young and needed to spread her wings. Marjorie was a little too possessive for her liking, but with an attractively low rent for a place in the countryside, a doting neighbour was not a steep price to pay. For now.

The melodic song of a robin outside the bedroom window stirred Eleanor from her sleep like it did every morning. She opened her eyes to the sunshine and robin song flowing in through the window. She had enjoyed the presence of birds ever since she had been a child. Eleanor knew from her voracious reading at the British Library, where she worked as an assistant librarian, that the robin was unusual among birds in that it sang all winter long as a means to advertise its ownership of a territory. Hidden behind the joy the robin brought her was a certain melancholy. She was alone after the loss of her parents, and with her level of education and social position, she could not pursue the dream of studying birds in postwar England. It was because of these inner doubts that Eleanor had taken a post as a librarian at the British Library. She was orderly, dependable, and in need.

Eleanor felt a pang of guilt that with the Second World War had come recruiting drives of young men to go the front. The irony of that tragic event meant that women were encouraged to step in to fill the void left by the departing men, and Eleanor had been offered a job as a librarian. She had obtained her High School Certificate at the age of eighteen, and now at twenty-two years old, she was well on her way to a career in the library. She tried to quell her guilty feelings by doing the best job possible. She had access to a world of books and knowledge that was now accessible to any young woman raised in a lower middle-class family, and she was going to take advantage of it. The library became a vehicle for Eleanor to obtain the knowledge, if not the diploma, of a higher education of her choice.

Eleanor rose from her bed, closed the bedroom window, and proceeded downstairs to get ready for another day at the library. She felt that the cottage walls and thatched roof that kept the rooms cool in summer added to the drudgery of English autumns; the coolness of the walls, the low ceilings and doorways, and the tiny windows contributed to her claustrophobia. She felt a longing to spend her time out of doors.

Eleanor poured water into a kettle, placed it on the stove, and went upstairs to dress. A few minutes later, the kettle whistled on the stove. She returned downstairs, poured the water into the tea pot, and prepared some breakfast. She was fastidious in her approach to life. After all, libraries could only function if the staff dutifully circulated books between readers and their proper place on the shelves. Attention to detail and preciseness were essential traits of a good librarian. She checked her watch and realized it was time to get moving. The bus that would take her to the train station would arrive opposite the pub in five minutes.

Eleanor knew all too well how London in 1946 was emerging from the destruction and despair of nighttime bombings, and a determination to overcome a potential invasion. She had heard how librarians had heeded the call of pending destruction by shipping many of the British Library's precious books to Wales for safekeeping, but hundreds of thousands had remained, in part because of their sheer volume and in part because of the war effort. She had participated in government-sponsored Holidays at Home where the libraries encouraged readership as a means to keep spirits up. She enjoyed reading, and as a young teenager, Eleanor had been horrified to hear how nighttime bombing raids had targeted London libraries. Libraries were beacons of culture, and in 1942, the bombs had damaged the British Library building and destroyed thousands of books in the ensuing fire. Also troubling for Eleanor, who enjoyed nature, was the bombing of the British Museum of Natural History and the resultant loss of the shell and botanical galleries. The only solace was that the most valuable collections had been previously whisked away to safe storage. Eleanor had only been eighteen and recently recruited by the library when the bombs had hit, but her outrage had been particularly strong when she had read of damage to the bird exhibits at the museum.

Despite the government's public relations campaign to bolster British resolve in the face of the attacks, many of the British, including Eleanor, had been terrified. She felt a cold chill run up her back as she recalled the fear in the faces of her parents and hundreds more seeking cover in the underground as air raid sirens had blared across London. In her mind's eye, she saw families with small children crammed into the space – adult men and women, and teenagers frightened to death as the deep thudding of bombs had rained down. She relived in her mind the moment the sirens had ended and she had emerged to see the shells of buildings in rubble and on fire. Through the smoke and smell of shattered brick, the fire brigades had been trying to put out fires and recovering the injured and the dead bodies. Like so many others, Eleanor was haunted by these images. She took a deep breath while straightening her back. *For now*, she thought, *the fear of bombings has ceased and the vestiges of life before the war have all but vanished.* Food was rationed, and Eleanor thought how lucky she was to have a kindly neighbour in Marjorie Quimby, who had offered her low rent for a cottage in Rabbit's Burrough where she could plant a small garden in an allotment left over when the Victory Garden campaign ceased.

Eleanor stepped out of King's Cross station, dropped a few letters into the postbox, and quickly strode to the library. She arrived promptly, just like every other day, and after hanging up her coat, she got to work reshelving books. Although the work was tedious, Eleanor could look forward to her tea break to read the latest news in newspapers from around the world. She also could keep up on the latest news in science and the arts from the periodicals that arrived daily.

She made a habit of perusing the scientific journal *Nature* for the latest news in science. Sometimes, there were articles by scientists on birds, but regardless, Eleanor had a voracious appetite to learn.

While perusing the journal, Eleanor read that the British Museum of Natural History had been restored and reopened to the public. The report was nothing more than a list of acquisitions, but what caught Eleanor's eye were the collections of birds and their eggs from various collectors from exotic lands.

Eleanor slumped back in her chair, closed her eyes, and began to imagine a life as a collector for the museum. The idea of being a free woman travelling abroad in exotic places to pursue birds brought a certain excitement to her. She had just finished reading in the newspaper about a massive tsunami in Hawaii. She wondered if the museum had any birds from Hawaii and began to imagine the life of a collector amidst the turmoil of a tsunami.

She was abruptly awoken from her day dreaming when she realized her break was up, but all day long she wondered and dreamed of a new life. Near closing time, she took out several books about Hawaii to read at home in her leisure. If she could not go on a collecting trip, she could imagine it. With books in her bag, Eleanor boarded the train for home, imagining that her bag was her luggage and she was not boarding a train but instead stepping on to a ship bound for the Pacific islands.

Arriving home in the stillness of a November evening, Eleanor spread her books onto a sofa and set about making dinner. She was thinking as much about food preparation as she was about opening the books on Hawaii. All evening long, with her dinner in her lap and in the glow of the wood burner, she pored over the books and news about Hawaii. She read about the island's endemic species, its geographical position, and its history of occupation. That evening, she retired to bed with dreams of something new in her life.

The following morning, Eleanor awoke once again to the song of the robin. He had become such a common sight in her garden that Eleanor decided it was time to give him a name. "What shall I call thee, fair robin?" she said out the window. The robin moved a little farther away to a distant fence surrounding her vegetable garden to continue singing.

"You seem to have figured life out much better than me," she said. "Perhaps I will call you Thales, the Greek father of science?"

Eleanor smiled to herself while closing the window to the cool autumn wind. She then followed the same routine to get ready for a day at the library.

That evening, Eleanor returned home to Rabbit's Burrough for a second night of reading and imagining. By then she had delved deep into her understanding of Hawaii, and as the night closed in, she stopped to reconsider.

A voice in her head said to her, *Why are you putting yourself through all of this? Sure, the idea of being a collector for the museum in a foreign land is a romantic idea, but there is more to life than imagination.*

Eleanor sat up. *Maybe I should just be happy to have a job in wartorn Britain and stop imagining something that is not going to happen. After all, a position at the museum would likely require a university degree, which I do not have.*

The inner voice spoke again. *Eleanor, you know you want to do something new. If you don't take the first step, you will regret it. You are young, and life is short.*

With doubts and encouragements sparring in her thoughts, Eleanor set off for bed, where she had a restless night. The following morning, the robin was singing again outside her window. "Good morning, Thales," she said. "What have you got to share with me today?"

The day seemed to fly by in a blur. Eleanor's mind was torn with her inner voice telling her conflicting views of what to do. By the time she got home, she was a mess. Marjorie Quimby had noticed it. Eleanor looked troubled as they passed in the lane between her house and Eleanor's cottage. *Something is on her mind*, thought Mrs. Quimby.

It was time to decide. Eleanor thought she might write to the museum to see if she could join an expedition, or at worst, they might give her some advice on how to participate. Or the museum might not reply at all, she thought. Her self-doubts were beginning to win when her ego jumped in. Perhaps she could volunteer and work her way up in the museum. That was it! The museum would have to reply out of courtesy if nothing else. Her mind was swirling. *What if they reply and politely say they have nothing to offer?* she thought. *How will I face that rejection? There is a very good chance I will be turned down.*

The very thought of a lifelong ambition being quashed was hard for Eleanor to imagine, but then, on the other hand, how would she ever know if she did not ask? She quickly stood up in disgust to pace, head down, mind in turmoil, trying to decide the next step.

I might not even like the job, she thought. *All those men and me, the only woman. And I haven't been beyond London, let alone some faraway land that I know nothing about.*

She burst out in anger, stormed into the kitchen, and stood by the counter, taking deep breaths. A voice in her head said, *Eleanor, calm down. Have a cup of tea and let the emotions pass.*

She turned to take the kettle from the stove, turned on the tap, and returned the kettle to the stove. She scooped a small amount of tea and waited for the kettle to whistle. The tea was soothing, and the time she spent making it was therapeutic. While sipping the hot tea, she made her decision: she would write. But to whom? She did not know anyone at the museum. She would draft a "to whom it may concern" letter and be done with it.

Eleanor pushed aside the books she had been reading and pulled the typewriter closer to her on the desk in the sitting room. She inserted a piece of paper and held her hands above the keyboard. She took a deep breath, began to type, and then stopped. Doubts began to enter her mind. What if they ignored her? Could she deal with the rejection of no reply? *The museum must get plenty of inquiries*, she thought. *Why would they take the time to reply to a young woman with no experience dreaming of joining their ranks?*

She tore the paper from the typewriter, crumpled it into a ball, and tossed it on the floor. *This is just a fantasy,* she thought. *I need to banish it from my thoughts.* But she could not leave it. Several tries later, she finally began to write.

E. Hutchinson, Robinsong Cottage,
Deacon's Lane, Rabbit's Burrough, Herts.

November 25, 1946

To whom it may concern,

I am writing in response to a recent report in the journal "Nature," in which I read of your acquisition of bird specimens and eggs. My interest stems from a childhood interest in birds and my position as assistant librarian at the British Library, of which the latter has allowed me to pursue my interest in the field of ornithology in my spare time. My ability to catalogue, attention to detail, and wide reading of the scientific and popular literature on birds have reinforced my desire to pursue a career studying birds. In particular, I would like to participate in an expedition so as to extend my experience to other lands and birds. Would you be so kind as to advise me on how best to proceed?

```
Yours sincerely,
```

```
E. Hutchinson
```

Eleanor sat upright and reread the letter. It was terse and to the point so as not to waste the reader's time. The letter was not perfect, but it would have to do. She folded it twice, licked and sealed the envelope, addressed it to the bird curator at the British Museum of Natural History, and went to bed.

The following morning, Eleanor rose as she always did to say good morning to Thales, who was dutifully singing outside her window, before she set off to work. She saw Marjorie tending her garden from behind the hedge.

"Good morning, Eleanor," she said.

Startled by the voice from the hedge, Eleanor fumbled with her mail.

"Oh, good morning, Marjorie," she said.

"You have quite a lot of mail today, Eleanor," said Marjorie.

"Why yes," Eleanor replied. She fumbled to put the mail into her bag. "Library correspondence."

"Well, have a good day," said Marjorie. "I might drop by later to see how you are getting on."

Eleanor gave a forced smile and picked up her pace, arriving minutes before the bus that took her to the train station. Before purchasing her train ticket, she reached into her bag, bundled up her letter among her other correspondence, and dropped them in the postbox. Somewhat nervously, she boarded the train and went off to work.

All that day and into the evening, Eleanor had doubts about what she had just done. She felt a tingle rise up her spine with the thought that the museum might reply with an offer to join an expedition. What would she do about her librarian job? What would she tell Marjorie? She smiled ever so slightly at the thought. *How exciting life might become*, she thought. The smile quickly departed, and she felt an emptiness in the pit of her stomach. *The museum might turn me down and brush me off or worse, not respond at all.*

Days went by without a response. She was having her worst nightmare come true. She couldn't bear the thought that her letter went ignored. *The museum likely gets hundreds of letters every day*, she told herself. *The staff is probably very busy. They wouldn't have time to reply to every request.*

Eleanor began to fret and, in her despair, began to imagine what a letter might contain if she was lucky to receive one. She composed it in her head and jotted down some of the points she hoped would be addressed. She imagined who might write to her. The director? Unlikely. A curator? Doubtful. Maybe a collector or a leader of an expedition? *I might have to wait a long time for one of them to respond*, she thought. She found herself imagining a letter arriving. She even imagined the letter being posted and it arriving at the Rabbit's Burrough post office, the postman putting it in his bag and delivering it to her door. Three days later, there was a knock at her cottage door.

"Just one letter for you today, ma'am," said the postman. There were no telltale signs on the envelope of who sent the letter. It was simply addressed "E. Hutchinson, Robinsong Cottage, Deacon's Lane, Rabbit's Burrough, Herts."

Eleanor smiled as she took the letter and moved to her sitting room to open it. She looked at the envelope and, with some satisfaction, tore it open and extracted the letter. Scribbled on a piece of paper read:

```
Gerald Benson, c/o British
Museum (Natural History),
South Kensington, London.

December 12, 1946

Dear E. Hutchinson:

Your letter, dated November 25, 1946,
has been referred to me for response. I
am leaving this evening on an expedition
to Hawaii, from where I will write at
length soon after I arrive. I am not an
official employee of the museum; hence,
this scribbled note, but you can reach
me by addressing future correspondence
to c/o the British Museum (Natural
History) on Kensington Street in London.
That way, the museum can expedite cor-
respondence through the Royal Mail and
diplomatic channels.

Sincerely,

Gerald Benson
```

Eleanor chuckled to herself. She was delighted in how it all had turned out. *Gerald Benson*, she thought to herself. *That is a good name for a museum collector. Thank you, Gerald.* She stepped outside to take a breath of fresh air. Off down the path that led to her vegetable garden, a robin sang. *This is the start of a grand adventure*, she thought.

CHAPTER 2:
Christopher

Eleanor often arrived early at the library to read the current news. She opened the *Times* to read that Foreign Secretary Ernest Bevin was urging Britain to maintain its colonial empire despite economic hardship after the war. The story in the *Times* was still in Eleanor's mind when she was cleaning up after dinner at the cottage that evening. Eleanor's inner voice, fuelled by her vivid imagination, made her pause and think about who Gerald might be. She scrubbed at a frying pan with gusto before stopping to stare at the wall. Her eyes moved across the kitchen before she went back to scrubbing the pan. *What if Gerald was more than a collector for the Natural History Museum?* she pondered. *Could he be using the front of a collector for the museum to hide a life of espionage?* She got a small smile on her face. Eleanor had wanted a more exciting life than her current post as an assistant librarian, but she was not considering espionage as a career. She wondered what she would do if MI6 contacted her. Was she unwittingly being drawn into a clandestine international intrigue? *Don't be silly!* she thought as she came to her senses. *Although it would be fun to imagine Gerald as a spy, I need to take him at face value.* The following day, a letter arrived in the post.

Gerald Benson, c/o British
Museum (Natural History),
South Kensington, London.

January 4, 1947

Dear E. Hutchinson:

I promised to reply once I had arrived
in Hawaii late last year, and I thank
you for your patience. The BMNH is keen
to get some specimens of the endemic
bird species on the island, which I
hope to do in the ensuing weeks. I am
hoping to add a few endemic Hawaiian
species of honeycreepers to the collection. The taxonomy and ancestry of the
honeycreepers are of particular interest
because of their uniqueness to Hawaii.
As Mr. Darwin explained, the separation

of organisms from their relatives over
long periods of time, combined with the
different environments they inhabit,
can lead to variations that eventually
become unique species. The same process
likely led to the evolution of unique
species in the Galapagos.

The honeycreepers are largely confined
to high elevations in Hawaii. Human
settlement brought changes to the land
and foreign species that, like so many
of the Pacific islands, inadvertently
decimated many of the native species.
My American colleagues have several fine
specimens of honeycreepers in storage
that they have generously offered the
BMNH as representatives of the honeycreeper family if I am willing to
prepare them as museum specimens. While
I am on the islands, I hope to get to
the highlands to see the birds live in
their native habitat. I understand a
new road has been built to the summit of
Mount Haleakala on the island of Maui.
There is an experimental forest called
Hosmer's Grove at about 7,000 feet ele-
vation where honeycreepers are reported
to be present.

Before I get too far ahead of myself,
I will address your questions in your
previous letter.

I don't wish to be presumptuous, but I
think it best if I describe the life of
a collector to give you a clear picture
of the profession and then make some
suggestions on how you might proceed
should you want to make a career out
of it.

To address the life of a collector,
I will begin with the present situation I am in here in Hawaii. The people
are very friendly, and there are roads
around the shoreline, making travel
easy. Getting into the highlands, other
than along roads such as to Mount
Haleakala, requires travel by horseback
or on foot. Camping skills are a must.
I spend much of my time in a tent far
from civilization.

In addition to the practical skills
I described, getting a post similar
to mine requires a university education. Without knowing you, I don't know
your level of education, so bear with
me when I say you will have to show a

high level of competence with birds to
be considered. Not to be deterred, my
advice is to get to know British birds.
Once you have developed your identi-
fication skills, you might be able to
accompany a local expedition near your
home. There are several books available
that are likely in the British Library.
Thorburn's "British Birds" and Witherby
et al.'s "The Handbook of British Birds"
are a good start. Visiting the BMNH
would also be a good step. There are
plenty of people who can answer your
questions there.

Please keep me posted on your progress.
Correspondence from home is always a
welcome distraction while travelling in
faraway places.

Sincerely,

Gerald Benson

While Gerald was in transit, Eleanor continued with
the daily routine of a librarian. She delved into more
books about Hawaii so she could correspond intelligently
with Gerald. She thought how clever of her to find Gerald
heading for Hawaii when she had just read the news story
about the massive tsunami that struck parts of the islands.

She was familiar with the bird guides recommended by Gerald, plus others. She was a librarian, after all. She had taken a few of them home but was bewildered by the number of species in the guides and the difficulty of seeing them. Eleanor could not afford a pair of binoculars, which hindered her progress, until as if by providence, she stumbled upon a book that would indirectly open a new world to her.

While researching the topic of tropical ecosystems in Hawaii, she saw a reference to Marian Sibylla Merian, a German naturalist and illustrator in the eighteenth century. She was intrigued by Merian, who had been born in 1671 in Frankfurt. As a child interested in nature, Merian had started to take art lessons. Eleanor was enthralled with Merian, who, three-hundred years earlier, had followed a dream of a naturalist and illustrator by travelling to Suriname in South America. Merian sounded like just the role model Eleanor was searching for.

Eleanor began to look through the card catalogue of titles held in the museum, and much to her delight, she found Merian's lavishly illustrated *Metamorphosis insectorum Surinamensium* from her travels to South America. Eleanor quickly put in a request for a copy, and the next day, she was granted access to the book, printed in 1726. The book was on a table where she pulled on a pair of cotton gloves. She opened the book to a smell of old paper. She recoiled not from the smell but from the meticulous illustrations of insects and observations of their life histories.

"My goodness," she said with astonishment. Page after page of illustrations made her gasp with excitement. She was becoming increasingly convinced that she could become a collector and now, perhaps, an illustrator of flora and fauna. Her late father had been an artist, and she had shown promise as a child with drawing and painting, just like Merian. *Maybe it's time to hone my art skills*, she thought.

On her first day off from work, Eleanor made her way to the Winsor and Newton shop, famous for making the finest watercolour brushes. She arrived at opening time at the new factory in Lowestoft, East Anglia. Nimble hands of makers of fishing nets were busily making watercolour brushes from the finest kolinsky sable. Her need for perfection would lead her to select a brush favoured by Queen Victoria and ideally suited to the detailed work she intended to produce. As she thumbed through a variety of their watercolour paints and sheets of paper, a salesman arrived. She described her intended use, and he provided her a notebook and tubes of paint to try.

At first, Eleanor was a little shy about showing her drawings and paintings to others; no one developed the skills of drawing and painting, especially with watercolours, without years of practice. She toyed with using the pencil to get bold and fine lines, and that was only the start. She discovered that copying only the essential outline and posture required careful observation combined with artistic composition. When the subjects were animals that seldom stayed put, she found the challenge became even greater. She learned that mastering the art required her to hone technical and observation skills along with an understanding of how animals moved. The muscles under the skin or feathers had to be considered to render a lifelike pose.

Eleanor struggled with all of these new skills, but she was determined and would not be daunted by the tasks. Gradually, she found she was catching on to the skills. With a few quick lines, she could capture the essence of animal movement. From her reading of animal anatomy, she began to understand how the bones and muscles gave the animal form, and with mastery of colour palettes and watercolour washes, she was starting to create wonderfully lucid depictions. She felt some pride in her work. Nonetheless, her attempts to capture in watercolours the birds in her garden proved challenging; the buntings, thrushes, finches, and Thales the robin would not stay still long enough to sketch them. What she needed were birds that did not move, and she knew exactly where to go.

Eleanor entered the British Museum of Natural History with art supplies in her bag and strode into the bird exhibit to sit on a bench. Before her in silent, unmoving poses were all kinds of birds in lifelike poses. *This is the perfect place to develop the skills to illustrate birds*, she thought. She opened her notebook and began to sketch. She could see how the wings emerged from the flanks of the birds, the position of the legs relative to the tail, and the eye socket relative to the bill. She examined the colour patterns and how light reflected off the feathers. The noises of crowds around her vanished from her mind as she concentrated on every detail.

"That's a very nice representation of a gannet, Miss," came a voice behind her. Startled, Eleanor turned to see a tall young man peering over her shoulder.

"I am sorry if I startled you, but I couldn't help but notice your artistry," he said. "Are you in art school?"

Eleanor felt a little embarrassed. She had not shown her attempts to draw birds to anyone before.

"Thank you. Do you like them?" she replied.

"Yes," he followed. "I wish I had your talent. I couldn't draw like that if my life depended on it." From his accent, Eleanor knew he was well educated and from a different social class, but she found him friendly and interesting.

"Oh!" the young man said. "I am so sorry. You are probably wondering who I am and how discourteous I am behaving."

"Not at all," she said. "I am practicing my drawing skills on the stuffed birds here because the darn things won't stand still in the wild."

"My name is Christopher," he said.

"Like the wren?" said Eleanor with an impish grin.

"Ashford, actually. Christopher Ashford," he said. "Would you like to see the specimen collection in the back of the museum?"

"Yes, indeed!" Eleanor replied. "That would be a real treat."

Christopher led Eleanor through the exhibit to a door he unlocked that opened into a corridor.

"I have the magic key," he said, holding the key before his face.

"You certainly do," replied Eleanor. Her remark went unnoticed or discreetly ignored.

"Are you an ornithologist, Christopher?" Eleanor enquired.

"Heavens, no," he replied, "but I enjoy watching them almost as much as I like to engage with the public."

"If you are as good at engaging the public as you are at bird-watching, maybe you should reconsider," she said.

"I think my family has other plans" he said with a wry smile.

They entered a large cavernous room reeking of mothballs. The smell nearly bowled Eleanor over.

"This is where the museum houses most of its bird specimens," Christopher said.

Rows of wooden cabinets, each with a pair of large doors with the Latin names of bird families attached in a slot, ran like a canyon for hundreds of feet in the dark room.

"I don't understand," said Eleanor. "The birds are in these cabinets?"

"Yes, millions of them, from all over the world," Christopher continued. "The museum has one of the largest collections in the world. Collectors are paid to collect and prepare specimens that are sent here for scientists to study. We have bird skins, their eggs, and bones. Some of the collectors are quite famous. Have you heard of Charles Darwin and Alfred Russel Wallace?"

She was about to ask Christopher if he knew Gerald, but thought better of it. She had never met Gerald and could hardly say she knew him.

"Charles Darwin, yes, but who was the other man?" Eleanor asked.

"Alfred Russel Wallace," replied Christopher. "He was – "

Eleanor stopped him short. "Don't tell me. I will look him up when I return to the library. It will be my home-work assignment."

"Very good," said Christopher. "Would you like to see inside a cabinet?"

"Very much so," said Eleanor.

"What family of birds interests you, Eleanor?"

This was the first time he had said her name. *He is quite charming*, she thought.

"Um, how about the robins?" she said.

"Ah, the family Muscicapidae. Interesting choice."

He began to walk down the rows of cabinets, reading the labels on the doors as he went. "Once you know the taxonomic order of birds, you can quickly locate the cabinet by its relative position. The Muscicapidae should be right here," he said while pointing to a lower cabinet. Christopher swung open the doors, letting the smell of mothballs waft by on the breeze. He pulled out a cabinet, and to Eleanor's surprise, there was a drawer full of robin specimens. Each specimen lay on its back, wings folded along its flank, head pointed forward, and legs folded as if in prayer across the belly. A tag was affixed to each specimen. Christopher reached in and removed one of the specimens from the cabinet.

"Would you like to hold it?" he asked.

The dead bird looked like a pale example of the sprightly Thales that sang to her each morning, but since this was her chosen field, she was game for an experience to further her cause.

"Please," she said.

The bird was surprisingly light. Its inner organs had been removed so that only the skin and a few bones remained. In their place was cotton batting that bulged out of the eye sockets but was otherwise concealed behind the feathers and stitched-up skin.

"To make a specimen, the collector has to learn the art of skinning birds. I have been told it is like removing a glove. The skin is peeled off the body, the brains are scooped out of the skull, meat is removed from leg and wing bones, and preservative is applied to the bare parts before being stitched up around a ball of cotton batting the same size as the bird's body," Christopher described in detail.

Eleanor straightened up. All she said was, "Oh."

Christopher replied, "At first it seems a little macabre, but once you have done a few, the procedure becomes, um, what you might say, everyday. If you are going to be an ornithologist at the museum, this is a skill you need to master."

All Eleanor could think about was the rows of dead robins. On one hand, she was saddened that so many robins had met their end this way, but on the other hand, her curiosity urged her to look at each specimen in detail. The plumages were all slightly different. There were specimens from all over Europe. She wondered if there were regional differences. Before her was an immense library of birds with stories waiting to be told.

"I must get back to the exhibition hall," said Christopher.

"I understand," replied Eleanor, "and thank you for taking the time to show me all of this. The visit has been very rewarding."

Christopher gave his business card to Eleanor before they bade farewell. She scribbled her telephone number on a piece of paper.

Eleanor arrived at Robinsong cottage at the end of the afternoon. She opened her front door, tossed her satchel on a chair, and proceeded to make a cup of tea. She smiled at the chance meeting with Christopher – she had warmed to him but doubted he felt the same about her. Nevertheless, she had made a few nice sketches and enjoyed seeing the inner workings of the museum. With a cup of tea in hand, she returned to the sitting room where she slumped in her favourite chair. She opened the satchel to take a look at her artwork. Her notebook was gone. She looked around her chair and then in the kitchen. She opened the front door to look around the landing. She thought she might have dropped it while fumbling for her keys. The notebook was nowhere to be seen.

While she was searching for the whereabouts of the lost notebook, the telephone rang.

"Eleanor," said the voice. "This is Christopher Ashford."

"Hello, Christopher"

"I have your notebook. You left it at the museum," he said. "I will be there tomorrow if you want to pick it up."

"Why, thank you, Christopher. I was all sixes and sevens trying to find it," she said. "I will pop around tomorrow, say about eleven?"

"That would be fine. You know where to find me," he said.

The following day, Eleanor made her way to the museum and promptly found Christopher.

"Here you go. Safe and sound," he said, handing over the notebook.

"I am very grateful to you, Christopher," she said.

"Why don't we get a cup of tea to celebrate?" asked Christopher. "Or better still, how about an early lunch? I know a nice Indian restaurant nearby."

Eleanor was not looking for a friend, but Christopher was quickly becoming just that. Despite her interest in him, she wondered if the feelings were mutual. After all, Christopher came from a well-established family and likely had plenty of women interested in him. Over lunch, they talked about birds and the museum. Eleanor thought Christopher was just being polite when suddenly he said, "Why don't you come with me to Oxford where I can show you the university and take you to my field site where I am studying birds? When do you have a day off?"

Eleanor was taken aback at the question. She wondered about his intentions. Was he interested in more than birds? Without time to think, she said, "I have Saturdays off."

"Okay, Saturday it is," said Christopher. "I will pick you up at the train station, say about ten?"

"That would be fine," said Eleanor before she could think about what she was doing.

"Plan to visit the woodlands and stay at our family home," said Christopher. "I will get you back to the station to get home with plenty of time on Sunday."

Eleanor smiled sheepishly. *What have I done?* she thought. *I only just met him, I don't know his intentions, I have hardly been out of London let alone to Oxford. The university, field work, train travel . . . my, oh my*, she thought.

But this is exactly what you want to do Eleanor, her inner voice said to her. *You want to travel and meet interesting people, see birds in places you have never been. And with a pleasant young man who seems to have taken a shine to you.*

"If you have further questions or need to reach me, ring me up," he said. "The number is on my card, and bring your binoculars." He laughed.

Eleanor strode out of the museum feeling bewildered. She had seen another element of the life of the ornithologist. Whether she could bring herself to collect birds and even consider skinning them was not clear in her mind, but the opportunities that the museum offered – to hold birds from around the world in her hands – thrilled her. More than ever, she wanted to be an ornithologist. She had had a taste for the life of the curator, the specimens, and the huge responsibility in their charge. Instead of being a librarian of published works, she yearned to be a librarian of nature. But first she needed to travel only a few hours from home.

She had heard Christopher say to bring her binoculars. She panicked with the realization that she did not own a pair, and the cost was something she could ill afford.

Moreover, the only binoculars available were of the vintage World War II variety. They were scarce and hard to find.

Eleanor's head was swooning when she finally arrived at Robinsong cottage. She had a smile on her face and a spring in her step, but deep inside, trepidation was rumbling. She nervously opened the door to her cottage, tossed her coat on a chair, and stood for a moment, hands on hips, thinking about how much fun lay ahead. Or if things went badly, her dream of becoming an ornithologist could come to an abrupt end. Her inner voices were arguing once more. She realized she was now committed to taking up Christopher's offer and hoped all would end well.

Eleanor's stomach was uneasy, so she made herself an egg sandwich and a cup of tea before retiring for the night. In the darkness, she imagined what lay ahead, hoping Christopher would meet her in Oxford as promised, where she would deal with his parents (and him!) and find out where all this would lead. She stared at the ceiling for what seemed an eternity with the excitement bubbling inside until quiet darkness closed over her and she fell into a deep sleep.

CHAPTER 3:

Oxford

When Saturday arrived, Eleanor awoke early, not wanting to miss her train. She made a cup of tea, forced some breakfast down her throat, picked up her bag, and stepped out of doors. As she locked the door, Thales sang to the gathering dawn.

"Thales," she said. "I am off on a big adventure today." Down the lane to the bus stop she strode.

From St. Neots to Oxford was several hours on the train, which gave Eleanor time to ponder what she was doing. She still did not have a pair of binoculars, which was like a badge to ornithologists. She could tell Christopher that she did not pack binoculars, which was true, although a little deceptive.

She watched the dawn mist dissolve into a sunny morning as the train made its way to London and then on to Oxford. Near 11 a.m., the whistle went while the train's steam hissed and sputtered above the deep notes of the engine, signalling her arrival at Oxford. Eleanor disembarked with her bag to a small crowd in which a beaming Christopher waved his lanky arm to get her attention. She smiled and felt an urge to give him a hug, but he was already reaching for her bag.

"Here. Let me carry your bag. I brought the new motor car for you to see," he said proudly. "She is parked behind the station. How was your trip?"

"Just fine," said Eleanor.

"Is this your first trip to Oxford?" he asked.

"Yes," she replied. "With work, I haven't had much time to explore."

"Well, we have a full day ahead of us," Christopher said, "and I have a few surprises for you too."

Eleanor smiled and thought to herself how much fun this was turning out to be.

"Here she is," said Christopher. "The new Triumph Roadster. Triumph has just released this model, and I was able to get my hands on one. Isn't she a beauty?"

The cream paint and chrome grille gleamed in the sun. Two large head-lamps looked like eyes. Eleanor's heart leapt. Her parents had not owned a car, and she had only been in cabs around London. She had never dreamed of riding in a car like this.

"I will put your bag in the boot, and you can climb into the passenger seat," said Christopher. Eleanor swung open the door to sit on the bench seat. The stick shift and pedals were the only things between her and Christopher. He climbed in, shifted into neutral, and turned the ignition to a roar as the cylinders fired up.

"I have hardly driven this car – it is so new – so you might have to tell me if I am going too fast," he said.

She felt the car shoot forward as Christopher released the clutch to race off down the road. The folded convertible top brought a rush of air through Eleanor's hair and across her cheeks. She had not felt so exhilarated in a very long time. A few people stopped to watch as the car zoomed by.

Down lanes, with the hedgerows just out of reach, they sped. Christopher downshifted on the corners and sped at breakneck speed along the straight stretches. Despite the car's modest power, it cornered delightfully and seemed born for the country lanes around Oxford. Eleanor could see Christopher was enjoying showing off his new car, but she felt a heightened sense of danger as a passenger in his car and wondered what lay ahead of them.

"I am going to take you to our home, which is only about fifteen minutes from here," Christopher yelled over the engine. "You can meet my parents, and we can get a bite of lunch before heading into Oxford. Are you okay with that plan?"

Eleanor was ready for anything – as long as she survived his reckless driving.

"Yes, of course. I am looking forward to meeting your parents," she yelled. "You haven't told me their names and what I should call them."

"My father is Anthony, and my mother is Elizabeth," he shouted. "They will be very welcoming, but don't call him Tony or her Lizzie."

Inside, her inner voice was trembling. Christopher was from a very different social class. As soon as she spoke, the family was going to detect her London accent and know where she was from, her level of education, and her family station. She was going to have to rely on Christopher.

"I hope your parents will accept me," she said.

"Of course, they will," returned Christopher. "I have already told them about you, and they are looking forward to meeting you in person."

She swallowed hard and held on as Christopher sped around a corner.

True to Christopher's words, the Ashfords' country home came into view a few minutes later. He downshifted, swung left through the entrance gates, and slowly drove along a pebble driveway to the front of the house.

"I am taking this part slowly," he said with a grin, "so as not to give Mother a heart attack."

Eleanor gave a difficult smile that said she was on the side of his mother.

Her heart began to race as the car came to a halt. She had never been to such a house in her life. She noted that Ashford Manor had been built with the local stone, its art-deco roof making a powerful statement of ease and sophisticated wealth against the clear blue sky. Leaded windows and solid wooden doors interrupted the rigidity of stonework. Surrounding the house were extensive grounds with flower beds, and a tennis court discretely located behind a row of towering elms and ashes reflecting the owners' lifestyle.

Eleanor stepped from the Triumph with Christopher just as the front door swung open. "Welcome to Ashford," cried out a tall woman in a knee-length skirt, cashmere sweater, and a flowing scarf.

"Mother," said Christopher, "this is Eleanor."

"Hello, Eleanor," she replied. "I am Elizabeth, but everyone knows me as Lizzie."

Eleanor glimpsed at Christopher, who shrugged and smirked.

"Hello, Mrs. Ashford," Eleanor replied, "Christopher has told me a lot about you."

"I am sure he has," she replied "and please call me Lizzie."

Eleanor felt very uncomfortable with the informality and thought it might be an attempt to try to better understand each other. At least for now, Eleanor thought she would just see how things unfolded.

"Christopher," Elizabeth ordered, "don't just stand there with that big silly grin. Get Eleanor's bag and show her to her room."

"Ah, yes," he replied and dutifully lifted her bag from the boot of the car.

"Follow me and I will show you where you will be staying."

"Now, Eleanor," Elizabeth said, "I want to hear all about your work at the library. Giving people something to read during the bombing was so important. Londoners might not have been able to escape the bombs, but they could, for a brief moment, escape in their fantasies through books. You played an important role."

Eleanor smiled. "That's very kind of you, Mrs. Ashford."

"Lizzie," she corrected.

"Lizzie," Eleanor repeated.

Elizabeth accompanied Eleanor into the house, taking the brief opportunity to look her over. She felt a slight tinge of envy at Eleanor's youthful good looks, but she didn't miss that Eleanor's clothing was off the rack. Under the welcoming gesture, Elizabeth was assessing Eleanor's intentions with Christopher.

Eleanor briefly glanced around the inside of the house, not wanting to appear to be overly attentive. Inside, she was feeling overwhelmed. *This is how the others live*, she thought to herself. The walls were lined with dark wood panels. The house felt cool and smelled slightly of last evening's cigars. She could see a large drawing room on her left and a hallway paralleling a staircase leading to other parts of the house. Off to the right and adjacent to the landing was another doorway that opened onto the dining room. A geometric pattern of white and blue tiles led to a staircase where a wrought-iron chandelier lit up the landing and Christopher, who was about to climb the stairs.

"Come on, Elie. The day is getting on," called Christopher.

Elie? Eleanor made a quizzical face and set off up the stairs. *No one has ever called me Elie*, she thought.

"Here's your room," said Christopher, opening a door to a large bedroom. "I will get my binoculars and meet you outside the door in a few minutes."

"Christopher," she called out as he exited the door.

"Yes," he replied.

"I didn't bring binoculars, silly me," she said.

"Don't worry. I will find you a pair," Christopher said.

"One more thing," said Eleanor. "I've never been called Elie before and, well, I kind of like it, but only from you, okay?"

"Yes. It will be our little secret," he said and turned to run down the stairs.

Eleanor took a deep breath and turned to look at her room. It was simply furnished, but the room was bigger than any room she had slept in. A screen covered a fireplace at the far end of the room, and two large windows looked out over garden and forest below. The bed had a quilt and two pillows, and at the end of the bed stood a small table on which Christopher had dropped her luggage. A few pictures of what Eleanor surmised were family members hung on creamy yellow walls with oversized pure white baseboards.

She pulled out a pair of trousers and a jumper and removed her skirt and blouse. Once she was dressed, Eleanor took a quick look in a floor mirror when she heard the car honking at the front door. A quick touch-up of her lipstick, and she was out the door to meet Christopher. He sat in the car dressed in a tweed sports coat and a pair of corduroy pants, and his tuft of curly brown hair pushed to one side.

"We need to catch some lunch, and then I want to take you to the Edward Grey Institute at the uni," he said. "After that, we will go to Wytham Woods where I am watching nesting birds. There's no time to lose." In a cloud of blue smoke, they sped off down the gravel driveway and into the lanes of Oxfordshire.

The car sped along in the sun, and Eleanor was enjoying seeing the countryside zip past. She thought that Christopher's life was full of adventure and fun.

"Elie," Christopher spoke out. "All of this might be a bit overwhelming for you, so I thought we could buy a few things to eat in the village and have a picnic somewhere quiet, if you agree." Eleanor was a little taken aback. She would have to be on her guard, as Christopher might have other ideas.

"Alright, as long as I get to choose the location," she said.

"Great," he replied.

The car came to stop in a village that had a grocery where Christopher dashed in to purchase some food.

"I hope you are okay with my lunch choice," he said. "Next time, I will get the cook to prepare something for us."

Next time? Eleanor thought. *He has plans beyond today?*

"There is a nice spot I think you will approve of down by the river," Christopher said as he zoomed off in the Triumph. Not far from the road stood a large tree that cast its shadow over the riverbank. A few other people were nearby having their lunch, and so Eleanor smiled approvingly.

"This do?" asked Christopher.

"Approved," said Eleanor.

Christopher spread a blanket on the ground and set out the packages of food.

"We don't have oodles of time, unfortunately, if we are going to get to the uni and Wytham before dark," said Christopher.

Christopher spoke between bites. "Elie, may I ask if you have a man friend?"

She was quite taken aback at how quickly he wanted to know about her personal life. "Do you mean anyone I am serious with?" Eleanor replied.

"Yes," said Christopher.

"Why do you ask?" she replied.

"Oh, I was just wondering. You are quite an interesting person that I would think might have someone else in her life," he said.

"Do you think if I did, he would be happy for me to come spend a few days with a young man in Oxford?" she returned.

"I guess that means no," said Christopher with a bemused look. "Well, I hope we can be friends regardless of circumstances."

"I'd like that," she said.

Christopher looked at his watch. "We'd better be going."

They quickly packed up and were on the road to Oxford.

"What have you got planned for us now, Christopher?" asked Eleanor above the hum of the Triumph.

"We are going to the Edward Grey Institute," he replied. "Have you heard of it?"

"No, I haven't," she replied.

"It is fairly new, formed a few years ago as an institute devoted to bird research," Christopher explained. "Grey was a viscount, I think, and former chancellor who had an interest in birds."

"Is he the same Edward Grey who was foreign secretary?" queried Eleanor.

"I believe so," said Christopher. "Anyway, the director is a David Brown, who I imagine you have heard about."

"Yes, he's written about robins – one of my favourite birds," said Eleanor.

"I thought so," said Christopher. "He's giving a lecture this afternoon, and we are going to be in attendance."

Eleanor was thrilled. "Is that the surprise you talked about when you picked me up?"

"I thought you'd like it," said Christopher.

A few minutes later, they entered Oxford, parked the car, and walked to the Edward Grey Institute.

"I thought you'd appreciate this library, being a budding ornithologist," said Christopher as he swung open the doors. "Welcome to the Alexander Library devoted entirely to ornithology," he announced.

Eleanor gasped. Before her were shelves of books on birds from around the world and copies of papers published in international journals sent to the library by the ornithologists themselves. She could spend a lifetime going through all the books.

"We don't have time to dawdle," Christopher said as he turned to enter a lecture hall. Gathered in a small room were students and professors who had come to hear what David Brown had to say.

By this time, Eleanor's head was spinning. So much had happened in this one day that she had not had time to comprehend all that was going on around her. David Brown was speaking about evolution of birds on islands, but Eleanor was in no state to fully comprehend or even focus on what he was saying. She sat quietly in awe of what she was witnessing.

After Brown finished speaking, Christopher asked Eleanor if she would like to meet him.

"Oh no, Christopher. Well, of course I would like to meet him, but my mind is swirling right now," she replied.

"So sorry, Elie. I am such a fool. This is overwhelming for you, all packed into today," he said. "We don't have much time anyway if we want to go to Wytham."

"Wytham?" Eleanor asked inquisitively.

"Yes, Wytham Wood is not far away. It's a woodland that was bequeathed to the uni a few years ago, and it's where I am helping the research on nesting birds," said Christopher. "Professor Brown's research of robins began there. I thought you'd like to see where he did some of his work."

Some time in a woodland was just the tonic Eleanor needed. Far from the hustle and bustle of academia and the boundless energy of Christopher, she hoped she might unwind before the dinner that evening at Ashford Manor.

Before long, Wytham Wood came into view, and Christopher parked the Triumph. They climbed out of the car, and Eleanor put the binoculars Christopher had given her around her neck. They headed into the woodlots where bird nest boxes had been erected. The woodlot was alive with birdsong. Blackbirds sang from their perches, and chiffchaffs, blackcaps, and willow warblers twittered in the shrubbery. A great spotted woodpecker drummed far off in the forest. A two-note call of a great tit rang out from the forest's edge, and the bird appeared in Eleanor's binoculars. It carried coloured rings on its legs, which Christopher explained were to identify individuals.

"The bird boxes are designed so we can look inside and keep track of how well the family does," offered Christopher. "There are plans for this study to become a longterm investigation into reproduction by birds."

"What do you do, Christopher?" asked Eleanor.

"I am hoping I can join the team to get some experience handling birds and learning the skills of a field ornithologist," he said.

"My interest is more in the taxonomy of birds," said Eleanor, "but we could make a good team."

Christopher grinned. "You are so amusing, Elie."

They wandered around the forest glades and across the meadows, watching birds and pointing them out to each other. Eleanor felt like she was falling for Christopher.

When the day was coming to an end, Christopher and Eleanor returned to Ashford Manor in a whirl of wind, blue smoke, and engine sputters. Eleanor asked Christopher how the family made its money. "My father supplied machine parts for the war effort," he said. She went silent.

Christopher told Eleanor that the evening meal would be at 8 p.m. in the dining room. He would meet her there. She climbed the stairs, entered her room, closed the door, and collapsed on the bed. Her head was swirling, and dinner with the parents was yet to come. She closed her eyes and dozed off to sleep.

CHAPTER 4:

Dinner with the Ashfords

The clamour of evening meal preparations startled Eleanor awake, and she glanced at the clock. It was 7:15, much to her relief. She rose from the bed, stretched, and began to sort her clothes. She would wear a floral dress she had bought for the occasion. She was ready to go by 7:30, and with a deep breath, she opened the door and walked down the stairs to enter the dining room. Annie, the servant, was the only person there, and she quickly directed Eleanor to the drawing room across the foyer.

Eleanor thanked Annie and walked to the drawing room. On the far wall opposite where Eleanor stood, a fireplace was crackling. A large sofa ran parallel to the outside wall with enough space to reach the tall windows overlooking the front gardens. On the sofa, legs crossed at the ankles, sat Mrs. Elizabeth Ashford. Opposite the sofa stood a table with a wireless and a sherry decanter against the inner wall, in front of which were two wing chairs, the nearest one holding Mr. Anthony Ashford. He was dressed in a three-piece suit, and he was balding and a little portly. *Life has been good to him*, Eleanor concluded. Elizabeth was wearing a floral dress that was custom tailored and very befitting on her.

"Come in, and welcome to Ashford Manor," bellowed Mr. Ashford as he jumped to his feet. Mrs. Ashford turned to face Eleanor and, with a big smile, hoped that Eleanor had had a good day.

"Eleanor, I would like you to meet my husband, Anthony," she said.

"How very nice to meet you, Mr. Ashford, and yes, Christopher took me on a whirlwind tour of Oxford," she replied.

Anthony said, "Elizabeth was telling me about you, but now that you are here, I can ask you directly. You work as a librarian, is that correct?"

"Yes, at the British Library in London," she replied. "As an assistant librarian." Before she finished speaking, Christopher arrived.

"It looks like you have already done the introductions," he said. "Let me get you a drink. What will it be Eleanor?"

Eleanor was uncertain what to say, and Christopher came to the rescue.

"Sherry?" he said.

"Please" Eleanor replied, feeling relieved. "I am surprised that you have sherry with all the rationing."

Anthony said, "We had a good supply in the wine cellar before the war, which I am relieved has ended so we could restock." Eleanor had never drunk sherry before, and when she took a sip, she was taken aback by its dryness.

"Mrs. Allen says that the evening meal is nearly ready, and we don't want to keep the cook waiting, do we?" said Anthony. "Step this way, Miss Hutchinson."

Eleanor entered the dining room, where a servant was placing food on a buffet. The warm room was filled with the aroma of the food. She had never smelled such aromas before, and just the scent was a treat during the time of rationing. There were place settings of silver with several forks and spoons placed around a dinner plate. A smaller plate was to her left and a longstemmed wine glass stood behind the plate. A large floral centre arrangement dominated the middle of the table.

"Please take a seat, Eleanor," said Mrs. Ashford.

By now, Eleanor was feeling very awkward. All of the conversation, the home, and dinner had a protocol that was foreign to her. What she referred to as "dinner" was called the "evening meal." She asked for directions to the toilet and was informed the *lavatory* was down the hall on the left. It was a foreign language that not-so-subtly identified social class and privilege. She tried to play the part, but inside she was trembling. Her inner voice said, *I feel like I am drowning.*

Christopher sat down beside her and proceeded to tell his parents about their activities throughout the day. Eleanor watched the body language and couldn't help but feel she was being assessed. The servant arrived with a bowl of soup, filled Eleanor's bowl, and then proceeded to Elizabeth, followed by Christopher and then Anthony. Eleanor awaited to see what she was supposed to do. *Which spoon do I use?* she asked herself. Christopher took the soup spoon and proceeded to shovel the soup into his mouth. Elizabeth was daintier, which Eleanor tried to emulate. The spoon fell out of her hand into the bowl where she tried to rescue it as a servant passed her another spoon.

"So," Mr. Ashford began, "I understand from Christopher that you work at the library. Do you have other ambitions?"

"I hope to get a job at the British Museum, but I fear that I will be found unqualified," said Eleanor. "Our society does not always make decisions on merit, unlike what I heard happens in America and Canada."

"Well, Eleanor," said Anthony, "we all have roles to play to make society function."

"It is not the role I question, Mr. Anthony. It is who gets to play them," she says.

"My word, Christopher. Your Eleanor is a very astute young lady," Anthony replied.

Eleanor buckled with his patronizing but decided not to push the point. Christopher and Elizabeth were looking less than amused.

Anthony continued. "A good example of our roles is the very work you did as librarian. You played a key role in keeping spirits up during those dreadful bombings by lending out books to take people's minds off the tragedy around them. We fortunately were able to move here to

Ashford Manor to escape the terror, but I read that Mr. Darwin's former home and a wing of the library were seriously damaged. It must have been harrowing for you, Eleanor."

"It was indeed, Mr. Ashford," she replied and then went silent. She looked at her hands on her lap and choked back a tear. Mr. Ashford could see a tear in her eye. "I am sorry if I touched on a delicate subject."

Eleanor looked up and began to speak. "Many people lost their lives and all their belongings to the bombs. I lost my parents to the night bombs."

All of the Ashfords stopped eating and stared in disbelief.

"Oh, my lord," said Anthony. "You poor thing."

She continued, "Yes, many of the lucky ones huddled each night in the underground as the sirens rang out. I was a teenager, and when the siren wailed, my parents told me to run as fast as I could for the underground. I never saw them again."

Eleanor stopped abruptly when she saw the family thunderstruck by what they just heard. "Oh, I am so sorry," she said. "I have ruined our dinner. Mrs. Allen is going to be annoyed. I am sorry."

Elizabeth was the first to speak.

"It is important to talk about your traumas, Eleanor," she said. "We lived here out of harm's way, and the bombings seemed distant. You have brought the trauma that so many faced into focus. Don't apologize. Now, let's just eat up and enjoy what is left of the evening."

The others fell silent and stared at their dinner plates. Eleanor felt terrible that she had ruined the evening but felt it was important for the Ashfords to realize how fortunate they were. After a lengthy silence, Anthony spoke.

"This has been a difficult evening for everyone. I think I might go off to the smoking room. Care to join me, Christopher?" he said.

They rose and walked out of the dining room in a stifled silence. Elizabeth then rose and asked Eleanor to join her in the drawing room. Elizabeth sat down on the sofa and gestured for Eleanor to sit beside her.

"You know, Eleanor, the tragedy you went through I can only imagine, and to speak about it takes great courage. You need to see that you can be strong in situations that might make others uneasy. I am quite proud of you, even if this is the first day of our meeting."

Eleanor had never been spoken to like this before. Elizabeth seemed truly concerned about her. It was what Eleanor imagined a mother would say to her daughter. Elizabeth and Anthony had no other children besides Christopher, and perhaps she was looking for a young woman to hold as her own.

Eleanor thanked Elizabeth for her kind words and then requested to leave for bed. Elizabeth bade her good night and told her breakfast would be served in the dining room about 7:30.

Eleanor climbed the stairs, entered the room, and fell onto the bed. Her inner voice called out to her, saying, *This is what happens when you go beyond your station.* Then a counter voice pealed, *It wasn't all that bad because she would never be part of this society.* She wondered what Anthony and Christopher were discussing and how she would face them in the morning. She said to herself that what she needed to do was get back to writing to Gerald. She might even ask his advice on what to do under the circumstances.

The following morning, Eleanor awoke at dawn but was still exhausted from the previous day. She went to the lavatory and then dressed for breakfast. She descended the stairs to enter the dining room that stood empty except for Annie, the servant, putting food on a buffet. Eleanor looked around, and Annie showed her where to sit. Annie began to pour Eleanor a cup of tea.

"Oh, you don't need to do that," said Eleanor. "I can get my own tea."

Annie replied, "This is my job, Miss." A silence fell as Annie finished pouring the tea. Annie had not failed to notice Eleanor's London accent.

"You've come up in the world, Miss," said Annie resentfully.

Eleanor was stunned by the comment, which Annie followed with, "How did you manage *that*?" she said with an unpleasant smile. "A nice London girl like you."

"I work at the British Library and share an interest in birds with Christopher, nothing more," she fired back.

"What's this I hear," broadcasted Elizabeth as she strode into the room. Annie made a hasty retreat out a back door.

"Oh, nothing but idle talk with one of the servants," Eleanor says.

"They have no business chatting with guests," Elizabeth proclaimed. "I will talk to her later. As if you haven't been through enough already."

"Oh, yes," said Eleanor "Please accept my apologies for . . . "

"Now stop that. We agreed that it was important to do, and that was last night. We have a new day before us," replied Elizabeth.

"Good morning, one and all," said Christopher with arms open wide and a huge grin. Right behind him arrived Anthony. "Good morning, everyone. I hope you slept well Eleanor."

Before she could speak, Elizabeth said, "Of course she did."

"Eleanor," Christopher called out. "We will have to go in a few minutes to catch your train."

Eleanor said she would pack her things and meet Christopher at the door in a few minutes. "Thanks, Mr. and Mrs. Ashford, for all your hospitality," she said.

"You are always welcome here, Eleanor," said Elizabeth. "We enjoyed your company, even if it stirred us out of our complacency."

"Good day, Miss Hutchinson," said Anthony. "Safe travels."

Eleanor dashed up the stairs, packed her bag, and arrived at the front door just as Christopher arrived in the Triumph. Annie stood off to the side, staring at the ground. Eleanor avoided her and got into the car.

"What's up with Annie?" said Christopher. "She should have put your bag in the boot."

"Who knows," said Eleanor. "I have a train to catch."

At the station, Christopher helped Eleanor with her bag. "I hope we can do this again," he said.

Eleanor smiled, knowing that she could never fit into his world nor he into hers.

As she was about to step on the train, Christopher said, "You forgot your surprise, Eleanor."

He handed her a package as the train pulled out.

"What's this?" she asked.

"A surprise," Christopher said. As the train gained speed, she opened the brown wrapper to a find a pair of binoculars.

CHAPTER 5:

Fox and Crow

The Fox and Crow Pub was an extension of home for Eleanor and the residents of Rabbit's Burrough. The nineteenth century whitewashed stone walls with black eaves, window panes, and door were a beacon to the locals who wanted a pint and to hear the latest gossip. Balanced against grumbling and gossiping, Fox and Crow was also a place to celebrate special occasions and to get a meal and a pint, but most importantly, it provided a warm feeling of belonging. And so, it was on a cool spring evening that Eleanor saw Marjorie Quimby leave the solitude of her comfortable home for a few hours at the Fox and Crow, unsure which of the emotions would be on display.

Eleanor watched Marjorie adjust her woollen coat against the evening chill as she passed down Deacon's

Lane toward the pub. Marjorie knew that the black door of the pub was also a doorway to a hot meal because, on this evening each week, the Fox and Crow served a pork pie dinner. Arriving early was important if one expected to get a meal. Despite the recent end to rationing, many food stuffs were in short supply. In an odd way, rationing had made a meal at the pub even more tasty and gratifying. After all, many of the British had endured the bombing campaigns, and all had felt the severity of rationing.

Inside the pub, Marjorie could feel the warmth of a large fire crackling in a stone fireplace in the middle of the pub. Several people, some alone, others in couples, sat at tables near the bar and in a distant room. She made her way to the bar, where she was greeted by AnneMarie, the daughter of the publican.

"Hello, AnneMarie," said Marjorie.

"Evening, Marjorie," AnneMarie replied. "Here for dinner?"

"Oh, yes," said Marjorie as she looked about the pub for a place to sit.

"What'll it be then?" asked AnneMarie

"Your dad's delicious pork pie dinner, I think it will be tonight, dear."

"Something to wash it down?" asked AnneMarie.

"Yes, please," said Marjorie. "I'd like to a start with a G and T, if that can be arranged."

"Why, of course," said AnneMarie as she walked into the kitchen, where she yelled, "One pie," and then returned to the bar with a glass.

"Gilbey's?" AnneMarie asked.

Marjorie nodded and looked again for at a table near the fireplace.

"Here you go, Mrs. Quimby," said AnneMarie. "I will call when your dinner is ready."

Marjorie took her gin and tonic to a table between the fireplace and the window. She preferred this location where she could watch people passing on the street and entering the pub. After all, gossip was something she quite enjoyed although she would never admit it.

Several people from the village came into the pub for a pint or a meal. A few went to the back room to throw darts, but most sat on bar stools or sought out tables nearby. A couple of young people Marjorie didn't know sat in the corner looking love struck. She smiled ever so slightly and sighed, recalling her youth with her late husband.

"Good evening, Marjorie," came a voice to one side of her.

She turned to see Jack MacLaughlin, the village postman, standing beside her. Jack was several years younger than Marjorie. He was a veteran of the war but showed no outward scars of his time in Europe. Inside, he might have his own demons, but Jack seemed a reliable postman. He had a route he followed each day that included Marjorie's house and Eleanor's cottage, and the Fox and Crow was his favourite watering hole.

"Are you meeting someone here tonight?" enquired Jack.

"No," said Marjorie. I came in to enjoy a nice meal and talk to some nice people," she said with a smile.

"Would you consider me as one of those nice people?" he teased.

"I could bend the rule tonight, but only if you promise to be a gentleman." she replied.

"I always am," Jack said. "I will give my order and get a pint and then join you. May I get you anything?"

"Thank you, but no need. The pork pie is a good bet," Marjorie advised.

A few minutes later, AnneMarie came to Marjorie's table with a steaming pie dinner.

"Anything more, Mrs. Quimby?"

"Oh, a nice Malbec would go down well," she answered.

"Sorry, we are out of most reds, but I will see if there is some of the house red, if you like," AnneMarie said.

"That would be fine, thank you, dear. I understand how difficult it is to get supplies now the war is over."

Jack returned a few minutes later. He raised his pint of bitter and toasted Marjorie. "Here's to our friendship and companionship. May it never end," Jack bellowed.

Marjorie was a bit flummoxed by his loud voice but smiled demurely. She did find his ways boorish at times, but he was a great source of stories. Being a postman, he knew everyone in the village and most of their activities. Marjorie's natural nosiness found him to be a good source of gossip.

By now Marjorie was starting to feel the effects of the gin and tonic, and Jack was warming to his bitter.

"What's new with our Marjorie?" he blurted out.

"I was hoping to ask you the same question," she replied, "but since you asked, I thought you might like to hear the latest news about my tenant, Eleanor – in the cottage?" she said.

"Oh, yes, I know Miss Hutchinson, but not well. She is gone to work on most days when I do my rounds. Is she not well?" Jack enquired.

"As far as I know, she is perfectly healthy. She keeps to herself, which is not good for a young woman."

Jack asked, "Did I hear she lost her parents in the war?"

"Yes, during the bombings one night – as they ran for the shelters. That's why I offered her my cottage – to help her get her feet on the ground," said Marjorie.

"That is sad indeed," Jack said.

"I have taken her under my wing, so to speak – you know she is interested in birds?" Marjorie said.

"No. I was not aware of that. There are lots of birds in the countryside. They sing to me as I ride my bike on my deliveries."

"Eleanor has a librarian job in London," said Marjorie.

Jack took another drink of his bitter.

"Am I boring you Jack?" asked Marjorie.

"No not at all," he replied.

She cut a piece of pie that went into her mouth on the end of a fork. Jack did the same with his meal.

"Are you worried about her, Marjorie?" asked Jack.

"A little," she replied. "Mostly because I don't know all that she is doing."

"Well, she has to work, which must eat up most of her day. Is there something else?" he enquired.

"Yes," said Marjorie. "She says that, from time to time, the library requests that she travel all over the country to pick up books and manuscripts donated by patrons," said Marjorie.

"What's wrong with that?" Jack said. "I wish I could get away to see the country too. Not that I am unhappy with my postie job. I enjoy giving people news when it is good. Especially you, Marjorie," he chimed.

"What I wonder, Jack – and this is just conjecture – Eleanor might have a secret rendezvous with someone."

"You mean a lover?" Jack whispered.

"I don't know," said Marjorie.

"What's wrong with that, Marjorie? Eleanor is a young woman and quite attractive, so I would think there are plenty of men interested in her. That's only natural."

"Well, yes," said Marjorie, "but she does not have a mother or father to confide in. She is pleasant to me but does not tell me anything about her personal life."

Jack took another drink of his bitter and returned to eating his pork pie without saying anything.

"Jack," said Marjorie, "do you know something?"

"No, not really," he replied.

"Not really?" said Marjorie. "You do know something, don't you."

"Well, not until you mentioned it," said Jack.

"Mentioned what?" Marjorie exclaimed.

"It might be nothing, but Eleanor is getting quite a few letters," said Jack. "For someone who lives alone, she seems to be getting a lot of correspondence."

"What kind of correspondence?" pried Marjorie.

"It's nothing, like I said, but she gets letters addressed to her with no return address on them," Jack offered. "Not every day or even every week, but there have been several."

Jack then went on the defensive.

"Marjorie, this is personal, and I probably shouldn't have told you this. And for all I know, they are just letters. I don't think they are anything. And I don't think you should go asking her. I might get in trouble for telling you this. You know the postmaster would not be pleased, and I could lose my job. I wished I had never told you this. This is what too much bitter can do to me."

Marjorie was all ears at the news Jack had just told her. She had seen Eleanor leave with envelopes. Her curiosity was piqued.

Marjorie and Jack finished their meals, and he decided to leave early.

"The first mail arrives early in the morning, so I had better get a good night's sleep," he said.

"Have a good sleep Jack, and it was very nice of you to stop by," she said. Jack rose from his chair, put on his coat, and headed for the door.

Marjorie slowly sipped what remained of her house wine. She mulled over what Eleanor might be up to and how she might find out. She was genuinely concerned about Eleanor's wellbeing, but she also felt a pang of guilty pleasure in hearing the news from Jack. The fox had just outwitted the crow.

CHAPTER 6:

Letters from Hawaii

A week had passed before Eleanor felt completely rested after her trip to Oxford. She had not heard from Christopher and assumed he was busy with his studies. She also had not heard from Gerald and wondered how he was faring. She poured herself a cup of tea and sat down at the typewriter and began to type.

Eleanor Hutchinson, Robinsong Cottage, Deacon's Lane, Rabbit's

Burrough, Herts.

May 25, 1947

This time she decided to use her full Christian name. *It is time*, she thought, *for Gerald to know that E. Hutchinson is a woman.* She smiled and had just begun to compose the letter when a knock came at her door. Eleanor quickly pulled the letter from the typewriter and slipped it into a drawer. She stood up, straightened her skirt, tussled her hair, and walked to the door. When she swung open the door, Mrs. Quimby was standing on the step with a tray of biscuits.

"I thought you might like some biscuits for your tea, Eleanor," she said.

"Oh, why thank you," replied Eleanor.

"You look a little pale dear," said Mrs. Quimby.

Befuddled, Eleanor replied, "Your knocking at the door just startled me, that's all."

"I thought I could hear a typewriter. Did I interrupt something?" Mrs. Quimby asked.

Visibly shaken, Eleanor replied, "Oh, that. I try to keep up with my correspondence by writing letters away from the library."

Mrs. Quimby smiled and stood silent for an uncomfortable moment.

"Would you like to come in for tea, Marjorie?" Eleanor asked eventually.

"If it would be no trouble," Mrs. Quimby said.

"Come in and do sit down while I get the kettle on," said Eleanor.

Mrs. Quimby walked into the drawing room, eyed the typewriter, and glanced on the desk to see if there were any letters while Eleanor went into the kitchen. A few opened envelopes addressed to Eleanor lay at the end of the desk. Marjorie eyed them with a cocked head. There were no return addresses on them, just as Jack the postman had said.

Eleanor arrived with a tea pot, two cups with saucers, and a small amount of sugar and milk on a tray, catching Marjorie looking at the envelopes on the desk. Marjorie jumped, back startled at getting caught.

"I am sorry I can't offer much sugar and milk," Eleanor said. "Rationing is making them hard to come by."

"No worries, dear. I prefer mine black," said Marjorie.

An uncomfortable silence was broken by Mrs. Quimby.

"How are you getting on, Eleanor?" she asked.

"I am fine, but thank you for asking. You remind me of my mother," Eleanor said.

"Dear, I didn't mean to upset you," Mrs. Quimby said. "You were away overnight the other weekend, and I was worried about you, but I guess I need to realize you are a grown woman capable of looking after yourself."

Eleanor thought that Marjorie's comment was a leading question and that she was hoping Eleanor would instead give her some new gossip. She thought, *Should I tell Marjorie about Christopher? Perhaps I should. What harm could there be?*

"I was invited by the Ashford family in Oxford to visit their home and attend a lecture at the university," Eleanor said.

"Oh my. That is quite a privilege for someone in your station, Eleanor," Mrs. Quimby said. "How did that come about?"

"It was a chance meeting of Christopher Ashford at the British Museum where I was sketching birds," said Eleanor.

"Oh, you have a young man in your life then, Eleanor?" queried Marjorie.

"It is not like that, Mrs. Quimby. We just share a common interest in birds," Eleanor retorted.

"And correspondence?" asked Marjorie.

"Mrs. Quimby, this is my personal life, and I prefer to keep it to myself. I appreciate your concern, but there is nothing that should worry or concern you," Eleanor said. "If there were, you would be the first person I would come to for advice."

"I am sorry, dear. I didn't mean to pry," said Mrs. Quimby. "I am only interested in your wellbeing."

"I appreciate your kindness, Mrs. Quimby. I see the gardeners have done a nice job of your garden," Eleanor said, trying to change the subject.

After some small talk, Marjorie rose from her chair.

"Well, thank you for the tea, and I promise not to pry into your life, Eleanor," she said.

"Good day, Mrs. Quimby, and thank you for the biscuits," returned Eleanor.

She closed the door and took a deep breath. "That woman!" Eleanor said, exasperated. She looked out the window to make sure Mrs. Quimby was out of earshot before returning to the typewriter. She hadn't replied to Gerald's letter in January partly because she was busy but also because she didn't want to seem too needy. She took a deep breath. "Now, where was I?"

Eleanor Hutchinson, Robinsong Cottage,
Deacon's Lane, Rabbit's Burrough, Herts.

May 25, 1947

Dear Mr. Benson,

Thank you for your letter about your
time in Hawaii. Your description of
the island explains your desire to
collect there.

I looked up the birds you mentioned in
the bird guides in the library and can
see that they would make a great addition to the collection. I was familiar
with Darwin's early investigations of
Galapagos finches but not the honeycreepers of Hawaii. I was also aware of
the tsunami in that part of the world
from news reports in the London Times.
I am hopeful the destruction does not
hamper your efforts.

I thought you might be interested in
hearing about how my foray into orni-
thology has progressed. As if by chance,
I met a young man named Christopher
Ashford on a visit to the British
Museum. I had gone there to sketch

birds so that I would become more familiar with them. Christopher introduced himself as a volunteer guide at the BMNH, which led to an invitation to visit his field study site in Wytham Wood in Oxford. I took up his offer and, through his connections, was able to attend a lecture by Professor David Brown from the Edward Grey Institute. His approach for studying birds in the field appeals to me, and I am at loose ends on whether to consider a career as a taxonomist or a field biologist. I was hoping you might give me some advice.

I have taken out some of the bird guides you suggested, from which I am slowly learning the birds around my cottage. Even with the assistance of binoculars, the task has been quite daunting.

One of the highlights of this new avocation is an interest in European robins. I have a territorial male outside my cottage that sings each morning. I mentioned this to Christopher, who gave me a copy of David Brown's newly published book, "The Robin's Life." I am reading it now and getting up to speed on this ever-so-popular British bird.

```
I would like to thank you once again for
your advice.

Sincerely,

Eleanor Hutchinson
```

A few weeks passed, which allowed Eleanor to get back into her daily routine. She rose in time to catch the bus and train before passing the postbox where she posted letters to Gerald. Her day was spent alone, mostly shelving and cataloguing books. She had plenty of time to think, and she wondered how long it would take for a letter from Gerald to arrive at her home. She did a little research on the Royal Mail deliveries and concluded that it was about time a letter from Gerald would be forthcoming. If he had received her letter and had the time and inclination to write, that is. A few days later, Jack, the postman, slipped the third letter with no return address into Eleanor's letter box.

The day at the library had been quite slow. With improving spring weather and longer days, library visits had declined. Despite the quiet day, Eleanor was feeling quite tired when she unlocked her front door. In the letter box was a letter. Her smile broke out into a quiet chuckle. She placed the letter on her kitchen table, put down her purse, and removed her coat before putting the kettle on the stove. She tore open the letter and laid it aside as if she already knew what it contained. She went to the lavatory and returned as the kettle began to whistle.

Gerald Benson, c/o British
Museum (Natural History), South
Kensington, London.

Dear Eleanor:

Thank you once more for your letter. I
was very impressed at how much you knew
about Hawaii and its birds. The British
Library deserves some of the credit,
but you are keeping up on the latest
news too. My collecting was profitable
despite my short time here. I arrived
shortly after the tsunami, which left
its mark on some parts of the islands,
but I was able to complete my work. The
Americans were very helpful in this
regard by providing me with specimens
and a laboratory to prepare the specimens. I also visited the Bishop Museum
in Honolulu to see a feather cape called
an 'ahu'ula by native Hawaiians that
belonged to King Kamehameha. The cape
was made from thousands of feathers from
the native honeycreeper known as the
mamo with a few feathers from the 'i'iwi
in the mix.

The BMNH has now suggested I shift my
efforts to the Amazon and Galapagos

Islands, and so by the time you get
this letter, I will likely be on the
high seas, somewhere in the Pacific.
I promise to write when I arrive in
South America.

Now, to address your question on whether
to embark on a career in field work
or in taxonomy in the museum, at this
stage, my advice would be to learn your
birds from some seasoned birdwatchers.
Whether you choose field work or taxonomy, you will need to have skills in
the countryside.

Please let me know how the meeting went
and keep me up to date on the news
from home.

Sincerely,

Gerald Benson

The following day, Jack was doing his postal rounds
on his bike. He stood the bike against Marjorie's gate and
began to fumble through his bag in search of mail for
her. She had anticipated him coming and was waiting at
the door.

"Only one letter for you today, Marjorie," said Jack. He
smiled and handed her the letter.

"Thank you, Jack," she smiled.

"How's your tenant doing?" Jack enquired with a smile.

"Well, quite well, I should say," offered Marjorie.

"I dropped off another letter to her yesterday," he said quietly from behind his hand.

"I had tea with her, and I can tell you it is all in innocence," Marjorie offered.

"Nothing a little, you know . . . " He winked.

"No, Jack. Eleanor is not like that," Marjorie retorted. "Off you go, Jack, and behave yourself."

CHAPTER 7:

Peter and Patrick

Eleanor loaned out several bird field guides from the library in an attempt to identify the birds around her garden. She had become proficient at recognizing the common species, but she had a long way to go to be able to converse intelligently with ornithologists. She found the task somewhat daunting, and she did not have much spare time to devote to learning them. Luck was about to change all that.

Marjorie had seen Eleanor with the binoculars that Christopher had given her. She watched as Eleanor alternated between scouting out birds and glancing in a field guide.

"Eleanor," she shouted from her garden patio, "may I have a word with you?"

Eleanor put down her binoculars and walked closer. "What is it, Mrs. Quimby?" she enquired.

"I know you are interested in birds from what you told me, and I see you have binoculars and a field guide. Are you trying to become a birdwatcher?"

Eleanor replied, "Yes, but it is much more difficult than I imagined."

Marjorie said inquisitively, "Have you met Peter from the RSPB? He lives in the village and knows birds very well."

"Do you mean the Royal Society for Bird Protection?" asked Eleanor.

"Protection of Birds, the Royal Society for the Protection of Birds," corrected Marjorie.

"Yes, of course," said Eleanor.

"Well, do you?" asked Marjorie.

"Do I what?" Eleanor replied.

"Know Peter?" Margorie was getting a little exasperated.

"Oh, sorry. No, I do not know him," Eleanor said.

"Then I will introduce you," said Marjorie. "He lives in the village. He is holding a garden party on Saturday."

Saturday came around, and to Marjorie's word, Eleanor got an invitation from Peter to join the garden party. The day was sunny and warm when Eleanor walked up the lane to Peter's cottage at the opposite end of the village. His cottage had a thatched roof with whitewashed mud and daub walls. The doorway was sufficiently small that Peter and most guests had to duck their heads to enter. Outside, there was a small terraced area that served as a patio, and beyond the cottage was an open grassy area where the garden party guests had assembled. Inside a long tent were tables and chairs for about thirty guests. Colourful banners hung in the tent, and bouquets of flowers adorned the tables with equally colourful place settings standing on either side of the tables.

Many gaily dressed guests were present when Eleanor arrived, including Marjorie, who was off to one side gossiping with one of the neighbours. The vicar was in attendance, passing along God's grace and forgiveness to those in need. Only two people felt the need it seemed. Jack MacLaughlin, the postman, was present and with Mr. O'Halloran, the post master. The two were telling postal jokes and may have just had too much to drink. Eleanor couldn't be certain. AnneMarie from the Fox and Crow was serving drinks, and a caterer Eleanor did not recognize was arranging food on the table.

Despite rationing, the locally grown food helped fill the table. When times warranted it, the village would rally to make sure everyone was taken care of, like the time the pigs had got loose from their enclosure and roamed the streets, terrorizing small children. By the time the owner, Mr. Allenby, had discovered the prison break, his entire drove and the piglets had been running hither and yon. The village had banded together to send out search parties armed with pots and pans, and before the day was over, all the wayward pigs had been rounded up. The locals called that fateful day All Hogs Day from that day forward. That day, as it turned out, was today and the reason for the garden party. Bill Bigglethwaite and his Hog Band, appropriately dressed in pig suits, blew their trumpets, strummed their guitars, squeezed their accordions, and bowed their fiddles with joyful tunes all the while belting out rowdy lyrics.

"You must be the young lady in the cottage at the other end of the village," a voice said. Eleanor turned to see a thin man in his thirties with wavy hair and a cropped moustache who was sporting a cream-coloured linen jacket and matching slacks.

"I am Peter," he said. "Peter Saunders. I hear you are interested in birds."

"Why yes, and nice to meet you," replied Eleanor. "I understand you work for the RSPB."

"That's right, when I am not holding garden parties," he exclaimed.

She was already warming to Peter.

"Listen, Eleanor," said Peter. "We have just purchased our first nature reserve at Minsmere in East Suffolk. There are a handful of avocets breeding there. They were, for all intents and purposes, extinct in the UK, and we hope this reserve will reverse their fortunes. We plan to drive down there tomorrow, if you'd like to join us. We can do some birding and hopefully see the avocets."

"Who is 'we'?" asked Eleanor.

"Oh. I'm sorry. Patrick is a friend. He has the motorcar and, importantly, the petrol."

"Is he with the RSPB too?" queried Eleanor.

"No. Government," returned Peter.

Eleanor thought Peter seemed to be a nice fellow, and his RSPB moniker gave her some relief that he could be taken at his word. She could do with a bird-watching tutor, and Peter seemed a good fit.

Peter began, "I know this is quick notice but – "

She cut him off mid-sentence. "Why, yes," she said.

"Great. We will pop over about 8 a.m. tomorrow so we have the afternoon to explore Minsmere. We might be back after dark. See you then."

He quickly turned on his heel and was greeted by other colleagues from the RSPB.

Eleanor watched with admiration at how easily he fit in with people. Perhaps it was the drink, or Peter might have been a natural socializer. In any case, tomorrow seemed like it would be a fun day for her.

Sunday morning came early for Eleanor. She wolfed down some breakfast and packed her binoculars and bird book into her bag with a sandwich and flask of tea just in time to hear Peter arrive outside her door. She stepped out into the cool air to see Peter waving to her from the passenger seat of a Wolseley driven by a smart-looking and slightly older man.

"Good morning, Eleanor" Peter said as he stepped out of the car. "Let me assist you with your bag."

Eleanor climbed into the rear leather seat as Peter put her bag on the seat from the opposite door.

"Eleanor this is my good friend, Patrick," he said. "We go back to uni days. Are you excited about today?" Patrick looked at her in the rearview mirror and gave a partial smile of acknowledgement.

Eleanor was very excited about the day. She had never ventured into East Suffolk or even seen the North Sea. She was also excited to see new birds under Peter's tutelage.

"Our journey is going to take a few hours but Patrick here knows the way and is an excellent driver," Peter said.

The car sped off down the lane, onto the main road through the village, and before long was making its way through the countryside off to the northeast through rolling hills and arable land.

After a few hours of driving, the threesome entered East Suffolk.

"Ah," Peter said, "this is Constable country. Are you familiar with his work, Eleanor?"

She was familiar with not only Constable's work but many of the celebrated British artists. Her father had encouraged her interest in art by taking her to the galleries in London. "Yes, I am familiar with him and his art," she replied. "I like to paint and draw, but I am no Constable,"

"Pity" Peter crowed, "I was hoping you'd dash off a sketch for me."

Eleanor laughed. She was warming to Peter. He seemed so at ease in all situations and was a gentle soul with a shared passion for birds. But who was Patrick, who was quietly absorbed in driving?

"Patrick," she asked, "how do you know Peter?"

His glance caught Peter's, and then the two faced forward while Patrick replied.

"We've known each other since uni," he said. "Peter had a passion for birds, which I do not have, but perhaps that is a good thing. We appreciate good music and often travel together around the UK. Now the war is over, we hope to get to the continent."

"You don't live in the village then?" Eleanor asked.

"No, my work keeps me tied to a desk in London," Patrick replied.

"What do you do?" she asked.

"Oh, just some government work. Boring stuff," he replied.

"I can concur with that!" said Peter. "It was near impossible to get you to come to the garden party."

"Your offer of a bed was all I needed," he jested. Peter smirked. Eleanor did not.

"Which department of government do you work for?" Eleanor persisted.

"Foreign Office," Patrick replied curtly. "I understand you are with the library."

Eleanor said, "Ever since my parents were killed during the bombings, I have lived alone."

"I am sorry to hear that, Eleanor," Patrick said. "Do you have any family?"

"No. I suppose I am a lone ship without a rudder," she said.

"Are you good at keeping secrets?" Patrick said.

"Secrets?" Eleanor exclaimed. "Why do you ask?"

She thought Patrick might have got wind about the letters from Gerald. She hoped not because they contained her personal ambitions and exposed her inner needs, which were for Gerald's eyes only.

"I just wondered," Patrick said.

Peter jumped in. "I wish Patrick was better at keeping secrets." They both smiled, and Eleanor felt she was on the outside of a long-term friendship the two men had. She sat back in her seat to watch the countryside fly by.

The drive wound through the Suffolk countryside to arrive at a narrow lane through a forest.

"We've arrived," said Peter. "Patrick will drop us off here and catch us up later. He has some business to attend to."

They climbed out of the car, pulled on their jackets, and slung their binoculars around their necks.

Peter began, "The RSPB has just signed a management agreement to make Minsmere a reserve, and I wanted to get a feel for the lay of the land to better understand the plans for creating the reserve. There is a nice mix of reed beds, lowland heath, wetlands, woodlands, and shingle beach. It is this variety of habitats that make it so attractive to birds. Right now, the reserve is off limits without a permit, but I can see the day that visitors will want to see the reserve. If that day arrives, we will need to have carefully planned where they can go to see birds without disturbing them. This gives me an excuse to go bird-watching," he quipped with a smile. "I will need to talk to some of the people who will be managing the site later today, but we can watch birds until then."

They walked along the edge of one of the reed beds where Eleanor saw a few ducks paddling about in a pond.

"What are those birds, Peter?"

"Shelducks, I think," he said as he raised his binoculars. "Yes, shelducks," he confirmed. "Perhaps I should give a you quick lesson in bird-watching. There are some tricks that will assist you in learning one from another."

"That would be wonderful," returned Eleanor.

"Okay, then," started Peter. "Birds in the field guide are usually listed in their taxonomic order, which will interest you since you have a fascination with the BMNH. At the front of the guide are the waterbirds, such as divers, grebes, ducks, and geese. Then you come to the seabirds and shorebirds near the middle, and the latter half is where you will find the songbirds. So, let's practice on the ducks you can see over there in the wetland. Can you describe the duck out there?"

Eleanor described the colours of the body, head, and bill.

"That's a shelduck," Peter said. "You have now identified our first bird. Only about six hundred more to go!" He laughed.

Eleanor and Peter continued their walk around the wetlands. He patiently helped her identify each species they saw. He described how the habitat the bird was in could help identify it from similar-looking species. He showed how male and females of the same species can sometime look quite different. He told Eleanor to focus on the colour of legs, bill, and feathers.

"Listen to the calls too," he said. "A lot of bird-watching is actually bird listening."

Eleanor was feeling quite overwhelmed with all that bird-watching entailed and was impressed at Peter's encyclopedic knowledge.

Suddenly, Peter stopped in mid-sentence and pointed over the wetland. "Look, Eleanor," he exclaimed. "An avocet!" He was nearly jumping up and down with excitement. "That is the reason we acquired Minsmere. The avocet was close to extirpation, and if we get things right, we might be able to bring it back as a regular breeding bird in the UK."

Eleanor could feel his infectious enthusiasm and was delighted to share this moment with him. "Saving species from extinction is the greatest legacy we can do in a lifetime, in my opinion," said Peter.

He was clearly thrilled to be part of the campaign and to tell Eleanor about his feelings.

"Too bad Patrick is not here to see this," she said.

"Patrick is not as interested in birds as me," said Peter, "but it would be nice to show it to him. We can tell him all about it later."

They carried on along the reed beds, across the heathlands, and into the woodlands. Eleanor's list of birds, all new to her, was growing quickly. She thought she would never remember all the names nor be able to identify them.

After a few hours, Peter bade Eleanor goodbye. "I will be about an hour with the management folks and then will catch up with you back at the car park."

He turned and walked away down a woodland track. Eleanor turned the other way and went in search of robins. She was now familiar with their songs, and before long, she had found a singing male. The day was warm and sunny, and she felt a little drowsy after the early morning start. She pushed on to get a good look at the robin. A male was on his perch singing in the sunshine not far away. She sat down and rested elbows on her knees to steady her binoculars in her hands. She intently watched the bird sing repeatedly. She made a note of his red colouration and pulled out her watercolours to try to match the colour. The robin was popularly known for its red breast, but in reality, Eleanor could see the breast and face were more orange than red. Eleanor mixed Winsor yellow and deep red to match the colouration of the robin she was watching in her binoculars. She noted the orange colouration was trimmed with grey and the body was a contrasting drab olive colour.

Eleanor moved on down the track to find several more robins whose colouration she closely observed. Many other birds were singing out of sight or flitting through the shrubs and trees so fast she could not identify them.

By the time she got back to the car park, the sun had moved across the sky, but Peter had not arrived. She began to wonder about Peter and Patrick. They seemed so nice to her, especially given her modest social position. She wondered about the two men's relationship and what the enigmatic Patrick was up to. He was much more reserved and kept his feelings close to his chest, unlike Peter, who was ebullient and always a fine gentleman.

She had not been waiting long when Peter appeared from down a lane.

"Did you see anything new?" he asked Eleanor.

"Not that I could identify, but just getting out into the countryside was worth it," she replied. "I spent some time watching robins singing their hearts out. I have become fascinated with them after reading David Brown's book."

"That's a bit too academic for me," said Peter. "The ornithologists and conservation-minded people are a different breed."

"That's a shame," replied Eleanor, "given the common currency of birds. How was your meeting?"

"Oh, fine," said Peter. "There is a lot of work to go and even more opinions, but I think we are making good progress. Now, where is Patrick?" he pondered.

A distant purring of a Wolseley Eight came out of the west, and Patrick wheeled into sight. Peter and Eleanor climbed in, and Patrick began to return along the lane he had just arrived from.

"Everything go well, Patrick?" Peter asked.

"Yes. You?" Patrick replied.

"Indeed, Eleanor got to see lots of new species. Right, Eleanor?" he said.

"Yes, we saw an avocet, Patrick," she said.

"Very good. Then the trip was well worth it?" he said.

As the car sped along the country road, Peter began to doze in the front seat. Eleanor was also feeling drowsy too but kept her mind on the countryside. Patrick glanced at Peter and could see from his breathing that he was in a deep sleep. He then glanced in the rearview mirror to catch Eleanor's eyes.

"Have you decided to make a career studying birds, Eleanor?" Patrick enquired.

"I would like to, but it is not going to be easy as a woman and in my present situation," she replied.

"Yes, I would think being an ornithologist might make things difficult, especially to make ends meet," Patrick probed.

"I don't need much since I live alone and have no dependents," Eleanor said, "but I might not even get the chance."

"Well," Patrick said. "Have you considered working for the Foreign Service?"

Eleanor was shaken by the question. Of course, she had not. Why would he ask?

"No, I had not," Eleanor replied. "Why do you ask?"

"I was just wondering," he said.

His gaze returned to the road for a moment and then quickly glanced in the rearview mirror to catch her uneasy expression. She turned away and so did he. The only sound was the purring of the engine.

After a moment of silence, Eleanor said, "I read that Mr. Bevin is supportive of reestablishing Britishness in the world. I suppose that has implications in your work?" she queried.

Patrick dodged the question. "Not really. The Foreign Service is very large and involved in many things."

"The world is changing, Patrick." Eleanor emphasized "Patrick" to make her point. "Women were finally given the opportunity to step up into men's jobs during the war, and we showed we were equally capable."

Patrick said nothing and kept his eyes on the road.

"My father was a wonderful man," Eleanor said. "Kind, caring, and very patient, but my mother had the intellectual capacity to do great things. The tragedy was that it was not just my mother that was held back but our entire family. Because she was a woman, she was expected to stay home, leaving my father as the sole source of support. He worked hard, for which I am eternally grateful, but my mother had the abilities to become someone. That affected me so that we did not have the means for a full education and a fulfilling life. Many families are trapped in this dilemma. I am trying to change that," she said.

"Those are quite revolutionary ideas, Eleanor," Patrick finally said.

"They are not revolutionary, Patrick," she retorted. "They are revelatory. They are the facts."

Patrick went silent again. He was feeling quite uneasy because of his entitled background and position in life, but he did not show it. He thought Eleanor was a force to be reckoned with.

Meanwhile, in the back seat, Eleanor's thoughts were playing with her emotions. She had just told off a man in an important position from a privileged background how the unfairness had played out. He could easily turn any faint hope she had of becoming an ornithologist into a roadblock. Perspiration beaded on her head.

"Patrick," she finally said, "I apologize for my outburst, and if I offended you, that was not my intention."

Patrick looked in the rearview mirror and smiled.

"Not at all," he said. "You've given me something to think about."

He glanced once more in the rearview mirror to catch Eleanor's reaction and then turned his gaze back to the road in front of him.

Night had fallen by the time they arrived at Eleanor's cottage. She thanked Patrick and Peter for taking her to Minsmere and making the day special for her. She shook Peter's hand and then Patrick's, who fixed his grey eyes onto her. She turned away, and he let go of her hand. The cool of the night air rushed in as she opened the door.

"If you want to go bird-watching again, let me know," Peter called as the car backed out of Eleanor's lane. "You know where I live. Ring me up anytime."

She waved as the car drove off and then noticed a silhouetted figure over the hedge at a window in Mrs. Quimby's house. The following day, Eleanor pulled her typewriter onto the table, inserted a piece of paper, and began to type a letter to Gerald.

```
Eleanor J. Hutchinson, Robinsong
Cottage, Deacon's Lane, Rabbit's
Burrough, Herts.

June 20, 1947

Dear Gerald,

I so appreciate your letters. They have
been immensely useful and supportive.
I do hope you do not find my personal
needs too taxing. To assure you of your
time being well spent, I will relay the
successful visit to the RSPB.
```

By strange coincidence, I got an invitation to attend a garden party by Peter Saunders. You might know him. Peter is part of a group who are tasked with managing the RSPB's new nature reserve at Minsmere. The reserve was acquired recently as a plan to bring the avocet back in the UK. The coincidence was that Mr. Saunders lives in the same village as me and invited me to travel to Minsmere the day after his garden party. His good friend Patrick, who works for the Foreign Office, drives a very nice car and agreed to take all three of us to Minsmere. We got there about midday, which gave me enough time to see the reserve, learn about the plans for its management, and identify some new birds under Peter's careful eye. The time down and back allowed me to learn about the RSPB and get to know Peter and Patrick, but most importantly, I got to see another career option in ornithology.

Because of your advice, I am now versed in the world of taxonomy, field studies, and conservation. Deciding on which career path to follow is one reason I am writing you. If I can be so frank, your letters describe the adventurous

life I yearn for, but as I mentioned to
you before, I have neither the education
nor qualifications to even be accepted
to an interview. I also feel very much
out of place among many of the men who
run these organizations. Overcoming this
fear is something I need to do, but it
is not easy. I can deal with my own
anxieties but would very much appreciate
advice on how to overcome the shortfall
in qualifications. Your advice would be
gratefully accepted.

Sincerely,

Eleanor Hutchinson

Eleanor spent the rest of the evening writing her library
correspondence. The next day she posted her letters in the
postbox on her way to the library.

CHAPTER 8:

Passage to Guayaquil

Eleanor was having a tea break at the library on a warm afternoon. She smiled at her many new adventures, although the residue of the encounter with Patrick still lingered. She sought solace from butterflies in her stomach arising from the memories of her outburst with Patrick by allowing her mind to drift to her time with Christopher, their chance meeting at the museum, and his invitation to Oxford. She smiled when she thought about his parents, Lizzie and Anthony, and how she and they fell over each other in feeble attempts to understand class distinctions. She imagined how all this came about because of the courage she mustered to write to the museum and to correspond with Gerald. He was non-judgemental and always encouraging, never condescending, and seemed to time his letters just when she needed them most.

She loaned out Josef Conrad's *Heart of Darkness* and that evening was carried away into the adventurous world of a tramp ship en route to South America from Asia amid pirates, intellectuals, scoundrels, and millionaires. Her life seemed very humdrum in comparison, but in her imagination and the safety of her cottage, she could travel the world.

The next day, Eleanor pulled out a world atlas to trace a likely route Gerald would be taking. She also researched how long the trip would take and thought that he should have arrived in Ecuador the previous week. She smiled in anticipation of a letter. She then searched the library shelves, where she found Robert Murphy Cushman's *Oceanic Birds of South America* and W. B. Alexanders' *Birds of the Ocean*. Seabirds were exotic and romantic. She had read Coleridge's *Rime of the Ancient Mariner*, Stevenson's *Treasure Island*, and Melville's *Moby Dick*, and as she read, Eleanor's imagination carried her onboard the ship. She imagined standing at the railing with Gerald, watching noddies, albatrosses, shearwaters, petrels, and a host of other birds wheel around the ship. She could feel and smell the fresh air biting at her face, but she was warm in her parka and exhilarated with time with him. Whitecaps spread as far as the eye could see, and out of what seemed like nowhere, an albatross appeared on balsa-thin wings. Tiny petrels dipped and alighted on the water as if the ocean was a garden pond. Near the South American shore, the tropical air brought frigate birds that alighted in the rigging or glided effortlessly in the slip-stream of the ship. She put down the book and realized she was still in the UK. As if Gerald was listening to her thoughts, his fourth letter arrived a few days later.

Gerald Benson, c/o British
Museum (Natural History), South
Kensington, London.

July 15, 1947

Guayaquil, Ecuador

Dear Eleanor:

I arrived a few days ago in Guayaquil
on the Pacific coast of Ecuador. The
crossing took many days, which gave me
time to catch up on my correspondence
and collecting. I got the specimens
from Hawaii off in the post before I
departed, and so now my sights are set
on the Amazon River and perhaps the
Galapagos. To be honest, I found the
time at sea a mixed blessing. I felt
quite nauseous from the motion of the
ship and ate only sporadically, but as
the days passed, I started to get my
sea legs, as the crew calls them. These
nimble seamen scurry about on deck in

all kinds of weather. I did manage on
several occasions to get on to the deck
where I could watch the seabirds. For
much of the journey, we were occasionally visited by an albatross that came
and went out of nowhere. I spent much
of my time below decks in my quarters
because of sea sickness, but as time
passed and I started to feel a little
better, I was able to make it to the
galley for regular meals and to get to
know some of the crew and passengers.

I learned that our ship had been char-
tered to arrive in South America. Tramp
steamers, like the one I found myself
on, can carry unusual cargo and passengers. Among the passengers was Diego
from Panama, who was an elegant man
about forty years of age wearing a tailored suit and sun-hat of fine plant
fibres. He had a well-kept beard and
wore dark sunglasses. He was in international trade. He had come to Asia
in search of new markets of some sort
or other.

Then there was Doctor Bedard, who had
served in the Pacific war as a medic.
He was a quiet man often lost in his

thoughts, and he spent a great deal of time just staring out to sea. I wondered privately if he was naturally reserved or if the horrors he had seen haunted him.

A Mr. Bellwright was the opposite of Dr. Bedard and kept me entertained with stories of his escapades during his travels in Southeast Asia. I was never entirely clear what he did there and that might be for the better. He was travelling with Mrs. Bellwright, although neither wore a wedding ring.

My greatest pleasure was meeting a Mr. James Barrett, who shared an interest in natural history. He is a Cambridge man who enjoyed an itinerant life where he could watch birds that fancied him. James spent a year in the islands around Malaysia in search of the Chinese crested tern. The last sighting was in 1938, and there are fears it might now be extinct. I would have liked to have got a specimen before it was gone, but I might have been too late. James joined the ship to South America in hopes of finding something that will fill his need for adventure. I never found out

how he funded his travels. The captain
and crew were a mix of races, all male
and hard working.

Whether we were in calm or stormy seas,
they kept the ship on course for our
destination. I wished I could have been
allowed time to hear their stories, but
if they weren't in the wheel house, on
deck, or in the engine room, they were
asleep in their berths. I would see them
come and go in the galley during meals,
but there was no time for idle chatter.

As I mentioned, albatrosses accompanied
us for much of the voyage. I saw several
whales too, blowing far away, and as
we approached the South American continent, we came upon very large flocks
of guanay shags. The same species made
famous the Guano Islands off Peru and
Chile as sources of now greatly depleted
supplies of fertilizer. The source of
the guano is of course the shags that
are drawn to vast schools of fish that
assemble off the coast due to favourable
ocean currents along the South American
shores. The ocean currents apparently
nurture plankton for great abundances
of fish that in turn attract the shags.

The current is named after a nineteenth-century naturalist, Alexander Humboldt, who, among other things, explored the Andes.

My simple accommodations in Guayaquil provide for all my needs. Meals are available twice a day, and I am free to roam the city and surrounding area. I am near the equator where the days can be very warm. The museum wants me to go the Galapagos. The Americans have an air base there, which I might work out of. The museum also wants specimens from the Andes and the Amazon, so I am going to have my work cut out for me.

I also received your letter dated June 20th. I am delighted to hear that your visit to the RSPB was a success. I do not know Peter or Patrick, but from what I read, the encounter was very fruitful.

You asked for my advice on what to do given your qualifications for a position in ornithology. The required qualifications will differ between museum work like I do (and which you seem most interested in), an ornithologist in academia, and a post at the RSPB. All three

of these positions will require a strong
background in ornithology, and I suggest
you keep your options open. You already
have met Christopher at the BMNH and
Peter at the RSPB, so now focus on the
academics. Have you attended a British
Ornithologists' Union meeting? The club
meets regularly, often in London. I am
not sure if you have to be a member, but
in any case, I would think they would
change the rules if you showed up in
person. Be prepared for some discus-
sions going over your head and don't be
deterred. From your letters, I think you
can give as much as you get!

Best wishes,

Gerald

Eleanor smiled as she read the letter. Her research had
prepared her to know more of where his travels took him,
what he saw while he was there, and even what experiences he had had.

She felt as if she had been with him all along, despite
being half a world away.

Gerald's urging to attend the British Ornithologists'
Union meeting quickly quashed the good feelings she had
about his journey. She knew she had to attend a meeting
for the reasons he gave, but she was full of dread and

misgivings. The meetings would be mostly comprised of men, and intellectuals at that. Mingling among such a crowd would intimidate most people, and especially a young woman with limited education, meagre knowledge about birds, even less knowledge about the recent advances in ornithology. *Gerald is right*, she thought, and the next day, Eleanor looked up the date and location of the next meeting in London. She had made up her mind to attend.

CHAPTER 9:
The Ornithologists

At the library, Eleanor began to research the British Ornithologists' Union. She learned that the BOU, as it was known in ornithological circles, published a journal called *Ibis* for all topics in ornithology. The library had a subscription and Eleanor spent hours perusing its pages. She smiled when she read how the venerable society was established in 1858 and had a long history as a venue for ornithologists to meet and discuss current topics about birds. She had got to know names of the famous ornithologists from reading the *Ibis*. Their meetings were where they might expect criticism and discussion, and that worried Eleanor. The opportunity to meet leaders in the field and to share ideas with like minds made the meetings both combative and collaborative. Young Eleanor was seeking the latter.

Eleanor arrived at a hotel in South Kensington where the meeting was to be held. She gazed at the facade and large front doors. The hotel was more upscale than anything Eleanor had experienced before, which only heightened her anxiety. The hotel's frontdesk staff directed her to the meeting room, where a short queue of gentlemen was waiting their turn. *Most are nattily dressed*, she thought, *and their conversations are either earnest, jovial, or sombre.* She joined the queue to wait her turn. She heard a distant rumble of voices from the crowd of people in attendance.

"Your name, please," a voice said as Eleanor reached the table. A very efficient woman seated behind the table was staring up at her with a pencil in her right hand and her index finger on the left, ready to run down the list of members. Eleanor noticed a name tag sporting her name,

"Mrs. S. Knott."

"Eleanor Hutchinson," replied Eleanor.

"I don't see your name here. Are you a member?" she asked.

"No," said Eleanor. "I just want to hear some of the lectures."

"Well, that is not allowed by the rules," the woman said forcefully. "You have to be a member or be invited by a valid member. I presume neither of which applies to you. You can become a member over there." She pointed to a table with another woman sitting by herself.

Eleanor glanced in the direction to her left and thought Mrs. Knott was well suited for her job as keeper of the membership.

"Thank you, ma'am," Eleanor said as she moved to the membership table.

"Do you wish to take out a membership, Miss?" enquired the woman behind the table.

"What does that entail?" Eleanor enquired.

"You will need to be nominated by a member and pay an annual fee of one pound, plus a guinea for a subscription to the *Bulletin*," she said.

"I do not have a nominator, and the membership fee would be quite a hardship for me," Eleanor said. "I was hoping I could just sit in the lectures to decide if I wanted to join."

"I am sorry, Miss, but these are the rules. I cannot change them," said the woman.

"She will be my guest," came a voice from behind Eleanor.

She turned around to see an older man, quite slim with a mane of hair and a bushy moustache, standing behind her.

"But sir," Eleanor said, "that is very generous."

He replied, "The club charges a fee to pay for its expenses and not to exclude anyone. Shirley here is just enforcing the rule." He nodded toward Mrs. Knott, who gave a forced smile.

Shirley Knott? How could her parents be so cruel? Eleanor thought.

"What is your interest in birds Miss . . . ?" He paused to signal he wanted her to tell him her name.

"Hutchinson. Eleanor Hutchinson, sir."

"Please add Eleanor Hutchinson to the list of guests," he said to the membership clerk.

"How is it you are interested in birds?" he asked Eleanor.

"Each morning, I am serenaded by a robin outside my window. He is so familiar that I gave him a name," she said.

"And what is that name?" he prodded.

"Thales," Eleanor replied.

"Ah, *nosce te ipsum*. Know thyself. What an interesting choice of a name for a bird," he said.

"You know your Greek philosophy."

He was puzzled that her East London accent did not align with the university training she seemed to impart.

"I work as a librarian at the British Library where I have plenty of books to read," she said as she smiled.

"Ah," he replied. "How pleasantly unusual a creature you are, Miss Hutchinson. Now, let me tell you what is about to happen in there." He pointed to the meeting room. "After some introductions, various ornithologists will get up to speak about some of their discoveries from around the world. They will be describing some new species, perhaps, and suggesting a change of taxonomy for others. You might find that part quite tedious. There will also be a few talks about other subjects that might be more appealing. From my years of experience, the young men will try to impress the senior members. They will lob easy questions so as not to embarrass the senior members. It is all a bit of a charade. The keynote is by Professor Brown from the Edward Grey Institute about his new ideas on clutch size in birds."

Eleanor spoke up. "I attended one of his lectures at Oxford a while ago."

The older man was surprised. "You are well on your way then," he said. "Now, run along and find a seat. The place is filling up fast. I will take care of everything here."

Eleanor smiled, thanked him, and slid past the table to reach the meeting room entrance. She noticed out of her eye that Mrs. Knott glance her way, unsmiling.

The meeting room was a standard hotel space with large columns down one side, a line of chairs in rows, and a lectern at the far end. A screen stood behind the lectern where illuminated slides could be projected. The room was already filling up when Eleanor entered. The audience was mostly men interspersed with a few women, and most had taken their seats and were in deep conversations about birds with unpronounceable names and arcane topics that Eleanor could not follow. Others were standing around the outside of the chairs, also lost in deep conversations. *I've never seen so many ornithologists in one place at one time*, she thought.

There were plenty of young men around Eleanor's age, mostly dressed in tweed jackets with leather elbow patches. From their demeanour, they were sons of wealthy and established families, likely from Cambridge or Oxford. They were clustered in a loose group along the right-hand side of the room. A few had noticed Eleanor enter the room and not so subtly encouraged their mates to look her way. She decided to take a seat at the end of a row on the left side of the room where they could not gawk at her.

The meeting also attracted many amateur and professional men and a few women from afar. Two young men from museums in America and Canada, a gentleman from the Bombay Natural History Society, a representative of the Australian Ornithological Union, and many Europeans gave the meeting an international flavour. A common interest in birds had brought them together, and they would leave with a better appreciation of each other.

The room filled up quickly, and she noticed the elderly gentleman who had generously taken her on as his guest enter the room, look around from right to left, and then spot her. He smiled and went the other way, acknowledging colleagues as he went. She wondered who he was. He hadn't offered his name, but he was clearly a man of influence from the response of the crowd in the room.

The meeting began and proceeded pretty much the way the elderly man had said it would. At first, Eleanor was intrigued by the talks from ornithologists who had discovered or rediscovered species from Africa, Asia, and South America. Her mind briefly went to Gerald; *he would have been right at home in this crowd*, she thought. These were his people, as it were, and Eleanor was hoping to follow in his footsteps. But after many speakers had droned on about their findings, she began to feel out of her league.

Mercifully, a tea break was called, which she used to stretch her legs and give her weary backside a rest. The clamour grew to a roar as the ornithologists embarked on conversations between themselves. A few of the men assembled around the morning speakers shook hands or held fierce debates. *Colleagues are not always friends*, she realized.

A luncheon was served buffet style in an adjacent room where Eleanor stood like a wall flower against a wall. She was not terribly social, especially in a room full of anonymous men. A few young men passing her by smiled and glanced over their shoulders before engaging in a schoolboy chatter. She rolled her eyes.

In the afternoon, the anticipated lecture by David Brown began. Professor Brown was a tall man with red hair and a receding hairline. He had been a nature enthusiast long before getting a post at Oxford. He had also become a supporter of studying birds in the wild, which intrigued Eleanor. They shared humble beginnings, which he never lost sight of. He gave her hope.

Professor Brown spoke about a new idea on why birds lay a certain clutch size. Most species, he pointed out, laid a few eggs while others laid many eggs in their clutches. One reason being proposed was that the size of the clutch was determined by the parent's ability to feed the nestlings. It was a fresh idea and got Eleanor thinking. It clearly also made some of the young men think too. Just as the elderly man had said, a young chap from Cambridge raised his hand to ask a question.

"Clutch size varies between nests of the same species," he began. "Clutch size also varies with season. How do you explain these observations?"

The answer was obvious to Eleanor, and she smiled as she recalled the elderly man telling her about the charade. Professor Brown replied that some parents were better provisioners than others, thereby explaining the difference between individuals of the same species, and that food supplies presumably diminished over time, thereby explaining the seasonal effect.

Eleanor had a question and gingerly raised her hand. The moderator took several questions from men in the crowd, and Eleanor was getting exasperated that she was being ignored. Her arm began to ache, and she switched arms but to no avail. The moderator called out that the question period was over and there would commence a tea break.

Eleanor was peeved that she had been ignored and sprang to her feet. She belted out in a loud voice, "I have a question!" The room fell silent. The young men looked her way. Some giggled and held their heads low so as not to be seen. All around her was the gaze of the world's foremost ornithologists. There were more university degrees in that room than she had ever met. Suddenly, she got very nervous about what she had done. A clammy feeling ran up her back, and her stomach turned. She thought she would vomit and swallowed hard.

The moderator broke the silence. "This is uncalled for, Miss!" he roared. "You will have to ask Professor Brown your question at the tea break, if he cares to do so."

Professor Brown interrupted the moderator. "That will not be necessary. Please, what is your question?"

In her East London accent, Eleanor began to speak. "Thank you, Professor Brown, and I apologize for my outburst. Wouldn't a simple test of your idea be to experimentally add eggs to a normal clutch to see if the parents were capable of raising all the young?" She sat down and glanced at the young men whose eyes were glued to her. They had stunned looks on their faces.

Who is that woman? they wondered.

"That is a very good question, Miss. I hope to do just that in the next breeding season."

He turned from the stage with the moderator while mumbling something unintelligible to him. Eleanor rose to go to the room with the tea. There were mumblings all around her. Few acknowledged her, and those that did wore stiff silent smiles. The young men were all in a twitter. None would break the ice and introduce themselves. She felt very much alone and thought that once again she had over stepped her position. *The young men know how far they can go, but not me*, she thought.

Eleanor approached the table with the tea. The others had joined in, but none were going to acknowledge her. She reached for a tea cup when a hand touched her forearm.

"Well done, Miss Hutchinson," came the voice.

She turned to see the elderly man who admitted her as a guest. He was gone as fast as he had arrived. She cracked a small smile, poured her tea, and found a wall where she could drink in peace.

After finishing her tea, she quietly placed the cup back on the table and slipped out of the room silently and alone. Mrs. Knott saw her go but said nothing. Eleanor walked quickly through the hotel lobby and into the rain falling on the street. She was finally free of the social life of a group of people she hoped to join professionally but thought that she would never socially pass muster. *No matter how hard I work or how passionate I am for this line of work, I will never break through the social barrier*, she lamented.

All the way home, she dealt with the uneasy feeling that she would have to resign herself to a librarian job. On the train, she imagined twenty years in the future and she was still at the library, perhaps now in charge of a section but having done nothing much in her life. She needed someone to talk with. *I will write Gerald*, she thought.

By the time the bus stopped in Rabbit's Burrough, twilight was fading to darkness. The pub was alive with laughter. *The ale is flowing tonight*, she thought. She could make out Mrs. Quimby chatting with Jack, the postman, as she walked by. The lane was dark, and the crumbling macadam was slick from the recent rain.

Eleanor turned onto the path that led to her front door, fumbled to find the keys, and was soon back in the comfort of her own place. She flicked on a light switch and tossed her coat and bag over the sofa before walking into the kitchen. She lifted the kettle off the stove, filled it with fresh water, and clicked on the blue flame on the stove. She then sat down on a chair and began to weep.

It seemed that all her hopes and dreams were not going to come to pass. She had met some wonderful people – Christopher, Peter and Patrick, and the anonymous elderly man today – but she was not from their social class. She knew things were changing in Britain; women were getting jobs and moving up in the ranks. Cambridge had just hired Dorothy Garrod, she recalled – their first woman professor. But Eleanor felt her humble beginnings had become her albatross.

Following a dinner of canned peas, spam, and leftover mashed potatoes, Eleanor took a second cup of tea into the drawing room. She turned on the single bulb lamp-stand that cast a warm cosy glow through its sepia-stained lamp-shade across the room to a log burner whose crackling fire provided warmth, light, and sounds. From the sofa, she could see her typewriter. She looked away and then back at the typewriter. *It is calling me*, she thought. Gerald, who had helped her navigate this far, might just be her ticket to solving her insecurities. She pulled out the typewriter, thought for a moment, and then began to type. She couldn't find the words for the first sentence. Her emotions were running high, and after a few tries, she thought it best to wait a few days until she was on an even keel with her thoughts and feelings.

Gerald had mentioned he was planning to visit the Galapagos, so Eleanor set to work as she had done before to research the islands and learn more about what he was experiencing. She thought it a good distraction from the emotional events at the meeting of the British Ornithologists' Union.

She opened the world atlas to the Galapagos Islands. She saw the islands strewn across the equator about six hundred miles from the South American continent. A story in the London Times informed her that a former US air base had just closed, and the islands' two thousand residents were having to find new ways to make a living. She then opened Darwin's account of his visit to the islands in *The Voyage of the Beagle*. She closed her eyes to dream of striding across the barren islands in search of flightless cormorants, Galapagos hawks, mockingbirds, and Galapagos finches. In the London Times, she read that Ecuador had joined UNESCO the previous year, which she thought would have pleased Peter.

The islands seemed distant and bizarre enough to have arisen from Edward Lear's imagination. Who else would conger up a place with tame animals, flightless birds, giant dragonlike iguanas, and strudellike lava islands?

That evening, at home alone in her cottage, Eleanor felt refreshed and sufficiently calm to write that letter to Gerald. She confidently set the typewriter on the table, wound in a sheet of paper, took a sip of tea, and began to type.

```
Eleanor J. Hutchinson, Robinsong
Cottage, Deacon's Lane, Rabbit's
Burrough, Herts.

September 15, 1947

Dear Gerald,

I receive each of your letters with
great anticipation. I so much enjoy
```

reading about your adventures, the birds you see, and the people you meet. Summer is coming to an end here, and the birds are on the move once again.

I took your advice to attend the British Ornithologists' Union meeting earlier this month. There, I met many fine gentlemen who shared a passion for the taxonomy of birds. Admittedly, I was a little overwhelmed at the level of detail these men (and women) had of their subjects.

Of particular interest was Professor Brown's talk on clutch size in birds. Have you heard what he is proposing? He has been recording the clutch size of birds in Wytham Woods, which I was able to visit with Christopher last spring. Professor Brown believes that the number of eggs in a clutch is determined by the number of young the parents can raise. His proposal is a novel idea that generated many questions. A reason I am telling you all this is that I made a bit of fool of myself by demand-ing time for a question. I overstepped my position, especially as a guest at the meeting, in demanding to be heard.

If you saw the reaction of the audience, you would understand my dilemma.
Professor Brown was kind enough to take
my question. I asked if he had experimentally enlarged any of the clutches to
see if the parents could not raise them
all, as he proposed. He thought my idea
was a good one, and he was preparing
to do just that. My worry is that I am
developing a reputation that might not
bode well in the ornithological circles.
I am beginning to wonder if a career as
an ornithologist might not be possible,
regardless of my aching desire to join
the ranks.

Well, that is enough about me. I look
forward to hearing about your latest
adventures in the Galapagos. I have been
reading about them at the library, and
they sound quite surreal. I am quite
envious of you, Gerald, and some day
hope to be able to have similar adventures. Until then, I will imagine your
world through your delightful letters.

Sincerely,

Eleanor Hutchinson

Eleanor read the letter once more, smiled and sealed it in a letter addressed to Gerald c/o the British Museum (Natural History). She sat back in her chair and began to imagine his response. What would he say about her personal trials and tribulations? Was she asking too much of someone she had never met? Her mind drifted to the Galapagos, the tortoises and tame birds, and the few grainy black and white pictures in books. She wondered about his trip from Guayaquil and the landing at Puerto Ayora on Santa Cruz Island. She was inspired after reading about the Norwegian Borghild Kristine Rorud, who lived in tent near Puerto Ayora to follow her passion of collecting botanical specimens for the Norwegian Museum, two of which were new to science. She felt a pang of insecurity that if a Norwegian teacher had enough compunction to travel to the Galapagos to live in a tent, surely Eleanor could do the same. The next day, Eleanor posted her letters on her way to the library. She wondered how long a letter would take to reach him and then for him to reply. A month? A month and a half?

Eleanor kept to her routine of working during the day, writing correspondence in the evening, and posting letters the following morning on the way to the library. A month had passed, and posting letters reminded her that it was about time for a letter from Gerald. A few days later, when Eleanor arrived at her cottage, a letter from Gerald lay in her letter box.

R. W. Butler

Gerald Benson, c/o British
Museum (Natural History), South
Kensington, London.

October 20, 1947

Dear Eleanor:

Your letter arrived a few days before
I returned to Guayaquil after a week
in the Galapagos. My visit was quite
short - I had hoped to visit several
islands, but that was not a simple
task. I managed to find a small ship
in Guayaquil that would take me to
Indefatigable, or what the locals call
Santa Cruz Island. The ship was providing supplies for the thousand or so
islanders that live there. After the
US air base closed on South Seymour,
the islanders found a source of income
and a regular supply of fresh food from
the mainland gone. The captain - an
Ecuadorian named Francisco - informed me
that the voyage would take about five
days, when he would unload his supplies
at Port Ayora and immediately return to
Guayaquil. He said that he would return
in about a week's time with new supplies, whereupon I could get a return

trip to Guayaquil. I agreed, and we set
off straight out into the Pacific.

Our arrival was met with great anticipation by the residents in Puerto Ayora.
Fresh supplies from the mainland were
in short supply, and many of the townspeople arrived at the dock to watch
the unloading. True to his word, after
refilling his water supplies, the
captain set sail the same day and was
soon out of sight. The economic downturn
turned out to be a godsend for me. Two
young men with little to do were more
than keen to help collect specimens.

Puerto Ayora overlooks a small bay on
the south shore of Santa Cruz. Simple
buildings run along a main road from
the wharf where we tied up to unload our
goods. Many of the Galapagos Islands are
very dry, with exposed lava and little
water, the locals informed me, unlike
the lush vegetation growing on Santa
Cruz. There are palms and grasslands
and, most importantly, fresh water to
supply the town. The weather is warm, so
I brought a tent along, which served as
my accommodation while searching around
the island. Several species of birds

were added to my collection, including
some Galapagos finches, a small dark
heron that resided on the beach, several
swallow-tailed gulls, a large brown
pelican, and a dove with a ruddy-brown
head and breast, a lovely blue colour
encircling the eye, and scarlet legs. I
think it is in the genus Zenaida. A few
seagoing iguanas were so tame I easily
secured a few specimens.

I was especially pleased to make the
acquaintance of the mockingbird given
its historical importance in Mr.
Darwin's formulation of the theory
of evolution through natural selection. Each island has its own race of
mockingbird, according to Mr. Darwin,
that differ slightly in measurements.
I can now see why he did not realize
these differences or their significance
until after his voyage. I would have
liked to have had more time to visit
the other islands in the archipelago.
There are reports of a flightless shag
on Narborough, which the locals refer
to as San Fernandina Island, and a
resident penguin. One could spend a
lifetime exploring the oddities of these
islands, but after about two weeks had

lapsed, Captain Francisco's ship entered the harbour. I assembled my collections while my two companions packed my tent and clothing, and carried it to the dock. I paid them for their services while the captain finished unloading his supplies and re-watered the ship, and by late afternoon, I bade farewell to the Galapagos. The return voyage took seven days due to some windy weather, but I arrived safely in Guayaquil to find your welcome letter.

I sense that between your words of concern, there still burns a passion to become an ornithologist. I feel the same passion and, to be honest, also sometimes question my choices. My suggestion is that you put the BOU meeting behind you for now. What is bothering you will dissipate in the minds of many who were there as they get on with their lives. In the meantime, I suggest you continue to learn your birds and meet fellow ornithologists who you might accompany into the field on an expedition. Experience travelling is an essential part of much of ornithology, whether collecting specimens or conducting field work.

My plan is to travel to Quito in the
high country where I will make excursions into the Andes. From maps I have
seen, I could access the high country
with a few days' journey from the city.
Alexander Humboldt apparently travelled
there over a century ago, so I will try
to follow in his footsteps.

Please continue to write and keep
me informed with your progress. The
museum, Royal Mail, and diplomatic services are very efficient in exchanging
our correspondence.

Sincerely,

Gerald Benson

Eleanor smiled with some satisfaction. Like all of
Gerald's letters, they arrived just when she needed
them most.

CHAPTER 10:

A Little Mularchy

When Eleanor arrived for work at the library the following day, she was met by her superior, Miss Bradshaw.

"May I speak with you for a moment please, Eleanor?" Miss Bradshaw asked.

"Yes. What seems to be the matter?" asked Eleanor while hanging up her coat.

Miss Bradshaw led her into her office and closed the door.

"Please sit down, Eleanor," she said. "It is nothing to worry about, my dear."

Eleanor was relieved and wondered what Miss Bradshaw had in store.

"I've been watching your progress here at the library, Eleanor," she began, "and have been impressed at your punctuality, efficiency, and studiousness – I am not sure 'studiousness' is the correct word, but what I mean is how you apply yourself to reading such a diversity of subjects."

Eleanor wondered where this all was going. Had Miss Bradshaw learned about her letters to Gerald? She had written them from home on her own time, so she couldn't imagine her having any concern.

"We have been offered a donation of two important titles from a patron in Scotland," began Miss Bradshaw. "The donors are important patrons of the library, and we want the titles they have offered to us for our collection. The library has accepted the donation, but the donors have stipulated that they be picked up by the library rather than depending on the mail service. This is where you come in, Eleanor."

"Me?" questioned Eleanor. "This sounds like a great deal of responsibility for an assistant librarian."

"To the contrary, Eleanor," returned Miss Bradshaw. "You are the perfect person. Besides being very capable and thorough, I understand you have spent time with the Ashfords, so you can navigate among people of, shall I say, the upper classes. Moreover, you are single, so you have no demands from a husband or family. And I understand you like to watch birds. I don't need to tell you that Scotland has plenty of birds. So, what do you say?"

Miss Bradshaw was as competent as Eleanor, was also single, and ran a tight ship. Those were the qualities the library was looking for in a head librarian. Eleanor wondered how Miss Bradshaw knew so much about her private life.

Eleanor protested weakly. "Those are kind words, Miss Bradshaw. I try to do the best job possible. But why wouldn't you go? After all, you too are good at your job and single, and if these donors are important to the library, why would you risk our reputation on a junior librarian?"

Miss Bradshaw quickly answered Eleanor. "I am needed here. So, the task is yours. The library will reimburse you for your travel, of course, but keep the receipts. I estimate the travel and visit will require three days. I will allow up to four days to allow for unexpected complications." Miss Bradshaw then raised her hand to one side of her mouth. "Such as a chance to go bird-watching."

Eleanor could not refuse. Here was her chance to see Scotland, meet some interesting people, and watch birds all on the pound of the library. She already knew the birds she would hope to see. Robins, of course. She wanted to determine the brightness of the red breast of the males ever since reading about the variation in the UK. She had noted the colour of the robins at Minsmere using her watercolours as a means to illustrate the degree of colouration. She was anxious to do the same elsewhere in the UK. Scotland was calling.

"What is it they are donating to the library?" asked Eleanor.

"Two books. A first edition of Fanny Burney's *Evelina, or the History of a Young Lady's Entrance into the World*, and *Persuasion* by Jane Austen, 1817 edition."

Two young women in a social class comedy. How apropos, thought Eleanor.

"The family you will be visiting is the Spratts. Here is their address and telephone," said Miss Bradshaw, handing Eleanor a slip of paper. "You will need to take the train to Edinburgh, where you can then transfer to a train to Inverness. The Spratts will be waiting for you there. Just let them know which train you will be travelling on."

"When are they expecting me?" asked Eleanor.

"Sometime this weekend," said Miss Bradshaw. "One more thing. The Spratts are important donors. I need say no more."

Eleanor rose and stepped out of Miss Bradshaw's office. She could hardly contain her enthusiasm. It might not be Hawaii or the Galapagos, but travelling to Scotland was a thrilling adventure. Or so she thought.

Eleanor could hardly wait until the weekend arrived. She had contacted the Spratts about her expected time of arrival. All she had to do was pack her things and catch the train.

The Flying Scotsman was puffing a head of steam when Eleanor arrived at King's Cross station. The fresh new British racing green paint on the locomotive was a not-so-subtle hint that this train was built for speed. The run to Edinburgh was only eight hours long, where she would get a ringside seat of the English and Scottish countryside.

She boarded the train, selected a seat, and sat down with a mix of uncertain feelings and excitement. Two blasts from the train and the carriage lurched forward. Before long, the train was gaining speed. The countryside so familiar to Eleanor quickly fell out of view, and she found herself gazing out the window. This was a new experience onboard the famous train crossing unfamiliar territory.

The train arrived in Edinburgh early in the evening. She was able to make the connecting train to Inverness, arriving there about ten in the evening. It was now dark, and Eleanor was a little concerned about stepping off the train in Inverness to look for someone she did not know. She thought about Gerald and his travels, which steeled her to what was to come. Mr. Spratt had said his son Bernard would be waiting for her arrival. Nevertheless, she began to think about what to do should he fail to show up.

The worries and fear fell away when she stepped off the train. There on the platform stood a young man nervously searching.

"Eleanor?" he asked sheepishly.

"Yes," she replied.

"My name is Bernard. I will drive you to our home in Mularchy," he said. "The car is just outside the station." He made no eye contact and hesitantly shuffled as if to tell Eleanor to follow him.

She slung the bag over her shoulder.

"May I carry your bag, Miss?" Bernard asked.

She shifted the bag into his waiting hand. She felt his hand graze her hand, and she stared into his face. He was shuffling the bags and still made no eye contact.

Nervously, Bernard started to walk to the car, and Eleanor followed a little behind him. He was not the talkative type, but he was pleasant.

The car was parked in the darkness not far from the station.

"How far do we have to drive, Bernard?" she asked.

"Sixteen minutes. Our home is eight miles from here," he said.

"You are very precise, Bernard," she said. "I like a man who is precise."

Bernard smiled and drove on. In silence.

After several minutes of silence, Eleanor asked Bernard what he did for a living.

Bernard replied. "I live with my parents. I like birds."

"Birds!" exclaimed Eleanor. "So do I. What kinds of birds do you have here, Bernard?" Suddenly Bernard opened up.

"I have records for 213 species at our home," Bernard said. Most of the species are resident passerines, and in spring and summer we get passage migrants. Some of the species, such as the fieldfare and redwing, breed outside the UK and pass through northern Scotland on migration." Bernard talked nonstop about birds for the rest of the way to their home. He never made eye contact, but Eleanor was impressed with his encyclopedic knowledge. By the time they reached the gates, Bernard finally stopped to manoeuvre the car onto the driveway.

"Thank you, Bernard, for telling me about your birds. I would very much like to see any robins you have about your home," said Eleanor.

"There are plenty of robins here, Miss," he said.

"Do you think you could show me some of them?" Eleanor asked.

Nervously, Bernard said he could do that for her.

"I will be here only a day or two," she said. "Let's find some time to go bird-watching, shall we?"

"I'd like that," he said.

The car proceeded down a gravel driveway. At the end of the driveway stood a Tudorstyle house with a large front door. A few lights were on in the upstairs rooms and over the door, which swung open, and an older man stepped out.

"Hello, Mr. Spratt," said Eleanor. "My name is Miss Eleanor Hutchinson from the British Library."

In a strong Scottish brogue, the elderly man said, "You've got the wrong man. I am Brown, the butler. May I help you with your bags, ma'am?"

Eleanor felt her face turn red with embarrassment.

"Thank you, Mr. Brown, but I can carry my own bags," she said.

Brown said nothing and stepped aside.

Bernard said nothing, despite Brown looking right at him for instructions.

"I will show you to your room then," said Brown. "When you come down stairs, the cook will have something for you to eat."

Bernard was already through the front door.

Eleanor was feeling out of place already. She said to Brown as they climbed the stairs, "I am sorry, Mr. Brown, but I am used to carrying my own bags."

Brown said nothing, opened the door to her room, showed her where to place her bags, and departed before he had to converse with Eleanor. She sighed and waited a few minutes for Brown to get out of sight before proceeding down the stairs. Bernard was nowhere to be seen. She looked into the drawing room and the dining room. They were large rooms with heads of stags and crossed swords over a coat of arms. She turned back to the stairs to follow a passageway toward the rear of the house. There was a distant light, and voices drew her toward it. As she stepped into the lit room, she saw Mr. Brown pinching the backside of an older woman, who smacked his hand. Eleanor realized she was in a kitchen where the older woman was attempting to place cheese and crackers on to a plate, if Mr. Brown wasn't so forthright.

"Oh, I am sorry, my lady," Eleanor said. "I was looking for Bernard."

"I ain't no lady, and Mr. Spratt ain't 'ere," she said. "I's the cook and will bring ye some food in the drawin' room shortly." Mr. Brown made a hasty retreat out the back door.

Eleanor turned on her heel and quickly walked back to the drawing room. She thought, *Two faux pas in ten minutes was not so bad. What was it Miss Bradshaw ordered me not to do?*

Eleanor was relieved to find Bernard in the drawing room. "Mother and father are already off to bed. We will see them first thing tomorrow morning." The room went silent.

Just then, Mrs. Brown brought in some food and drinks for Eleanor.

She looked at Eleanor and said, "I 'ope this'll do ya for now, Miss."

"It will be fine. I hope you were not pinched for time," Eleanor quipped.

Mrs. Brown let out a loud laugh but caught herself short with her hand over her mouth. She quickly departed her laughter reverberating down the hallway. Eleanor nibbled some cheese and crackers in silence.

Bernard spoke first and nervously. "I am going to bed. Breakfast is at 7:30 in the dining room," he said and hastily vanished up the stairs, leaving Eleanor on her own.

She thought Bernard to be a little odd, but he was gentle and seemed nice. She thought that he likely had had few interactions with young women.

CHAPTER 11:

The Party

The following morning Eleanor was awoken by voices downstairs. After cleaning up for a new day, she pulled on her favourite skirt and blouse, brushed her sandy hair, and pinched her cheeks a few times in the mirror before descending the stairs to the dining room. She entered the dining room where Mr. and Mrs. Spratt and Bernard were sitting around a large oak table. Breakfast was on a table to their left, and on the right were very large windows that let in the morning sun.

Mr. Spratt was first to see Eleanor, and he rose with open arms, which was a cue for Mrs. Spratt to do the same. "Come in and welcome, my dear. Don't be shy. I hope Bernard treated you well," said Mr. Spratt while Mrs.

Spratt said, "Oh, what a smartlooking young lady you are, Miss Hutchinson."

Eleanor was flummoxed by the ebullience of the Spratts and the juxtaposition of their non-conversant son, Bernard. "Why, thank you," she said.

"We have a full day ahead for us, Miss Hutchinson," said Mr. Spratt. "You can spend the day with us here. Miss Bradshaw told us you were interested in birds, so Bernard can assist you in that department. This evening, we will have a grand masquerade party to celebrate our donation to the library. The entire town has been invited, and you will be the guest of honour. I hope you will be up for it?" he asked without expecting a reply.

"It's been a long time since we had such a gala," said Mrs. Spratt. "You will be treated to Scottish hospitality."

Mr. Spratt was a small man, about sixty years old, and was trim, likely from a life of nervous energy. His frock of hair erupted in a chaotic bundle matched by an unruly grey beard. He wore a tweed jacket, a checkered red and blue vest, and a tie embroidered with tiny red grouse. Mrs. Spratt wore a floor-length flowing floral kimono that trailed behind her as she breezed across the floor. Her long flowing and greying hair splayed down her back. On her feet were embroidered slippers and on her fingers were three oversized rings. She held out her hand to Eleanor.

"You must be famished," she said. "Bernard, get Miss Hutchinson some tea."

Bernard rose from his seat, still chewing a mouthful of toast, took a teapot from the buffet sideboard, and began to pour a cup of tea from behind Eleanor.

"Thank you, Bernard," Eleanor said. He did not reply and returned to his seat. He finished his breakfast without uttering a word.

Mrs. Spratt began. "Today is going to be hectic in preparation for the gala tonight," she said. "Guests will arrive starting about seven and will continue into the wee hours."

Mr. Spratt interrupted. "You don't need to know the details, Eleanor. In fact, we don't either!"

Both Mr. and Mrs. Spratt laughed.

"Everyone will be tippy before long anyway," he chuckled.

"I will stay out of the way," Eleanor said. "The library is so delighted to be receiving your generous donation."

"The pleasure is ours," Mrs. Spratt replied. "We have no need for the books, which I understand have gained in value, and so we thought we should put them in a safe place where others can read them."

"How kind, Mr. Spratt."

"Dougal, please," Mr. Spratt said. "And Marjorie is my wife's Christian name."

"Is this your first donation, Dougal?" Eleanor asked.

"First donation of books. Marjorie believed that everyone should be entitled to a good education, and so we have also supported schools here in Scotland," he replied.

"I suppose the Spratts know a lot about schooling," quipped Eleanor with an impish grin.

"Oh, did you hear that, Marjorie? Miss Hutchinson here knows of our support for schools," said Dougal.

Eleanor tried to contain her smile.

"Now get some food into that wee body of yours, and we will find something to entertain you. Would you like a tour of the house?"

"That is very kind, but I don't want to get in the way," said Eleanor. "I might just go bird-watching, if you agree."

"Oh, yes," said Mr. Spratt. "What a good idea. Bernard can take you, can't you, Bernard?"

Bernard looked up, a little startled, and nodded.

Shortly after breakfast, Eleanor and Bernard left the house to search for birds in the surrounding grounds. Eleanor had told Bernard she was particularly interested in robins, and Bernard knew exactly where to find them.

"Why are you interested in robins, Miss Hutchinson?" he asked.

"Please call me Eleanor," she said. "Robins' breast colouration is thought to change across the UK. Robins in the southwest around Kent and in Europe are paler than robins farther north. A professor at Oxford thinks the pale ones are winter migrants from Europe that come to the UK after breeding. I have a colour swatch I made to match the colour. Here, I will show you it." She rummaged in her bag and pulled out the orange and red colour swatch she had made at Minsmere.

"This is the colour of robins at Minsmere," she said.

Bernard said, "I think ours are as bright or maybe brighter, but we should check." They spent a while searching out several robins and discussing the brightness of the breast plumage.

"If we go down along the seashore, we might see a few woodcocks, sedge warblers, reed buntings, and black-caps," said Bernard.

Eleanor found Bernard much livelier on his own and in his element, and she marvelled at his knowledge of local birds. They spent the morning looking for more robins and adding a few more new species to Eleanor's growing list. They stopped for a quick lunch in a nearby coastal town before returning to the woodlots and forest edges favoured by robins. After a few hours, Eleanor had grown quite pleased with the number of robins she had seen and especially the number of documented breast plumages she had accumulated. They decided to call it a day and head home for the evening festivities.

"Bernard, what can I expect this evening?" Eleanor asked.

"Oh, it will be a lot of fun. Mother and father will invite a lot of guests. There will be food and lots to drink. The entire town could show up, for all I know. Some of the people will do crazy things."

"Like what?" asked Eleanor feeling both apprehensive and curious.

"It is hard to say because every party is different," replied Bernard. "I generally stay out of the way."

His last sentence made Eleanor a little worried.

As they approached the house, a bevy of activity was underway with vehicles and people buzzing about. A large ivy-covered archway stood just inside the gates with what looked like a naked Roman god at its zenith. Inside the house, there were people coming and going with enormous floral arrangements, costumes and dresses on hangers, and tables and chairs brought in for the occasion. The great hall was full of balloons, and crepe paper twirled into a corkscrew shape hung between the walls. Tables adorned with white linen cloths formed a line along one wall, and a small stage was already in place where musicians were setting up their instruments. Mrs. Spratt was racing about in her flowing kimono, correcting the staff and asking when various items for the party would arrive. Mr. Spratt was nowhere to be seen.

"Oh, Eleanor," called out Mrs. Spratt. "Did Bernard show you some birds?" But before she could answer, Mrs. Spratt said, "Mrs. Brown will have a meal for us at about six o'clock. It will not be anything special, and she will serve it in one of the back rooms away from the activity here. Millie, when did you say the musicians would arrive? James, not over there. Put those flowers on the table." Off she went in a whirl of her floral kimono with her long wavy hair trying to keep up as she strode across the hall. Mrs. Spratt was in full command and had no time for Eleanor.

By six o'clock, Eleanor had found her way to the kitchen, where Mrs. Brown directed her to a side room where she had put out a simple meal.

"These parties are very taxing on you, I imagine, Mrs. Brown," she said.

"Aye, dear, but they are me job, and I quite enjoy the merry making," she replied with a knowing smile. "Not everything that goes on is ever remembered," she said with a wink.

"How does Mr. Brown feel about the parties?" she asked.

"T' be honest, 'e's not much for them, being a strict Presbyterian," Mrs. Brown said. "I told 'im to just let the chips fall where they may, but 'e said it is not God's way." By now, Eleanor was feeling a little uneasy. What did Mrs. Brown mean? She would have to be on her guard?

Mrs. Brown left for the kitchen, and Eleanor helped herself to the food. Soon Dougal arrived by himself. Eleanor noticed he only had a few crackers and cheese on his plate, so she passed him some sliced meat.

"Thank you, Miss Hutchinson, but I can't eat any fat," Dougal said. "Marjorie doesn't eat meat." Suddenly, Mrs. Spratt arrived in a whirlwind of flowing kimono all in a panic. The guests would soon arrive, and she was not dressed. She asked Mrs. Brown to make sure all the food would be ready no later than eight o'clock and disappeared down the hallway.

Eleanor returned to her room, wondering what was in store for that evening. She had come to Scotland simply to pick up two books and found herself immersed in, well, she wasn't quite sure what. She found herself wondering about Gerald somewhere distant in South America and far from this silly world. He was probably hiking in the Andes or canoeing down a tributary of the Amazon, contributing to science and the advancement of humankind. He couldn't advise her, even if she could reach him in the moment. She was on her own this time.

Eleanor had only brought a floral dress and high heels in case she needed them. She wasn't expecting a grand masquerade party in the rural countryside of Scotland. The din from downstairs was growing, so she pulled on her dress, slipped her feet into her heels, took a quick look in the mirror, and with a sigh, swung open the door. Beyond the balustrade, the first guests were arriving. Soon the crowd swelled, and Eleanor stood behind the Spratts as each guest was welcomed. Each guest wore a masquerade costume and had a nonsense name. A man who introduced himself as Mr. Kirk was dressed as a reverend, which seemed an unlikely guest at such a party. There was Mr. Bond who said he was a banker, and the town's two publicans, an ailing Mr. McEwan and the stout Mr. Guinness. A man dressed as a fisherman with rod and creel said his name was Pythagoras. When questioned by Mrs. Spratt that he looked like a fisherman rather than a mathematician, he replied he was not a fisherman but an angler. An upright young man in an army uniform said with a smile that he was Captain Furlough, "On leave," he quipped. A man looking very Russian said he was an author and went by the pen name Warren Peece. One woman sporting a blue rosette in her lapel said she was a conservative politician. Her name was Eileen Wright. A Mr. Webb was dressed up like a giant black spider along with requisite eight legs, and his wife was Madame Butterfly, wings and all. Mr. Webb looked Eleanor over as if she were his intended victim and said, "And prey tell, who might you be, dear?"

Eleanor replied, "I am a librarian," to which Mr. Webb returned, "Oh, now I think of it, you do look like a librarian."

Eleanor replied, "You misunderstand. I *am* a librarian, from the British Library."

Mr. Webb said with a smile, "And I am the King of England," as he whisked Madame Butterfly away.

Also in the line of guests was a nubile young woman named Angela dressed appropriately as an angel with wings, a halo, and a plunging neck line. *She looks more devilish than angelic*, thought Eleanor. A Mademoiselle Dupont arrived wearing a chic ensemble, likely from a Paris couturier. She said she lived in France and was a bridge between nations. She looked the demure Eleanor over from head to toe.

"Did I overhear that you are the librarian, my dear?" Mademoiselle Dupont asked. Eleanor replied that she was, to which Mademoiselle said she too might have a donation to make to the library, but this was not the time or place, before breezing away as if carried on air.

And so the crowd swelled with more and more guests. Among the throng, Eleanor caught the eye of a young man, handsome and confident. He was wearing a sports jacket with a matching vest, trousers, and a white shirt with the collar up to expose a neck tie. A chrysanthe-mum sprouted from his lapel, and a cigarette smouldered between his manicured fingers. He looked dangerous to a single woman. She glanced away. *Where is Gerald when I need him?* she thought.

Inside the hall, the crowd had grown to over one hundred guests of all walks of life. The noise from all the chatter was deafening. Eleanor remained near the back of the hall where she could observe the goings-on. From far away, she heard the faint wail of bagpipes. The sonorous pipes grew closer and closer until the hall rang with the song of the highlands. In paraded two pipers, followed by Mr. and Mrs. Spratt dressed in matching tartan kilts and jackets. He wore knee high socks, she expensive nylons. Where he had a tam, she wore a cap.

The Spratts made their way to the front of the hall, and the two pipers came to a military stop and ceased blowing the pipes.

"Welcome to Mularchy," shouted Mr. Spratt. The crowd let out a roar.

"Tonight, we celebrate the arrival of Miss Eleanor Hutchinson from the British Library," he hailed.

"Oh no. Oh no," said Eleanor.

He waved at Eleanor who shyly waved back with all eyes turned on her.

"Marjorie and I also welcome each and every one of you to Mularchy," he shouted.

Suddenly, from behind a curtain, sprung a nimble young man dressed in a red bodysuit, a cape, and a black mask.

"Sit down, you old fool," yelled the jester while pointing at Mr. Spratt. "No one wants to hear speeches. They want to have fun." He pulled out a bottle of hot Tabasco sauce and took a swig. His eyes lit up, and the crowd roared with laughter. The jester leapt about the room, hiding behind his cape and emerging to try to kiss the young women before making his exit.

Four trumpets from the upper gallery blasted as the huge doors to the hall swung open. Four men in highland dress carried a roast pig into the hall, followed by a team of servers.

"Eat, drink, and be merry," shouted Mr. Spratt, and the crowd descended on the food and drink tables.

Eleanor had not seen anything like it before. Here were people of all walks of life throwing out convention to have fun. It was a far cry from her life at the library, but she wasn't sure she was comfortable with it.

As the crowd devoured the food, a band started to play, and a few of the guests started to form a circle. Some wore kilts or tartan skirts while others were in dress attires and costumes. Eleanor had not seen such an eclectic group of people in one place. The young dandy she had seen entering Mularchy House walked over to her.

"Would you care to dance?" he asked.

"I don't know how to dance, sir," she said.

"I will teach you. No one here cares how well they dance," he said, holding out his hand. "My name is Reginald. It is a pleasure to meet you, Eleanor." He stared into her eyes, and she turned aside his glance.

Reginald led Eleanor into the circle where the Spratts were already standing. They were delighted to see Eleanor join the country dance.

"Just follow what the others do, and you'll soon catch on," said Reginald.

The music started, and the dancers began step dancing in tune to the beat. Eleanor turned the wrong way and stepped on the wrong beat several times but eventually could follow the others. When the music stopped, she thanked Reginald and went straight to the drinks table. She needed to drown her emotions.

The night wore on with nonstop dancing, revelling, eating, and drinking. Everyone was having a great time. Eleanor noticed that Bernard was nowhere to be seen. She took her leave of the hall and, with a drink in her hand, stepped out on a porch overlooking the garden and the grounds beyond. The moon was nearly full, casting a light onto the distant garden. She could hear voices and laughter in various locations. In the dim light, she saw Angela stumbling back toward the house on the arm of a young man, her wings in her hand and her halo discarded in a flower bed.

Suddenly, Reginald appeared behind Eleanor with a start.

"The moon is beautiful tonight, Eleanor," he said.

"Yes, it is," she replied.

"Are you staying the night here at Mularchy?" he asked.

"Yes, the Spratts have kindly provided a room on the second floor for me," she replied.

"Well, I hope I will get to see more of you before long," he said.

Eleanor was feeling quite uncomfortable with Reginald.

"Well, enjoy your evening, Reginald," she said as she turned to leave.

"I hope I do," he said with a grin.

Eleanor just wanted to get away from him. She returned to the house, and when no one was looking, she scaled the stairs to her room. She noticed light glowing under the door of Bernard's room and thought she might knock to see how he was doing but thought the better of it. She needed her rest for the long journey home tomorrow.

She slipped into her room, got into her night clothes, and pulled ajar the tall windows that opened on the dark garden below. The noise of the party was faint from her room as she climbed into bed. She took a deep breath and stared at the ceiling.

Quite some time passed before she heard a faint voice. She thought whoever it was had called her name. She listened intently to be certain she was correct. Then she heard a pebble hit the window next to her room.

"Eleanor. Eleanor," the voice called in whispered tones. It sounded like Reginald.

She rose to see a silhouetted figure on the ground a short distance away. Eleanor hid behind the sheer curtains to try to see who the figure in the shadows was.

"Eleanor. Eleanor. Where are you?" the voice called out. *It's that damned Reginald*, she thought.

Reginald stood on the ground, staring up at the lit window. He could see a silhouetted figure through the curtains. His heart leapt as the figure approached.

"Eleanor. Let me come up to your room," he whispered.

Suddenly, Bernard appeared on the balcony. Reginald had chosen Bernard's room by mistake and quickly melted into the shadows.

In the next room, Eleanor saw the whole escapade. "Thank you, Bernard, thank you," she whispered to herself while closing the window. She giggled as she returned to bed and soon was off to sleep.

CHAPTER 12:

Return to London

The following morning, Eleanor awoke, visited the loo, and was getting dressed when she heard Chopin's Nocturne being played on a piano downstairs. She smiled and went downstairs. The music was coming out of the great hall, which had been the site of a raucous party the night before. She peered into the room and saw Bernard sitting at the piano lost in the music. His fingers moved easily across the keyboard. She stayed back to let him finish and then applauded.

Bernard was startled to see her, so she reassured him how much she appreciated the music.

"Where did you learn to play like that?" she asked.

"I taught myself. I just listen to the music and then play it," Bernard said matter-of-factly.

"That makes it all the more impressive," Eleanor said. "What else can you play?"

"Most music, if I can hear it first," he said.

"You don't read music?" Eleanor said.

"I am starting to learn how to read scores, but I enjoy just playing it," he said.

"You are very talented, Bernard," she said.

"Thank you, Miss Hutchinson," he replied and went back to playing as she turned to walk to the dining room.

Breakfast was served on the sideboard. Porridge, fried eggs, tomatoes and bacon, brown toast, and tea steamed on the sideboard. The thought of fried eggs, tomatoes, and bacon swimming in fat did not appeal to Eleanor on the best of mornings but especially not after the previous night of partying.

Eleanor took a piece of dry toast and a cup of tea.

Mr. and Mrs. Spratt arrived in a more sombre mood than the previous day.

"I hope you enjoyed the party last night, Miss Hutchinson," said Mr. Spratt.

"Yes, thank you and your hospitality too," she said.

"We like to hold these parties for the whole community to build spirit to assist everyone and enjoy their company independent of their position in life," said Mrs. Spratt.

"It will be quite the cleanup for everyone today," said Eleanor.

"Yes," said Mrs. Spratt. "Now, let's see. We need to get you the two books wrapped up and make sure you get to the train in time. You have a long ride back to London. I will see if Bernard is available."

After breakfast, Mr. and Mrs. Spratt led Eleanor into their library. The locked door opened on a floor-to-ceiling set of shelves. Eleanor suddenly felt quite at home.

"I could while away a lot of time in here," she said.

"You are welcome anytime," Mrs. Spratt said while Dougal climbed a ladder to an upper shelf, removed two books, and descended to a table in the middle of the room. He showed the two books to Eleanor and wrapped them in brown paper.

"On behalf of the Spratt family, I would like to present to you the two titles we agreed to," he said.

"On behalf of the British Library, I gratefully accept your generous donation," she replied.

Both smiled.

"Don't take your eyes off these books until you get to the library. You probably know they are worth quite a lot of money, and no one would want to see them go astray," Mr. Spratt said.

"Oh, stop it, Dougal. Miss Hutchinson knows full well how valuable these books are. Now, let's get Bernard to drive you to the station."

Brown had retrieved Eleanor's luggage and placed it in the boot of the car. Bernard was sitting in the driver's seat with the engine running.

"Bon voyage, Miss Hutchinson, and do come again soon," shouted Mrs. Spratt as they pulled away.

As the car neared the station, Eleanor said to Bernard, "I want to thank you for taking me bird-watching and serenading me this morning with your piano playing, Bernard. You have a lot of fine talents."

"Thank you, Miss Hutchinson," he said without making eye contact. "I had fun."

He brought the car to a halt and stepped out to get Eleanor's bags. He passed them to her and said, "Here you go, Miss Hutchinson. I hope you have a safe journey."

She took the bags and pressed a kiss against his cheek. "Thank you for rescuing me from Reginald last night," she said.

Bernard looked puzzled and took a moment before he climbed back into the car and drove off. Eleanor walked to the ticket agent, purchased a through ticket to London, and wrapped her arm around the bag containing the precious books.

A young man dressed in an army uniform walked toward her. She thought she recognized him from the party.

"Hello, Miss Hutchinson, was it?" he said. "You were at Mularchy House last night, were you not?"

"Yes," said Eleanor. "You are?"

"Captain Furlough at your service ma'am," he said, coming to attention.

"I understand you are travelling to London," Furlough said. "I am too and would be happy to accompany you if you are willing."

"Some company would be lovely," she said.

The train steamed up to the station where Eleanor and Furlough got onboard. They found some empty seats and put their bags on the ground before them. The bag with the books she kept close to her side.

"What's in the bag, may I ask?" said Furlough.

"Oh, just some books the Spratt's are donating to the library," she replied. "What brings you to Scotland, and why are you off to London?"

"The Spratts are old friends who invited me to join their party. They have been such kind people over the years. I convalesced with them after taking some shrapnel. London is my home," said Furlough.

"Well, we have a long train ride," said Eleanor. "Plenty of time to get to know each other."

"Indeed," said Furlough.

The train arrived in Edinburgh right on time, and Eleanor and Furlough transferred to the Flying Scotsman for the journey to London. The previous late night was catching up on Eleanor and Furlough. Both struggled to stay awake. Eventually, the movement of the train had its soothing effect, and Furlough slumped into the corner of the carriage. His khaki jacket slumped open, revealing a pistol in a case strapped around his chest and hidden under the jacket. She was shocked and turned away. *Why would he have a hidden pistol?* she wondered.

The same movement that sent Furlough off to sleep jarred him awake as the train nosed into King's Cross station. He quickly regained his composure and looked at Eleanor.

"I must have dozed off. Hopefully not for long," he said glancing down at the bag holding the two books.

"Not for long, Captain Furlough," she said.

"I will walk you to the library since I am going that way, Miss Hutchinson. That is if you don't mind," he said.

"That would be fine," Eleanor returned, and the two strode off in the darkness toward the library. Miss Bradshaw was waiting.

"Welcome to the library, Eleanor. Was your journey enjoyable? I presume you have the two books?"

Eleanor replied that she had an enjoyable time and had the two books in her bag. She turned around to see Furlough striding off down the road.

"Who is the gentleman, Miss Hutchinson?" Miss Bradshaw asked.

"He was at the Spratts' last night and kindly accompanied me to London," she said.

Miss Bradshaw gave an approving smile.

Inside Miss Bradshaw's office, Eleanor finally put down the bag with the two books. She was quite glad to be rid of them.

"Let's take a look shall we," said Miss Bradshaw.

She zipped open the bag, removed the books from their wrappers, and gave Eleanor a big smile.

"You have done very well, Eleanor," she said. "These will be a fine addition to the collection of titles. For your efforts, I will be giving you a day off tomorrow. Go home and enjoy the day," she said.

"Thank you, Miss Bradshaw," said Eleanor. She turned and walked down the steps, feeling quite content with herself, and before long was home in her cottage. She couldn't stop wondering why Captain Furlough was carrying a concealed weapon until sleep and Chopin replaced those thoughts in her head.

A few days rest were all that Eleanor needed to feel rested and ready for work. After the whirlwind trip to Scotland, the great Scottish party at Mularchy, and the unnerving return with Captain Furlough, she had not given Gerald much thought. She had come to realize that, although she had met many new people, several of whom she had got to know quite well, none seemed to know her as well as Gerald, who she had never met. He was her mentor and confidant who had only corresponded through letters. She had imagined how Gerald might look, but he had always remained aloof, buried in her subconscious mind.

Her every minute seemed full, and she felt a little guilty not writing to Gerald. *He is likely somewhere in the Andes*, she thought. He had mentioned Humboldt, and she began to research where Gerald might have tried to trace the famous explorer's footsteps.

Quito, she learned, was over nine-thousand feet above sea level, and the Antisana Volcano, where Humboldt had spent some time, was higher still and in the realm of Andean condor. The condor was the largest flying bird in the world, weighing as much as thirty-three pounds and having a wingspan of nearly eleven feet. Eleanor imagined what it would be like to be with Gerald in Quito, mingling among Spanish-speaking Ecuadorians in the markets and the Andes. *The birds must be astounding*, she thought. Eleanor closed her eyes, and soon she was with Gerald hiking in the Andes. That evening, Eleanor pulled out her typewriter and began to compose a letter to Gerald.

Eleanor J. Hutchinson, Robinsong
Cottage, Deacon's Lane, Rabbit's
Burrough, Herts.

November 23, 1947

Dear Gerald,

I received your letter dated October
20 and delighted in reading about your
time in the Galapagos. By the time you
receive this letter, you will likely
have already been to the Andes. I have
read extensively of where you are travelling so that I can get a good sense of
your travels.

A very fortunate opportunity arose
that I would like to share with you.
To my surprise, the head librarian, a
Miss Bradshaw, requested I travel to
Scotland to courier two books that were
being donated to the library. I took
up the opportunity to see a part of
the UK I had not visited before and to
see some of the birds in that part of
the country.

The donors were the Spratt family, who
were the most entertaining and jovial

couple I have ever met. They put on a
rambunctious party attended by hundreds
of people from near and far. They were
extremely kind to me and provided their
son Bernard to show me the local birds.
He was very well versed in the local
birds, far better than me, and he kindly
showed me several robins around the
estate grounds. I have created a colour
chart of the breast plumage brightness
using my watercolours, which seems to
work quite well. The trip was a bit of
a whirlwind, and I arrived back at the
library safe and sound with the donated
books in tow. Miss Bradshaw was very
pleased. I am following your advice of
visiting other parts of the UK to see
its birds, and the library connection
seems a good way to do so. I am hopeful
that Miss Bradshaw feels the same and
will give me more opportunities.

Sincerely,

Eleanor

Eleanor posted the letter the following morning, and
Gerald's letter arrived not long after.

Gerald Benson, c/o British
Museum (Natural History), South
Kensington, London.

December 7, 1947

Quito, Ecuador

Dear Eleanor:

Your letter arrived just as I returned
to Quito, and so I thought I would
write you a reply before leaving for
the Amazon, where I could be out of
reach for a month or more. I arrived
in Quito where I found a small hotel
that catered to foreign guests. The
city is over nine-thousand feet above
sea level, which allows it to escape
most of the mosquitoes and flies that
thrive at lower elevations, but I found
my breathing quite laboured. Since
Antisana, which is even higher, was my
desired destination, I decided to spend
a few days getting accustomed to the
thin air. The markets were a wonderful
distraction, and are where many native
Ecuadorians sell clothes, toys, and
food. I was able to purchase a jumper

made from alpaca, which proved very welcome at the high altitude.

My intentions were to collect some high-elevation birds, and so I set off on horseback on a fifty-mile journey that took several days riding. Eventually, I arrived at a cabin where the great Alexander Humboldt lived in 1802. The adobe walls and thatched roof were intact. Humboldt, you probably read, arrived at the idea of holistic inter-connectedness of life on Earth during his visit to the Andes.

The weather during our visit was bleak and snowy, despite this time of year being the dry season. I suffered badly from altitude sickness, unlike my Ecuadorian guides and porters. They were able to collect for me a caracara, an ibis with a black face and rufous plumage, a gull that might be new for the museum, a lovely flower piercer, and a lapwing. Their identity will have to wait until my return.

I was pleased to read that you were able to visit Scotland. I was reminded of the highlands while in Antisana where the

grass meadows resembled the heath-lands.
My wish for you is that you continue to
take advantage of travelling so that you
feel comfortable living out of a suitcase or a duffle bag. Such is the life
of the museum collector.

Please continue to write and keep me
informed with your progress. You seem
uncannily well versed in where I am
going and what I am seeing, but I should
expect no less from a librarian! It is
both a tribute to you and the great
British Library.

Sincerely,

Gerald Benson

CHAPTER 13:

Welsh Wild Places

The days came and went for Eleanor with little change to her routine. She had had a taste of travel, and the initial anxiety had been replaced with the thrill of seeing somewhere new. When she was not shelving books and documenting new titles, she was helping prepare a new secure location for the two new books the Spratts had donated. Miss Bradshaw felt it was important that the public be made aware of new additions to the library's titles. Eleanor's confidence in her abilities were growing, in part because of the support from those around her, but also because of her willingness to try. Gerald had played an important part in the remaking of Eleanor, but she still relied on his advice. Her experiences had sailed smoothly, aside from a few social stumbles, but she hadn't faced some realities of life. Until, that is, on a January day while overseeing the construction of a showcase for the two new books, Miss Bradshaw turned to Eleanor to ask her to meet in her office.

"I have something new and exciting to discuss," she said.

Eleanor's curiosity was piqued.

"Please close the door, Eleanor," said Miss Bradshaw as she moved behind her desk and took a seat. "Please sit down, Eleanor. Last year, your visit to the Spratts was highly successful. We got the books, and the Spratts were delighted with your company. They are considering sending more titles our way. But that is not why I asked you to come into my office. What I am about to tell you must swear to the utmost secrecy."

Eleanor was very curious, but she also felt a responsibility she might not want.

"Yes, I will tell no one," said Eleanor.

"Very well," Miss Bradshaw began. "There is another opportunity for an even more important donation to the library. A former employee of the library, a Mr. Gwyn Llewelyn, has offered to donate a book. Not any book but one dating to the late Middle Ages. The book is an illuminated manuscript on vellum enclosed in a gold-and-ivory-studded leather cover."

Eleanor gasped.

"The book is valuable, and so we will need to take some precautions," said Miss Bradshaw. "Are you prepared to undertake this mission, Eleanor?"

"If you think I am the right person, then yes, I am prepared to help," she said.

"Good," said Miss Bradshaw. "I will articulate the exact plans in a few days as the pieces fall into place, but for now this is what you will need to do. You will travel to Mr. Llewelyn's house in the Brecon Beacons of Wales where he will give you the book. I have spoken with Mr. Llewelyn, and he has offered you accommodations at his house since he does not live near town. I know Mr. Llewelyn, and you should feel right at home there. I would never put you in any danger, Eleanor. You will return immediately to the library, where you will hand over the manuscript. A special box and bag will be given to you for the transport. You will require three days: two days of travel and a day to visit Mr. Llewelyn. It is imperative that you not linger. I cannot over emphasize the importance of getting the manuscript back here. Do you understand?"

"Yes, I understand Miss Bradshaw," said Eleanor. "One question. Is it wise to be travelling by train with such an important book?"

"There are no worries about travelling to Mr. Llewelyn's house. On your return journey, there will be someone who will accompany you on the train to London. I am making plans now."

"And when should I plan to go to Wales?" she asked.

Miss Bradshaw replied, "In a few days' time. There are some details that I need to attend to first. I would prefer that your departure be as discrete as possible. I will inform you when you are to leave. You should have your bag packed at home, ready at a moment's notice."

"I am looking forward to the adventure, Miss Bradshaw," said Eleanor.

"I hope it is not an adventure. The quicker and quieter, the better," replied Miss Bradshaw.

"Yes ma'am," said Eleanor as she rose and turned to leave the room.

"Eleanor," said Miss Bradshaw. "Thank you."

Eleanor smiled and left the office. She couldn't stop thinking about what was in store for her in the next few days. *Who would have thought life as a librarian could be as exciting?* Eleanor pondered. *Gerald's life might be like this. If so, I want more of it.*

A few days later, Eleanor was on the train from London to Cardiff. She felt a mix of excitement, yearning to see the important manuscript and to be part of the legacy of bringing it to the library. She also felt uncertainty about her ability to carry it off, but there was no turning back now.

The train ride took several hours to reach Cardiff, where she caught a bus to Swansea arriving by midafternoon. At Swansea, she transferred to a bus that would travel north through the Brecon Beacons. She found the bus driver in a coach with the engine running.

"Pardon me, sir," Eleanor said. "Is this the bus to the Brecon Beacons?"

"Yes, it is," he replied. "Are you Miss Hutchinson?"

"Yes, I am," she was pleased to say.

"Very well. I have instructions to drop you off at the lane leading to Mr. Gwyn Llewelyn's house," he replied.

"How far is that?" Eleanor enquired.

"A little more than an hour, depending on how many stops we need to take," he said. "You just find a seat, and I will let you know when we arrive."

She thanked the driver and took a window seat to watch the Welsh countryside pass by.

The day was coming to an end when the driver hailed Eleanor to disembark.

"Just down that lane about a hundred yards you will come to a gate. A track will lead you to Gwyn's house," he said.

"We make this run twice a day, so just be sure to be on the roadside before 9 a.m., and the driver will pick you up," he said.

"Thank you," said Eleanor. "You've been very helpful."

She stepped off the bus onto the roadside and proceeded down the treelined lane toward the gate. The night was closing in, but she could still see the way along the gravel road. She pushed open the gate and began to make her way along the track that was barely visible in the twilight. Great oaks with massive limbs reached overhead. A tawny owl began to call nearby. A rustle in the upper storey of the trees startled Eleanor and she gasped. Against the flickering light, a hundred or more rooks had arrived to roost in the woods. Their raspy calls seemed like an omen of pending doom.

Just as Eleanor was wondering if she had made a big mistake, a light emerged down the track. It was moving toward her, and she soon realized it was a torch held by someone coming her way.

"Mr. Llewelyn?" she shouted.

"Oh, yes," came the reply. "Is that you, Miss Hutchinson?"

"Yes, it is, and I am glad to see you," she said.

"I thought I should come to find you, as it was growing dark," said Gwyn. "I guess the bus was delayed."

Gwyn was now in front of Eleanor, and in the reflective light she could barely glimpse his face. His navy blue gansey and dark corduroy trousers made his outline dissolve into the descending darkness. He was a man about sixty years of age whose sad weary eyes and greying hair and beard were caught briefly in the reflective beam of his torch. Gwyn stood at about five foot two, smelled of bracken and wool, and carried a broken heart stained by the passage of time.

"Perhaps," said Eleanor. "We did make many stops, including mine."

A Border collie was sniffing at Eleanor and craving attention.

"Kip, stop it," said Gwyn, pushing his muzzle away from Eleanor. "We don't get much company here. I will get you some tea. Let me carry your bag."

The cottage where Gwyn had lived since leaving the library stood on the edge of the forest. From the lane, Eleanor could make out a light in one of the windows, and the rising moonlight reflected off the slate roof tiles. Smoke rose from a chimney. Beyond the cottage, in the moonlit night, lay a wide valley and distant mountains. No other sign of human habitation could be seen.

Gwyn pushed open a large oak door that spilled light into the outdoors and across Eleanor's feet. She felt a pang of uncertainty as she stepped through the doorway where

Gwyn stood. She tried to reassure herself by recalling Miss Bradshaw's words that she had known Gwyn well and there was nothing to worry about. There she stood, a young woman with an older man she knew little about in a dark cottage out of earshot of any human. She was relying entirely on Miss Bradshaw's words.

"Let me take your coat," said Gwyn. He had a posh accent, which reminded her of the members of the British Ornithologists' Union meeting.

"Please sit down, and I will get you a cup of tea. The evening meal will be ready before long. Do you eat lamb, Miss Hutchinson?" he said.

"Yes, and please call me Eleanor," she returned.

"You can put your bags in the spare room, if you like," Gwyn said. "It is up the stairs to your left."

Eleanor picked up her bag and climbed the wooden stairs that creaked under foot to push open a dark wooden door. A small light was on in the small room. A simple but comfortable bed was located next to a window concealed by curtains. On the wall hung several small paintings of birds and a black-and-white photo of a young man in an army uniform, and in the closet hung clothes that she presumed belonged to him. She put down her bag and moved closer to the photograph. *I wonder who this is?* she thought. After a quick look in a mirror, Eleanor returned downstairs to a cup of tea. Meanwhile, Gwyn had put on an apron and was fussing in the kitchen.

"You have a peaceful location here, Gwyn," said Eleanor.

"Yes," he called back from the kitchen. "A bit far from things, but that is the way I like it."

"Do you have robins nearby?" asked Eleanor.

"Oh yes. There is one in the back garden that lives in my veg patch and several more along the forest edge. Why the interest in robins?"

"I have one outside my cottage in Rabbit's Burrough," said Eleanor. "I call him Thales, and he greets me each morning."

"Ah," called Gwyn. "Know thyself. That is a curious name for a robin, is it not?"

"I suppose so. I just thought it sounded nice," she said.

Gwyn raised his eyebrows and muttered a small chuckle. *There is more to this young woman than meets the eye*, he thought.

Gwyn entered the living room where Eleanor sat near the fire with Kip asleep at her feet.

"He's accepted you, Eleanor," said Gwyn. "He doesn't take to strangers very quickly. Kip is my early alarm to anyone coming down the track."

Kip looked up from his sleep.

"Aren't you, Kip? You hear everything long before me," said Gwyn.

"I can't imagine you get many visitors down here, do you, Gwyn?" Eleanor commented.

"No," he replied. "Most people turn around at the gate, but a few years ago, there were some birdwatchers looking for flycatchers. Kip stopped them in their track until I gave them permission to search around." Suddenly, Gwyn remembered something. "There was a couple of people just the other day that poked their noses down the track. I didn't recognize them, and they were dressed like city folks."

"Have you had any attempted burglaries, Gwyn?" asked Eleanor.

"No. Kip keeps them at bay if there were, don't you Kip?" he replied. Kip looked at him and wagged his tail. "Oh, that reminds me. I have the manuscript to give you. I don't want that to get burgled. Let me show where it is, and we will take a closer look after dinner."

Eleanor rose from her large chair by the fire and followed Gwyn into a dark-beamed room in the corner of the house with floor-to-ceiling bookshelves. The shelves were overflowing with books. There were English literature titles, histories of Wales and the United Kingdom, European war accounts, atlases of the world, and many more. A table in the middle of the room was piled high with books, and others were lying on the floor. Eleanor gasped at the number of books and their unruly state. She was a librarian used to order.

"This is quite the collection you have, Gwyn," she commented while stepping over a book of Shakespearean plays.

"Pardon the unruly mess," he replied. "It is not becoming of a former librarian." He smiled. "I will dig out the manuscript from its hiding place later, but for now, take a look at my collection. If you see other titles the library might like, let me know. I need to check on the lamb in the oven." Gwyn turned to go out the door.

Eleanor was impressed with the books Gwyn had amassed. She perused the shelves, making a mental note of some of the books that might interest Miss Bradshaw. On one shelf, she saw a framed photo of the same young man in military uniform that hung in her bedroom. Behind the photo was a collection of bird books. She ran her finger past *The Observer's Book of British Birds*, *British Birds and their Haunts*, and a series of ladybird books for young audiences that included *British Birds and Their Nests*, *Pond and River Birds, and Health and Woodland Birds*, but what interested her was how issues of a scientific journal called *British Birds* stopped in 1943. She thought Gwyn's eclectic taste might include birds. After all, he knew about the robins in his back garden. She then looked at the small bird paintings on the wall and realized they were original watercolours. The artist's name of Rhys Llewelyn was written in pencil. She began to wonder if Rhys was the young man in the photograph. *Rhys has to be a relative, perhaps a nephew?* she pondered.

"Dinner is ready, Eleanor!" came Gwyn's voice from downstairs.

"Coming," she shouted while turning from the library toward the creaking stairs and into the dining room.

"You have an impressive collection of books, Gwyn," Eleanor said.

"I acquired quite a few while working at the library, and then when I moved out here in '43, I started to buy more to entertain myself during long winter nights," he replied.

The dinner of lamb and vegetables was just what Eleanor needed. She hadn't eaten much since leaving London, partly because of the shortage of time and partly from her anxiety about going to Wales, which she had never been to before, to find an old man living alone down some unmarked track and stay the night in his house. Gwyn and Kip had put any fears to rest, and she tucked into the meal.

"I got the lamb from a local farmer and grew most of my own veg," he said. "Between gardening, reading, and hiking the moors with Kip, I have enough to keep my mind occupied."

Eleanor asked, "You live in a quiet out-of-the-way place, Gwyn, and although it is idyllic, do you not get lonely?"

"It is a lonely existence, but I have my reasons to seek solitude," he said.

Eleanor did not push for more answers and instead began to wonder about the story she had been told that Gwyn had left the library on his own accord. She wondered if he had been let go for something he had done. It had only been a few years ago, and he was still relatively young. Suddenly, it dawned on her that she might have been his replacement.

"When did you say you left the library, Gwyn?" Eleanor asked.

"Why is that important?" he replied.

"I just wondered because I have been there since 1944, about the time you left," she said.

Gwyn smiled and said, "You were probably my replacement." He chuckled. "We have more in common than I thought."

Eleanor thought that Gwyn seemed genuinely pleased, but he did not answer her question about why he had left the library.

After dinner, Eleanor helped Gwyn tidy up the dishes. They then retreated to the drawing room.

"I would like to offer you a nice drink," said Gwyn, "but with all this rationing, getting anything to warm your insides is near impossible. All I have is a little Scotch I keep for special occasions. Would you like a taste?"

"Please, but make it a small one," she said.

They both sat by the fire sipping Scotch. The warmth of the fire was a tonic to the eerie solitude.

"Let me not keep you in any more suspense," said Gwyn. "You've come all this way to see the mediaeval manuscript I have upstairs. Come along."

He walked into the library, drew closed the window curtains, and began to pull away a panel in the wall. He then removed a small box. Eleanor was surprised at the smallness of the box. Gwyn proceeded to open the lid, and with a pair of cloth gloves, he lifted a tiny pocket Gospel from its box. He placed it on the table and ever-so-carefully opened the book. The Latin text was written on vellum and illustrated with brightly coloured images. Eleanor was mesmerized. She had never seen anything so beautiful or so old or so tiny.

"How old is it, Gwyn?"

"I am not sure. Perhaps late Middle Ages," he replied.

"What a gem of a book," she said. "I don't know if I can take the responsibility to get it to London."

"Don't worry, Eleanor," said Gwyn. "No one gets up here, and someone will meet you at Swansea to assist you."

"Would you mind turning a few more pages?" Eleanor asked. "This is a once-in-a-lifetime experience for me."

Gwyn proceeded to gingerly open a few pages. The cursive text was exquisitely uniform. The illustrations were as bright as if they had just been painted.

"What was this book's purpose, Gwyn?" she asked.

"These pocket Gospels were meant to be carried just like a pocket bird guide today," said Gwyn.

"Both for heavenly beings," quipped Eleanor.

"You could say so," chuckled Gwyn.

"I would love to see more of it, but that can wait for when it is safely in the library in London," said Eleanor. "Let's put it away for safe keeping."

At that, Gwyn wrapped up the book, returned it to its box, and placed it behind the removable wall panel.

They returned to the drawing room to sit in large comfortable chairs where the firelight cast a glow onto their faces.

"Thank you, Gwyn, for showing me that very special book and especially for donating it to the library for all to see," said Eleanor.

"It will be a bit of a relief," said Gwyn. "I didn't get to see it much hidden away in the wall, and so I thought it best to find it a new home."

Eleanor turned to Gwyn, who was staring at the fire in the fireplace. "How did you come by it, Gwyn?"

"Back in the 1500s under Henry VIII's rule," said Gwyn "the Dissolution of the Monasteries began a purge of Catholicism. Many things, including these pocket Gospels, passed to collectors. I heard about this one when I worked at the library. An elderly woman, who was not much longer for this Earth, contacted me about many things she wanted to pass into safe hands. She had no heirs, was not keen on the government, and wanted me to have it. I couldn't say no. Who knows where it might have ended up. I know her wishes were not to give it to the government, but it is mine now, and I feel the library is its best home."

"Where did she get it from?" asked Eleanor.

"I recall it had been in the family a long time," said Gwyn.

"Have you any idea what it is worth?" asked Eleanor.

"I don't have an exact figure. Someone who specializes in these books would have to appraise it, but I would expect it would bring a pretty penny," Gwyn said. "There are plenty of people, some who are on the other side of the law, that would probably like to have this in their collection."

"I can assure you the library will have it appraised and notify you," Eleanor said.

Eleanor was becoming enchanted by the wildlands of Wales that had harboured many a scoundrel and fostered a rich tapestry of tales, venerating their past deeds. The land was so wild and hauntingly beautiful that it had become the foundation of Welsh culture. Through the evening, Gwyn captivated Eleanor with tales of the brigand Twm Sion Cati, who purportedly lived in a cave in the Upper Tywi Valley, the Roman invasion followed by the arrival of the Anglo Saxons, and King Arthur, who fought against them. He described the Monastic Rule of David that forbade the use of plough animals, and told her about the ascetic lifestyle of the monks condemned to drink only water and eat only bread and herbs. Illtud, Saint Teilo, and Saint David were among many other monasteries erected as a tribute to their God.

"I think it is time for me to turn in, Eleanor," said Gwyn. "You should have everything you need in your room. I will have breakfast ready at six tomorrow so we have time to watch birds before you leave at nine."

"Thank you, Gwyn, and thank you for your kind hospitality. This has been a special evening I will not soon forget," she said.

CHAPTER 14:

Tragedies of War

B y the time Gwyn had poked the fire and began to turn out the lights, Eleanor had climbed the squeaky stairs to her room. She closed the ill-fitted door as far as she could and turned on a small light near the bed. She got out her night clothes and, noticing that the door was slightly ajar, turned out the light before getting undressed for bed. She heard Gwyn pass by her door on the way to his room next door. Maybe having the door slightly ajar was a good thing so Gwyn might hear her if needed in the middle of the night. She pulled up the duvet and buried her head in a large soft pillow. The moonlight poured into the room, directly onto the photograph of the young man in military dress. He gazed at Eleanor with a smile frozen in time. It made her feel uneasy, so she pulled the curtains to block out the moonlight. Many young men, like whoever this was on her wall, had lost their lives, and she wondered what his story might have been. In the quiet moonlit Welsh countryside, she began to dream of Gerald.

In the early hours of the night, the calling owl went silent. Kip gave out a bark, which startled Eleanor. At first, she did not know where she was until she saw the window overlooking the darkened countryside. Two lights were shining down the track. Kip barked again. Eleanor rose and peered from between the curtains at the two lights. Then darkness once again filled the woods as the lights backed up and drove away. Kip whimpered and flopped down again by the door. Gwyn was undisturbed. She continued to watch for signs of people and wondered what she would do or what they might want. After a few moments, she heard telltale squeaking of the staircase's boards. Eleanor froze in terror. She stared at the door partly ajar. The footsteps ever so softly reached her door. A creaking sound as the door opened was all she could take, and she screamed. In came Kip, who nuzzled her hand.

"Oh, good grief, Kip. You frightened the life out of me."

Kip pulled back his ears and wagged his tail.

"It's fine, Kip, you were just doing your job," she said. He nuzzled her hand with his wet nose and curled up at the foot of her bed.

Downstairs, a light went on.

"Eleanor," called out Gwyn. "Are you alright?"

She rose, pulled her house coat around her, and walked down stairs where Gwyn was sitting on a sofa in the dark.

"Did Kip startle you?" he asked.

"Yes. He came into my room. I shouldn't have screamed."

"That is nothing to be ashamed of, Eleanor," Gwyn said.

"Did I wake you, Gwyn?" she asked.

"No. I don't sleep much these days," he said. "Here, sit down and we can talk for a while."

Gwyn poured her another small Scotch that she sipped ever so carefully, treasuring every drop.

"You asked why I moved to this remote location," said Gwyn, "and I never fully answered your question. The young man in the photograph in your room was my son."

Eleanor noted that he used the past tense.

"Was your son?" she asked.

"Yes," said Gwyn. "He died on DDay on the beaches of Normandy."

"Oh my," replied Eleanor.

"The anniversary is coming up soon," said Gwyn.

"Do you have any other children, and what about your wife?" she enquired.

"Elsie died before the war of natural causes when Rhys was a teenager," he said. "I raised him and was hoping he would go off to university. He was such a talented and bright young man." Tears welled in Gwyn's eyes.

"He loved birds, just like you Eleanor," Gwyn said, briefly turning toward her. "His bird paintings are scattered about the cottage. They are a reminder of him that I see every day."

Eleanor said, "So many young men lost their lives that day. I can hardly imagine what it must have been like."

"That is why I do not sleep well," said Gwyn. "I keep imagining what it must have been like for Rhys the few minutes before he died. I can see in my mind the landing craft pushing through the surf, full of nervous men, their bellies feeling nauseous and their bowels rumbling. Many knew that few were going to survive this day and prayed they would be spared. I can see the landing craft hit the beaches and the door drop to the sand. Ahead of the men, in the stench of fear on their breath, lay a stretch of sand over which lay bodies of dead and moaning men. The rat-a-tat-tat of German machine guns filled the air with screams and whizzing bullets. Men were scrambling to wade ashore past floating corpses. Those ahead ran for their lives, many falling as they went. Many were crying in fear. A few went crazy and charged up the beach roaring as they went only to be mowed down by the guns. My son, my only son, dear Rhys, had never seen anyone die before, and now beside him a bullet pierced the skull of a companion who fell instantly face down in the sand. I can see him lugging his kit and rifle ashore when a bullet hit. At first it seared him like a hot iron. He felt the blood trickle down his neck. He reached up to touch the blood that was pouring out. He faltered to his knees, and before he could say 'I love you, Dad,' he slumped into the sand. The sounds around him – the screaming men, the whiz-zing bullets, the death, the loss of life – were replaced by a peaceful sensation as life drained out of him into the sand to be washed away in the incoming tide. His body lay there for hours and days. Each tide lifted his corpse higher on the beach. A battle raged on the high ground above the beach. More soldiers poured ashore to die. Each young man gave his life to a cause they never fully understood."

Gwyn paused, took a sip of Scotch, and continued.

"When I got the news that Rhys was dead, my reason for living died too," he said. "My wife was gone, now my only son. I have no heirs, no one to leave my life's work to. No one to care about me in my old age." He paused once more.

"I also gave up on God," he went on. "How could a caring omnipotent God be so cruel to me who has lived an exemplary life? Why would he let others who live such terrible lives survive and have my dear son slaughtered on a foreign beach where I could not at least let him die in my arms?"

Tears were pouring down Gwyn's cheeks.

"That was why I left the library. I had to get away from people and immerse myself in nature. That is where we belong, not in some imaginary kingdom in the clouds. So, with an inheritance from my parents, I searched for a remote place close to nature and found this cottage.

"And that is why I am donating the pocket Gospel to the library," he continued. "I have no need for it, and I have no interest in religion. I have replaced Bibles for books of nature. Tomorrow, when the sun is shining, you will see why this is place is better than any heaven imaginable."

Eleanor sat in silence. She was lost for words. Her parents were gone, and she had needed to find a way to survive, but her plight paled in comparison to Gwyn's. She reached over to take his hand.

"Gwyn," she began. "I don't know what to say."

"I got a little carried away there," he apologized.

"You had to say it, and I am honoured to have been the one you chose to tell," she said. "I will not share this moment with anyone."

"We should get back to bed," said Gwyn. "The morning will soon be upon us, and if we want to see some birds before you catch the bus, we will need some rest." They returned to their respective rooms where Eleanor fell off to sleep.

The following morning, as Gwyn forecasted, began in bright sunshine. Eleanor could hear Gwyn downstairs preparing breakfast. She got dressed and flung open the curtains to let the light in and reveal a verdant green valley dotted with woodlots and moorland. An ochre sandstone hill cut a sharp horizon line against the blue of the sky and over which she could see a bird soaring. Outside a robin sang. She sighed a breath of Welsh country air and turned to descend the stairs.

"Good morning, Eleanor," called Gwyn in a cheery voice. "I hope you slept well" – he paused – "after my diatribe."

"You were very touching, and I was very moved by what you said. I now have a better idea why people sometimes feel they need to get away," she replied. Gwyn proceeded to plate her breakfast, and both sat together to eat.

"Gwyn," Eleanor began, "have you any plans for what you will do with your cottage when the day comes?"

Gwyn smiled. "Why? Are you interested in it?"

"That is not what I had in mind," said Eleanor, feeling a little embarrassed. "I would not be that bold. What I wondered was . . . Last night, you said you had given up on religion and turned to nature. If nature is so important to you, I thought you might consider giving your land to a conservation group. A few months ago, I travelled to Minsmere, where the RSPB has acquired a new reserve to save avocets and wetland birds. They might be interested in your land. You did tell me birdwatchers come here to see pied flycatchers."

"The RSPB?" queried Gwyn.

"The Royal Society for the Protection of Birds," returned Eleanor, "but there are other organizations too that might be interested."

"I had not thought that far ahead," said Gwyn. "I have been spending my waking hours mourning the loss of Rhys."

"Conserving the land for the birds Rhys so loved would be a legacy that would be a lovely tribute," said Eleanor.

"I will have to mull that over," replied Gwyn. "Let's get outside while you have time to see some birds."

Eleanor and Gwyn slung their binoculars around their necks and stepped through a back door into the sunshine.

"Those hills are known as the Elenydd, and they stretch as far as mid-Wales. On days like today, I often pack a lunch and trek up the slopes into the moorlands above. There are small lakes and bogs, and the view is stunning," said Gwyn. "Rhys loved to get up there in the clear air away from everyone. I suppose he inherited that from me."

"From my room, I could see a bird soaring over the hills," said Eleanor. "What do you suppose it was, Gwyn?"

"Most likely a red kite. It is a bird of the moorland and farmland. I have also seen peregrine falcons and occasionally a merlin," said Gwyn. "In the Arthurian legend, the Esplumoir Merlin has been described as a high place like this, perhaps with a cave, so maybe this is it," he jested. "Sometimes when I am up there, I think I hear Rhys's voice overhead, like Perceval hearing Merlin's voice as a shadow of a merlin passed by. Do you hear voices, Eleanor?"

"Yes," she confided but then checked herself. "Doesn't everyone?"

Gwyn led Eleanor passed his vegetable patch where she caught sight of a robin. She pulled out her colour chart to note the breast plumage intensity.

"This is the intensity range of colours I have seen around the UK," Eleanor said as she showed him her colour palette. "I use watercolours to match breast colour."

"You are both a scientist, artist, and bibliophile," said an astonished Gwyn.

He then led Eleanor along the forest's edge, where she documented the colour intensity of several more robin breasts.

"We'd better get back to the cottage so you can catch your bus," said Gwyn.

Eleanor felt a pang of regret. Regret that she had to leave the beautiful Welsh valley. Regret that she had to leave Gwyn in his sorrows. And regret that she could not spend more time watching birds and hiking the Elenydd.

At the cottage, Gwyn led Eleanor into the library, where he opened the wall panel, removed the pocket Gospel, and placed it into a tiny box. Eleanor thanked him again as she put it into a bag marked "British Library."

"I will inform you when I get your precious little book to the library," she said.

"Please do, and you are welcome to visit any time," Gwyn said. "I will not be so morose next time. You have cheered me up immensely. Here is a small token of my appreciation. Don't open it until you get home."

She placed the small package wrapped in paper into her luggage.

"The pleasure has been all mine," said Eleanor.

"I will walk you up to the gate," said Gwyn. "The bus will stop for you where the lane meets the road."

He swung open the front door. Kip slipped past him and trotted up the track toward the gate. Gwyn opened the gate to allow her to pass.

"Have a safe journey, Eleanor," Gwyn said.

"Thank you for all your kindness and hospitality. I hope your joy in the world returns soon," she said as she touched his arm.

Gwyn smiled and turned along the track toward his cottage with Kip running ahead.

CHAPTER 15:

Close Encounters

Eleanor looked up the lane. She recalled seeing car lights there the night before. Ahead, out of the shadows cast by tall trees and shrubs, was the main road where the bus was to arrive in about fifteen minutes. She made her way up the lane, her mind swimming with all the sadness of the previous night and the joy of the morning, sparring for her emotions.

When she arrived at the main road, there was no sign of a bus that was supposed to arrive from the north. She then looked south where a green car stood and where two men were smoking cigarettes with their backs to her. They were too far away for Eleanor to hear what they were discussing or to recognize their faces. One of the men noticed Eleanor and gestured to the other man, who turned to see her. They stamped out their cigarettes and got into their car.

Eleanor could feel that something was not quite right. Gwyn was out of earshot and too far away to run to for safety. She thought that it might all be a coincidence, and the men might just drive past. She looked quickly around, trying to decide what to do next, when she heard a car engine approaching. The morning air was cool, which sent a chill down her back. She felt her breakfast rumbling in her stomach. She glanced back at the green car slowly approaching when she heard another car coming from the north. She saw a black Wembley approaching, and she jumped out in the road to wave it down. The Wembley came to a halt, and Eleanor, in a panicked voice, quickly asked, "Can you *please* take me to the nearest town?"

"Hop in, Miss Hutchinson. It would be my pleasure," came the voice.

"Patrick," she shrieked. "Am I glad to see you."

Patrick drove past the green car where the two men turned their faces so as to not be recognized. Patrick glanced at them out of the corner of his eye.

"What are you doing here?" Eleanor asked.

"Didn't Miss Bradshaw tell you," replied Patrick, "you would be provided an escort to London?"

"She told me the escort would meet me in Swansea, not in the middle of Wales," said Eleanor.

"Change of plans," said Patrick.

"There's more to this than you are telling me, Patrick. Who arranged it, and why did the plan change?" she asked.

"I can't tell you everything, Eleanor," he said "but it was because of Mrs. Quimby."

"Mrs. Quimby? Now I am really confused," said Eleanor. Patrick gave a tiny smile.

"There are people out there who will pay handsomely for rare books like the one you have there," he said gesturing, to her handbag. "These books are treasures of British culture, and no one wants them to be stolen. The black market will go to lengths to get them."

"I understand all of this Patrick. What I need to know is how Mrs. Quimby is connected to this story."

"Mrs. Quimby saw an advertisement in the newspaper classifieds on the day you left. It was written in some sort of code that she realized was an alert to those two fine gentlemen back on the road about your visit."

"So, she called you and you came to my rescue?" said Eleanor facetiously.

"Something like that," said Patrick. "Now, tell me how your visit with Gwyn Llewelyn went."

Eleanor was beginning to see that Mrs. Quimby was much more than a nosy neighbour.

By late afternoon, Patrick and Eleanor arrived at the British Library, where they were greeted by Miss Bradshaw and a policeman.

"Come," Miss Bradshaw said, gesturing for them to enter her office.

"Constable, please wait at the door and let no one in," she said.

Eleanor, Patrick, Mrs. Quimby, Miss Bradshaw, and some library staff were present.

Eleanor was surprised to see Patrick and especially Mrs. Quimby.

"Hello, Mrs. Quimby!" she exclaimed. "What a pleasant surprise." Before she could enquire why Mrs. Quimby was present, Miss Bradshaw spoke.

"Eleanor," she said, taking her British Library bag from Eleanor's shoulder. "Let's see what Mr. Llewelyn has provided us."

As Miss Bradshaw removed a small box from the bag, she said, "Oh, this feels very light. Are you sure there is anything in it?"

"It is empty," said Eleanor to the startled Miss Bradshaw.

Miss Bradshaw stood upright, folded her arms, and said in a calm tone, "Would you like to explain yourself, Eleanor?"

Eleanor fumbled into her coat pocket and removed the pocket Gospel to the alarm and surprise of everyone.

"What has got into you Eleanor?" exclaimed Miss Bradshaw. "Do you have any idea how valuable that book is? You could have left it unattended or been pick pocketed."

"I can explain," said Eleanor, and she told the story of the car lights from the night she was at Gwyn's and how she would have encountered some badlooking men if Patrick had not arrived in the nick of time.

"I put the empty box in the library bag for that very reason," Eleanor explained. "If I was robbed, the robbers would get away with a box and not the real book. It was safely in my coat pocket. It is a *pocket* Gospel, after all."

"Brilliant," exclaimed Patrick with a huge grin. "I suppose we can thank God's grace for the outcome."

"I am not so sure about that," said Eleanor. *I at least deserve some credit*, she thought but did not say.

"Well, that is some clever thinking, Eleanor," said Miss Bradshaw, "if not a little unorthodox. Let's see what we have here then, shall we?"

Miss Bradshaw carefully opened the book while the others gathered around. Eleanor stepped aside to watch them stare with wonder at the ancient book before them. The library had gained a precious new title, and she had gained an experience never to be forgot.

After a small ceremony to thank Eleanor, Miss Bradshaw told her to take the rest of the day off. "Patrick will drive you home, and thank you once again, Eleanor."

Eleanor smiled and then turned to leave with Patrick.

In the car, Eleanor confronted Patrick.

"How is it you knew where I was and came to my rescue?"

"Do you mean how did I rescue a fair damsel in distress?" he quipped.

Eleanor got angry.

"I am not a damsel and I was not in distress," she yelled. "Why are you patronizing me!"

"I am sorry, Eleanor," said Patrick. "That was not called for. I have to tell you that your plan to separate the book and box was brilliant."

"Are you going to answer my question, Patrick, or are you going to sit there like a pompous ass?" she demanded.

"I am sorry, Eleanor. Things are not getting off well. Let me answer your question. Miss Bradshaw initially had planned for an escort at Swansea, as you stated, but decided that it would be safer if I picked you up. It's as simple as that," said Patrick.

"It is just as well," Eleanor said, "and I suppose I shouldn't be so harsh on you who just saved me from those two thugs in Wales." She thought to herself that maybe she was a damsel in distress, but she would never give Patrick the pleasure of thinking he was correct.

Eleanor continued, "I saw car lights in the lane outside Gwyn's last night that gave me the willies. That's when I devised the plan to separate the box and book."

Patrick let out a loud laugh. "Those lights were my car. I was just checking that no one was sneaking around Gwyn's hoping to rob him of the book in the middle of the night."

"Why didn't you tell me?" asked Eleanor. "I could have got a good night's sleep."

"I couldn't come knocking at your door at one in the morning just to say the coast was clear, now, could I?" Patrick said.

"Yes, that is true I suppose," said Eleanor. "How did you know I was in Wales?"

"Miss Bradshaw came to me when she decided to change plans. She knew we knew each other, and I had a car I was willing to provide," said Patrick.

Patrick and Eleanor reached Rabbit's Burrough by early evening. She stepped out of the car, reached into the back seat for her bags, and turned to Patrick.

"Would you like to come in before driving home?" Eleanor asked.

"No, thank you. I told Peter I would drop by," replied Patrick.

"Well, thank you again for all you have done, and I am sorry about what I said," she said.

"We are all tired, Eleanor. The pleasure has been all mine," said Patrick.

"Give my regards to Peter then," said Eleanor.

"Will do," said Patrick as he backed his Wembley out of the lane.

Eleanor opened the door to her cottage, picked up her mail, and set down her bags and coat. She thought that the past few days had been full of adventure, and although the near catastrophe with the would-be robbers had been unnerving, the end result was like something out of an Agatha Christie novel.

Eleanor made herself a cup of tea and looked into the fridge to decide what she might have for dinner when she remembered Gwyn had given her a small parcel. She returned to the drawing room where she had left her bags and pulled out the small parcel. It was wrapped in brown paper and tied with a cotton string. She tugged the knot loose and opened the paper. Inside was a tiny framed painting of a robin. She sighed and smiled when she saw it, and then she looked in the lower right corner. The artist's name written in pencil was Rhys Llewelyn.

CHAPTER 16:

Invitation from Kalmia

While thumbing through her mail, Eleanor remembered Gerald's letter about travelling to the Amazon where he would be out of reach for a month or more. Enough time had elapsed that she expected to hear from him soon. In the library, she began to research where he might go. From Quito, a road wound east, crossing the Andes before plunging into the Amazon basin. This was the likely route Gerald would take. Once he reached the eastern side of the Andes, he would reach a major tributary several hours later. In an atlas, Eleanor read that the Napo River was a major river he would likely reach.

Eleanor J. Hutchinson, Robinsong
Cottage, Rabbit's Burrough, Herts.

R. W. Butler

April 4, 1948

Dear Gerald,

The library requested I go to Wales to
pick up a late Middle Age pocket Gospel
that a Mr. Gwyn Llewelyn had donated.
I took up the chance to see Wales and
its birds.

Mr. Llewelyn is a very fine fellow
who lives in a cottage on the edge of
the Brecon Beacons north of Swansea.
He overlooks a wide valley that was
full of birds. The area is quite well
known for its pied flycatchers, of
which I was fortunate to see a recent
migrant. Mr. Llewelyn said April was
when they returned, so that was a fortunate sighting.

He has a piece of land that should be
conserved. I recommended he enquire
about it with the RSPB or other nature
organizations. I also saw a red kite
that was a new species for my list, now
at nearly a hundred species.

I am feeling much better at interacting
with people from all walks of life and

in my skills as a budding ornithologist.
Your advice and encouragement have made
all the difference. I am hoping that
someday I will have a job at the museum
similar to you but have doubts I will
meet the standard.

A project I began at my cottage that
continued on my travels is the colour
matching of breast plumage of the robin.
I might have mentioned in a previous
letter that robin breast colour differs
across the UK with the palest being
in the southwest and brightest north
of Hertfordshire. I have made a colour
swatch of the different breast plumage
colours of robins I encountered on my
travels, and I was considering writing
a paper for the British Ornithologists
Union journal, the "Ibis." I have never
written a scientific paper before, and I
am not certain about how to get started.
Perhaps you could share some advice? In
the meantime, I wish you well and that
your Amazon travels were productive.

Sincerely,

Eleanor

Eleanor put aside the envelope with the letter to Gerald to read her correspondence, most of which was addressed to the library. One envelope caught her attention because it was addressed to her cottage in Rabbit's Burrough. The writing was cursive and bold. The letter inside was from a Kalmia Rosenblum in Cumbria.

```
Kalmia Rosenblum, Lake View Cottage,
Brooksmere, Cumbria.

Dear Miss Hutchinson

I hope you will pardon my intrusion in
your life with this letter. I have heard
many good things about you and your
exciting life from your landlady, Mrs.
Quimby. Although we have never met, from
what Mrs. Quimby has told me, we share
the same zest for life. I am residing
in a cottage in the Lake District, which
is full of birds. My regular treks into
the mountains often result in seeing
unusual species. I would be delighted if
you might consider spending a few days
here where we can enjoy the mountains
together. If you like trekking, there
are plenty of places to see. I am free
most days, and if you are willing to pay
a visit, all you need do is ring me up.
```

With best wishes,

Kalmia

What an odd letter, Eleanor thought. *Someone out of the blue is inviting me to her cottage for some mountain trekking. She seems to know Mrs. Quimby, so that gives her legitimacy, but how does Mrs. Quimby know her?*

Later in the day, Eleanor saw Mrs. Quimby going down the lane, and she confirmed that Kalmia and her parents were among her friends. She encouraged Eleanor to take up Kalmia's offer. Mrs. Quimby provided Eleanor with a telephone number, and the visit was arranged to coincide with Eleanor's days off from the library in June. In the interim, she would carry on with her correspondence.

By early May, Eleanor thought she should have heard from Gerald. She had continued her correspondence with the library patrons by typing or handwriting letters in the evening and posting them the following morning on her way to the library when one day a letter from Gerald arrived not unexpectedly. She seemed to have an uncanny ability to predict when Gerald's letters would arrive and what to expect he would write. He had become such a familiar travelling companion in her mind as she moved about the country on library business. She could call on him whenever she needed support.

Gerald Benson, c/o British Museum (Natural History), South Kensington, London.

May 7, 1948

Quito, Ecuador

Dear Eleanor:

I have been remiss in writing to you,
partly because of my absence in the
Amazon and partly from an illness I con-
tracted while there. The illness seems
to have passed and I am on the mend.

The trip to the Amazon has changed my
mind. The diverse life forms boggle the
mind. From birds to insects, mammals,
and plants, the number of species overwhelmed me. I took the bus from Quito
across the Andes, where we stopped for
one evening in the misty forests on the
mountain slopes. I hope to return some
day to those forests because I suspect
there are many species new to science
living there.

I was able to find a few villagers
living along the Napo River to canoe me
downstream where we lived in the jungle
for several days. A highlight was the
morning hooting of howler monkeys and
the sight of brightly coloured macaws.

My guides showed me where scores of
colourful parrots gathered along a river
bank. Near our camp, I found a hoatzin
nest with two adults in attendance. They
look like colourful turkeys with feather
plumes on their crowns. There are hooks
on the inner wing of their chicks to aid
in climbing about in trees. I suspect
there is more living things here than
in any comparable place in the world.
This is nothing new. So many explor-
ers and naturalists before me have been
overwhelmed by the abundance of life. I
was able to collect many new specimens,
which should pay for my travels once I
get them to the museum.

We encountered some of the native
people, who were puzzled about our
appearance and purpose. My guides reassured them that I meant no harm, and
they left us on our own.

In the forest along a wet area, we
encountered an anaconda measuring over
eight feet that my guides said was
a small individual. I was initially
alarmed by its presence, but the snake
seemed uninterested and quite docile.

I am not certain where I will be travelling next. I might possibly stay here in
Ecuador. I have a large number of specimens that need to be packed up and sent
on to the museum, so you can continue to
write to me here, if you so wish.

To answer your queries about your abilities, from what you have told me, your
experiences have gone exceptionally
well. I would suggest you continue to
take opportunities to show your versa-
tility. You might consider a trip abroad
to show your skill at international
travel, especially in a nonEnglish
speaking country.

For the scientific paper, I can only
suggest you look at similar papers and
match the style. Avoid flowery language
- most editors want the facts and not
the frills. The procedure involves you
sending three copies of the manuscript
to the editor, who will read it and, if
deemed suitable, send it to a few peers
knowledgeable in the field to comment.
Their comments will weigh heavily on the
editor's decision to publish it or not.
Papers that are of interest but have

some flaws are sent to the authors to correct and resubmit.

Sometimes the reviewers can be vicious or unobjective, so be prepared, but many offer good insight that improve the paper. In this case, the editor will ask you to make the changes and resubmit, whereupon he might accept it or send it out for another go around. If a paper is unacceptable, you will be told. Some people find paper writing daunting and intimidating, but generally those that persevere succeed.

I wish you all the best in your paper writing, and I want to be the first to congratulate you when the paper is in print.

Sincerely,

Gerald Benson

CHAPTER 17:

The Heroes of Cumbria

Eleanor knew from the book requests how the public longed for heroic stories. *Perhaps it is their banal lives*, she thought, *that makes them yearn for more adventure than they are willing to pursue.* She also knew that the origin of these stories was sometimes based on real events that the teller then elaborated on and embellished. The storyteller was not the only culprit in this fabrication; often storytellers were encouraged by their audience, who sought some gratification from hearing how the story was told. Events became stories and stories legends that came to define a people, a village, or nationhood. It was when legends based on untruths became rallying calls for destruction that stories were most dangerous. Eleanor was particularly empathetic to quixotic comedies that exposed

the sadness of inadequacy. How a seemingly inconse-
quential event could take on legendary proportions was
what Eleanor was about to discover.

It was early June when Eleanor stepped off the train at
Lake Windemere to a waving Kalmia Rosenblum further
along the platform. Eleanor was carrying her small travelling suitcase and a duffle bag filled with what she hoped
would be suitable trekking clothes.

"Eleanor!" called Kalmia as she strode along the platform toward her.

"I knew it was you by the binoculars," she said with a
wide grin.

Eleanor glanced down at the binoculars hanging
around her neck.

"I've heard so much about you from Mrs. Quimby. It is
a pleasure to meet you in the flesh," said Kalmia.

"The pleasure is all mine," returned Eleanor.

"Let me help you with your bags," said Kalmia. "The
car is just on the other side of the station."

Kalmia was in her early twenties and about the same
age as Eleanor. She wore russet-coloured trousers and a
blue blouse beneath a jumper of naturally dyed colours.
Her wavy hair was dark and hung close to her shoulders, framing her tanned face out of which pierced blue
eyes that matched her blouse. Eleanor noted how both
Kalmia's matching colours and her tailored clothing stood
out among country people milling about the platform.
Eleanor was wearing a beige trench coat cinched tight at
her slim waist. She wore her floral dress beneath and kept

her sandy hair in place with a barrette. She hoped to get out of the dress and into trousers as soon as possible.

Outside the train station was Kalmia's Morris Ten. She opened the boot, put the bags in, and told Eleanor to hop in. Kalmia fired up the engine, and they drove off down the road in a cloud of blue smoke.

"We've got so much to discuss that I don't even know where to begin," said Kalmia. "First, I need to pick up a few things at the grocer, and then we have about a half-hour drive to Lake View Cottage."

"May I help with anything?" asked Eleanor.

"Thank you, but no. I will just be a few minutes," said Kalmia, stepping out of the car.

The town of Brooksmere was quaint with a few customers walking the street. The green grocer was located on the ground floor of a two-storey building. True to her word, Kalmia returned to the car in a few minutes with a bag of vegetables.

"For tonight's dinner," she said, holding out the bag. "I hope you like lamb."

"Yes, I do," Eleanor said as the car sped off down the road.

For nearly half an hour, Kalmia manoeuvred the Morris Ten along country roads.

"You are fortunate to be able to drive a car, Kalmia," said Eleanor, "with all the rationing."

"I seldom drive and only for essentials, such as replenishing my food stocks and picking you up." Kalmia returned. "I am so glad you came. I want to show you what I am creating in the cottage and then spend a few days trekking the hills, if you are up for it."

"That sounds wonderful," said Eleanor, unsure what it all entailed. "I have to admit, Kalmia, I am not well versed in trekking, so I am relying on you as my teacher."

"You will love it," Kalmia replied.

After about half an hour had passed, Kalmia turned off the main road to bump along a lane toward a cottage that looked across a valley to a distant lake.

"Welcome to Lake View Cottage," said Kalmia.

"How lovely, Kalmia," replied Eleanor. "This is your home?"

"Yes," she said, "along with a dog and the birds."

Small windows pierced whitewashed walls supporting a slate roof with overhanging eaves, which resembled an oversized rain hat. Leading to the cottage was a flagstone walk through flower beds of chamomile, St. John's wort, yarrow, blackeyed Susans, burdock, and madder.

"What a lovely bed of flowers you have, and what an unusual assortment," said Eleanor. "What is that plant, Kalmia?"

"That is weld or dyer's rocket," said Kalmia before pointing to a cluster of yellow flowers on tall stems. "Do you know this one?"

"No," said Eleanor. "What is it?"

"Woad is its common name or Asp of Jerusalem," said Kalmia.

"Are these medicinal plants?" asked Eleanor.

"Oh, maybe," said Kalmia. "I grow them for their dyes."

"Dyes?" asked Eleanor.

"Yes. Did I not tell you I was a weaver?"

"No, you didn't," said Eleanor. "I would love to see what you do."

"I will show you," said Kalmia.

They walked to the cottage where Kalmia let her Border collie Ozzie out the door. He greeted Eleanor with a wet nose before Kalmia could call him off. Kalmia then veered around the side where a shed with a wood stove stood. Next to the stove was a large pot stained a deep purple from years of use, and hanging around the shed were clusters of dried plants. An aroma of dried hay filled Eleanor's nostrils. An alchemy of bottles marked with alum, Glauber's salt, vinegar, washing soda, cream of Tartar, and other mordants and dye assistants stood on upper shelves. Eleanor thought she could have just stepped into a witch's lair except for Kalmia's youthful enthusiasm.

"I dye my own wool here and then spin it into skeins for knitting or weaving," she said. "Come inside and I will show you."

The inside of Kalmia's cottage was not unlike other cottages of that era with a low ceiling held in place with dark beams, small windows penetrating stone walls, a fireplace with a log burner centrally located, and furnished with well-used furniture. The air was warm from an Aga stove in the kitchen. What was different was the dyed wool hung to dry on clotheslines across the living room. More wool, but this time dried, lay in baskets waiting to be spun, and even more wool – dyed, dried, spun, and wound into skeins – filled shelves in a side room that also served as a studio. In the centre of the room stood a Jack loom with a colourful warp ready for weaving. All about the room were stacks of blankets and scarves, all made with natural dyes and woven by Kalmia. In the living room, beneath the strings of drying wool, were two chairs piled high with knitted sweaters, gloves, hats, and socks. Eleanor also found a sofa where she decided to sit.

"You have quite the cottage industry going here, Kalmia," Eleanor said.

"Oh, sorry for the clutter," she replied. "I will be shipping most of this out to towns around the Lakes in a few weeks. Can I get you some tea?"

The evening was warm, and so Kalmia suggested she and Eleanor eat dinner outside. She set up a table and brought two kitchen chairs out into the garden. "Do you use wool from Beatrix Potter's sheep?" asked Eleanor.

"The fibres are too coarse to take well to dying, but the fleece is made for surviving in the Lakes' mountains. The Herdwick breed she saved from extirpation is put on the fells around Christmas time, so they have to be hardy and withstand snow and cold," said Kalmia. "We will get up there tomorrow."

After dinner and a warm cup of tea, Kalmia described the terrain they would encounter the following day and the route she had chosen. She also showed the kit she had for her and Eleanor.

"We will be gone in the hills for three days and two nights. I have an extra pair of boots especially made for climbing these hills that I can lend to you, Eleanor. There is also an oilskin rain cape I made that will keep you reasonably dry if caught in a squall, and it can double as a waterproof wrap around your sleeping blanket."

Kalmia showed Eleanor how the oilskin cape wrapped around two rolled blankets that were then bent into an inverted U and secured around a knapsack.

"I also have a warm jumper for you to wear up there," she said while pulling out a naturally dyed sweater of sage, yellow, and russet with a turtle neck and rolled cuffs.

"You can unroll the cuffs if your hands get cold, or put on mittens," Kalmia said. "I have a matching wool cap for your head. And a scarf. A change of clothes, and that should be about it."

"What will we eat?" asked Eleanor.

"I have made up some simple meals we can eat as we go and a warm meal for dinner," said Kalmia. "Oh, yes, and a water container and cup to drink and eat from. Ozzie will come along for company. He needs to burn off some steam."

Ozzie's ears perked up with the mention of his name.

For someone whose cottage was so cluttered, Kalmia was unexpectedly organized for the trek. Eleanor thought the careful planning was the outcome of years of experience surviving whatever the mountains had thrown at her.

The following morning broke in a cloudless sky. Following breakfast, the two women set off on foot across the valley in search of robins on their way to a gate, beyond which rose an unpaved road that angled up the mountainside. Stone walls separated the valley from the hillside, on which a few sheep grazed. The trees in the valley quickly fell below the two women as they hiked up the road into the russet and green cropped vegetation of the hillside.

Kalmia and Ozzie were well versed in these treks, but Eleanor was feeling the pace. Kalmia slowed and, after about half an hour, stopped to look down the valley and to allow Eleanor to catch her breath. Eleanor gazed out across the hills and mountain ridges. Some very tall mountains stood to the north, overshadowing many lower ridges, each with a valley.

"Kalmia," Eleanor said, "this is stunningly beautiful. You are very fortunate to live here. All your troubles fall away when you come here."

"It is odd, perhaps, but when I am feeling I need a break, I climb the mountains," said Kalmia. "My demons often come along, harping in my head as I climb the hillside, but gradually I out pace them, and after a few days, they are out of sight." She chuckled. "But they always seem to be waiting down the trail when I return."

Eleanor smiled.

The two women continued to climb the mountain. Meadow pipits dressed in tawny and buff camouflage betrayed their presence by aerial displays, twittering a message to other pipits that this was their turf. Where heather grew, the gobbling calls of red grouse erupted, upset by the women's presence. A few wheatears flashed their white rumps as the birds launched into the air as if in defiance. Kalmia pointed out a buzzard soaring high over the hill.

After a few hours, the slope eased to a ridge that led off to the northwest. The wind sent a chill down the perspiring backs of the two women, but that mattered little to Eleanor. She had never been in the mountains nor had she witnessed nature on such a grand scale. Ridges and craggy mountains reached out before her. The song of meadow pipits carried on the wind serenaded the mountain. She took a deep breath and saw Kalmia looking out to the horizon.

"This view was worth a hundred treks up that hillside," said Eleanor.

"It is quite lovely, isn't it?" said Kalmia. "Let's keep going or those demons will catch up with us."

They spent the rest of the day following ridges, climbing to cols, and descending the other side. The trail was more of a sheep route that zig zagged along the high ground. They reached a point where they could see Scafell Pike off in the distance.

"That's Scafell Pike over there" she said, pointing with one hand. "It is the highest point in England at nearly three thousand feet. We won't be going there, you will be happy to know," Kalmia said with a grin. "I have another surprise for you." She beckoned Eleanor to follow her.

There was no obvious trail where Kalmia veered off the ridge to descend the mountain slope, but she and Ozzie seemed to know where they were going. The ground levelled before falling away again. As soon as Eleanor stepped over the edge, she gasped. A tiny tarn, pearl shaped and still, was nestled in an amphitheatre of heather and scree.

The two women and Ozzie made their way to the water's edge where Kalmia announced they would stay the night. The days were long, so there was plenty of time to set up a camp and make dinner.

Kalmia told Eleanor how she strived to leave no sign of their presence. They would prepare their meals on a large flat rock near the shore, she explained, and sleep between two boulders where there was some grass to provide a soft mattress.

"We can refill our water bottles in the tarn, but if you want to wash, use a tiny stream and pool over there where it leaves the tarn. You will find a sponge in your knapsack but no soap," she said.

While Eleanor prepared the bed rolls, Kalmia fed Ozzie and got their food out of her knapsack. She had converted a tin can into a miniature stove that used cardboard and wax as fuel. On top, she warmed mashed potatoes and boiled water for tea. She chopped up some vegetables she had bought at the green grocer and sliced some cold meatloaf. While she was preparing the dinner, Eleanor watched intently, admiring how it all seemed second nature.

"Kalmia," she asked, "how did you come to know Mrs. Quimby?"

"Oh, she and my mother are longtime friends from university days. They studied maths together at Cambridge."

"Maths!" exclaimed Eleanor. "I didn't know Mrs. Quimby was a mathematician."

"Yes," continued Kalmia. "They worked together during the war. Somewhere near where you live, I think. Mother would never talk about what she did."

"You chose a different career path then?" asked Eleanor.

"Yes. My parents lived in London prior to the war. We bought Lake View Cottage where we spent our holidays, and when the war broke out, we moved there for safety," Kalmia said. "I fell in love with the Lakes and the cottage. When the war ended a few years ago, they moved back to London. My father was looking to hire someone to keep an eye on the cottage, so I suggested I could remain there to save him money. All I needed to do was find something to support me while I was there, hence the weaving and knitting."

"How long do you intend to stay?" asked Eleanor.

"Until my passion for the Lakes dries up," Kalmia replied. "I think dinner is ready."

The two women ate their meal before the sun approached the horizon.

"I would like you to see the setting sun from up on the ridge," said Kalmia.

The two women set off up the slope across the level ground to arrive on the ridge just before the sunset. The verdant green vegetation and the tawny rocks created fingerprint shadows across the ground. The enhanced colours brought on by the low angle of the sun was a reminder that night would soon be upon them. Such sunsets were what intoxicated Woodsworth and Coleridge to pen their words and, legend had it, were when the fairies might appear. Eleanor was mesmerized. When the sun set, Kalmia said they should be getting back while there still was some light.

Darkness enveloped the camp, and stars appeared overhead. The two women climbed into their bed rolls, and soon Kalmia was off to sleep. Eleanor lay awake, thinking about all she had seen and heard, wondering about Mrs. Quimby and Kalmia's mother, and smiling at the beauty she had witnessed. The stars became brighter as the night crept over her so that she could see the Milky Way in a band across the sky.

The following morning awoke with the same clear weather. Kalmia lit the stove to boil water for tea while Eleanor visited the small washing pool below the tarn. When she returned, Kalmia had breakfast laid out, and they both ate in the cool air. Kalmia then took her turn while Eleanor cleaned up around the camp. With Kalmia back in the camp, they made their plan for the day.

"I thought we could leave most of our gear here," Kalmia said, "and go for a day hike. All we need is our knapsacks, some lunch, and water. The rest can be left right here."

The party of three retraced their steps back up to the ridge and continued along the trail they had used the previous day. Kalmia told Eleanor she was looking for stray pieces of lichen that she could use for dyes.

"Lichens are age-old sources of colours that you wouldn't believe by looking at them," she said. "The problem is that they take a long time to grow, and so I only take those on windfall limbs or broken free of their rock footings."

Just before lunch, Kalmia stopped Eleanor with her hand.

"Ozzie," she called, "come. Sit. Good dog. Eleanor, see that piece of lichen over there on the ground?"

Eleanor replied, "There is lichen everywhere. What are you talking about?"

"No, look along the edge of the cliff," Kalmia returned, pointing to a dropoff where a piece of lichen was quivering in the wind.

"That species produces a lovely dye. Stay here while I get it."

Kalmia took off her knapsack and lowered into a crouch while leaning away from the cliff edge. As she moved toward the precipice, her footing gave way, and with a scream, she slipped onto her backside and over the cliff.

Eleanor heard the scream and a tumbling sound down the slope.

"Kalmia!" she screamed several times.

"Oh, damn," shouted Kalmia out of sight down the slope.

"Are you alright?" shouted Eleanor.

"It's my ankle. I think I sprained it," yelled Kalmia. "Don't go near the edge. Go back along the trail where the slope is less steep, and then you should be able to reach me."

Eleanor did what Kalmia requested and soon she and Ozzie were by Kalmia's side.

Kalmia already had her boot off and was examining her swelling ankle.

"Is it broken?" asked Eleanor.

Kalmia slowly and gingerly rotated the ankle. "No, I think it is just a sprain."

"What should we do?" asked Eleanor.

"I don't think I can walk on it, so I am going to need some help," said Kalmia.

"What kind of help?" asked Eleanor.

"You and Ozzie are going to have to go back to Brooksmere and get the mountain rescue to get me out of here," said Kalmia.

Eleanor suddenly realized the seriousness of their predicament. She had half a day before sunset. Their camp was a few hours back along the trail, which was not easy to find, and she was not even sure of the trail they had taken from the town. She realized she had put all her faith in Kalmia to get them in and out of the mountains.

Kalmia was next to speak.

"Eleanor, there is not enough time to get to town. We will need to stay put overnight. I need you to go back to our camp and bring the gear here. We will stay the night, and first thing tomorrow, you will return to Brooksmere to get help."

Eleanor realized the huge responsibility Kalmia was giving her.

"I will go right now," she said.

"Eleanor," said Kalmia, "I will be fine, so take your time and try to be calm. Leave something on the trail where we saw the lichen so that you can find me when you return. It should take you about two hours to get to our camp and another two to get back here. That should be about 4 or 5 p.m. . . . "

"Are you sure you will be alright?" asked Eleanor.

"Leave me your knapsack with food, water, and warm clothes," said Kalmia. "You can use my knapsack back on the trail. Now off you go. Call Ozzie, and he will come with you. He knows the way."

"I will be back as soon as I can, Kalmia," said Eleanor as she clambered back up the slope and onto the trail where she found Kalmia's knapsack. She left a scarf on the heather to mark the point where she should turn off the trail and find Kalmia. She and Ozzie then started back along the trail in a hurried pace. Eleanor felt the pressure of finding the right turn off and then carrying all the gear back to Kalmia before nightfall. *What will happen if I fall or get lost?* she thought. *What would Gerald do? Where is he when I need him most?*

CHAPTER 18:

Seeking Help

About two hours down the trail, Ozzie veered off
down a slope that Eleanor recognized.

"Good boy, Ozzie!" she exclaimed.

Within minutes, she was back in their camp. Only
twenty-four hours ago, she had been marvelling at the
exquisite view of the tarn, which now lay there inert and
disinterested. She quickly bundled their things into the
knapsack, tied both blanket rolls in a Ushape around the
top of the knapsack as Kalmia had shown her, and started
to climb back up the slope toward the trail. Ozzie ran
ahead and stood on the main trail, waiting for instructions on which way she wanted to go. The return along
the trail began to look familiar now that she had hiked it
twice, and Ozzie trotted along as if it was all a lot of fun.

Eleanor was panting heavily and worried sick about Kalmia and even more so about how she was ever going to get back to town to find help. The hike to their camp, aided by Ozzie, made her feel a little more confident, but she knew the next day was going to be trying. She calculated that she was a full day's trek from Brooksmere, where she would have to overnight before leading the rescue party back to Kalmia the following day. She would be physically exhausted but knew Kalmia depended on her to succeed.

About three hours later, Eleanor thought she had arrived at where Kalmia had slipped over the cliff, but she wasn't sure. She couldn't find the scarf to mark the location. The cliff edges began to look the same. Then she spotted what she thought was the lichen that had lured Kalmia to the precipice, and there was the scarf.

"Kalmia," she shouted.

There was no answer. *She might be out cold*, thought Eleanor.

"Ozzie," she called, "where is Kalmia?"

Ozzie stared at her quizzically.

"Oh, come on, Ozzie. You found our camp. Now let's find Kalmia."

Eleanor shouted again with some desperation in her voice.

"Kalmia!"

All of sudden, Ozzie's ears pricked up. *He hears something*, Eleanor thought. And then he was off around the precipice and out of sight.

Eleanor was carrying an extra heavy pack and was not going to follow him. Instead, she made her way back along the trail to where the ground sloped more gently and worked her way toward the base of the precipice where she caught sight of Kalmia's sweater.

"Ozzie," called Kalmia as he licked her face. "Where's Eleanor?"

"Right here, Kalmia," she called out.

"I thought I heard you, but I guess you couldn't hear me, so I whistled for Ozzie," said Kalmia. "You made it! You are quickly becoming a mountain girl."

That was a much bigger compliment for Eleanor than Kalmia knew.

Eleanor dropped her pack beside Kalmia and asked, "How's the ankle?" Kalmia showed her a swollen and blue ankle joint.

"I am afraid I won't be walking out on this," Kalmia said. "But that is for tomorrow. Can you set up camp here? I will start some dinner."

Eleanor set up camp and together they ate dinner. The two women laughed as Eleanor told Kalmia about trying to find the camp with Ozzie's guidance. Darkness was closing in, and soon they were in their blankets. Eleanor fell into a deep sleep while Kalmia tossed to try to find comfort for her ankle.

In the early morning before the sun was up, Eleanor rose, stretched, and got dressed. She rummaged through the knapsack to find some breakfast. Kalmia stirred and sat up.

"It is barely light Eleanor," she said.

"I want as much time as I can to get to Brooksmere," she said. "I figure it will take eight hours or more. How did you sleep?"

"Not very well," Kalmia said, "but I am not going anywhere for the next two days. When you get to town, ask for Mr. Sneeze."

"Mr. Sneeze?" asked Eleanor. "Are you kidding me?"

"Arnold Sneeze is in charge of rescues, although there is not much call for it now that I think about it. In any case, he will mobilize a group to get me back safely."

Once Eleanor had eaten and got everything in place for Kalmia, she set off with her knapsack and Ozzie.

"Be careful, Eleanor," said Kalmia.

"I will be right back. Don't go anywhere," she said with a smile.

On the trail, Eleanor could feel the adrenaline kick in. She was off at a steady pace with Ozzie running ahead. She passed where the turnoff to the first camp veered off the main trail. She heard the pipits singing overhead and the neurotic red grouse grumbling in the heather. The hours passed. All she had to do was keep on the same course along the ridge until the trail dipped down the mountainside. By then, she imagined, she would see the town before it was dark.

Eleanor didn't know how long she had been moving when she saw a shepherd with his dog moving sheep along the fells. She waved and the shepherd waved back, so she stopped. He descended down the slope.

"Afternoon, ma'am," he said. "Is that Kalmia's Ozzie with you?"

"Yes, sir. Kalmia has had a fall and I need to get help," said Eleanor.

"What happened?" asked the shepherd.

"She slipped off a ledge and badly sprained her ankle. She can't walk on it, so I need to get some people to bring her out."

"Where did this happen?" asked the shepherd.

"I don't know the names of the places here, but I have been walking for about six hours," Eleanor said. "We stayed last night at a tiny tarn off the main trail that was shaped like a pearl. It is tiny. Kalmia fell off a precipice about two hours walk farther along."

"About six hours away, you say?" said the shepherd. "I think I know where that is. Where are you going?"

"I am going to Brooksmere to get help."

"If I can help when you come back, I will," he said. "Brooksmere is about four hours away. Godspeed."

Eleanor thanked the shepherd and set off with Ozzie. She felt reassured that she was on the right trail to get to the town. Four hours later, just like the shepherd had estimated, Eleanor arrived at the gate that opened to a road leading to Brooksmere.

It was late in the day when Kalmia started to consider what she would do if Eleanor did not get back to town. She might have taken a wrong turn. Although the ridges offered a natural route through the mountains, a traveller had to be able to read the signs of where others had gone when the track disappeared in the endless heather and grassland. One could easily veer off course and struggle to find the route. It had happened to Kalmia enough times for her to know the pitfalls. She also let her mind wander to the eventuality that she might get caught out in the rain. Her cape should keep her dry for a while, but if the rains persisted, she could find herself suffering from hypothermia.

"Excuse me, ma'am," said Eleanor to a woman coming back from shopping with a bag of vegetables. "Where might I find Mr. Sneeze?"

"Arnie, you mean?" she replied. "He should be at his watch repair shop next door to the grocer if he's not in the Fox and Chickens," she replied.

"Thank you," said Eleanor as she strode toward the high street.

Fox and Chickens, she thought. *I guess that is the pub.*

She turned down high street, passed the grocer, and entered the Watch and Clocks shop where a balding middle aged man with a moustache was fidgeting with the movement of a clock. Arnold Sneeze was about five foot four inches tall and heavily set. He raised his head at the sound of the doorbell and put down his jewellers' tools.

"Good day, ma'am. How can I help?" Arnie said.

"Are you Mr. Sneeze?" asked Eleanor. "The man in charge of mountain rescues?"

"Indeed," he replied with some enthusiastic concern. "What has happened?"

Eleanor explained how Kalmia was stranded, how she sprained her ankle and was unable to walk, and approximately how far away she was from town. Mr. Sneeze tossed aside his apron and said he would mobilize a team immediately. He ushered Eleanor to the door.

"Meet me at the community hall," he said, closing and locking his shop door behind her.

Eleanor looked up and down the street, wondering where to find the community hall, when the church bells began to peel. Store keepers and shoppers began to arrive on the street. Some stood with hands on hips, a cluster of women gathered like chickens at feeding time, and others shrugged as if they had no idea what was going on. Which was generally true. There seemed to be no reason for the church bells to peel in the late afternoon on a weekday. A crowd had now assembled on the street, and they began to walk toward the church.

"Probably some kids playing a prank," said one man.

"Maybe the reverend is practicing for Sunday," offered another.

By the time they arrived at the church, most of the town was either arriving or had arrived outside the belfry. The constable, for safety's sake, ordered everyone back while he entered the church to investigate.

A few minutes later, the bells stopped peeling. The constable marched Mr. Sneeze out through the great wooden door of the church to the evening light. Mr. Sneeze was protesting.

"Explain yourself, Mr. Sneeze," the constable said.

"Explain myself!" Arnie said irately. "Explain myself? You all know the ringing of the church bells indicates a pending emergency. It is clearly explained in the rescue manual that you all got." The crowd began to mutter. Some seemed to vaguely remember something about the bells, but there had been no emergency for well over a decade, and memories fade. A man in the crowd shouted out, "What emergency, Arnie? Is the sky going to fall?" The crowd burst into laughter.

"You might find it funny, but I have on good authority that Kalmia Rosenblum is in dire straits far off in the mountains," he retorted.

A gasp went out in the crowd, and there began a worried discussion.

"Now," yelled Mr. Sneeze. "I want every ablebodied man to meet me in the community hall in fifteen minutes. There we will devise a rescue plan."

The crowd quickly dispersed, discussing what each would do. The town was about to be mobilized under the direction of Mr. Sneeze. Mr. Sneeze lived for these moments, and although lives could be in danger, he knew events like this would hold him in good stead in the community. He might even be hailed a hero.

Fifteen minutes later, Eleanor arrived among a crowd of people at the community hall. There were many men willing to volunteer to join the rescue and many who were content to watch. Women were there too, some carrying young children, some wanting their offspring to witness the event, others wanting to gossip, but most wanted to do whatever they could to assist the effort. Mr. Sneeze rose in front of the assembled crowd. He was wearing a brightly coloured jumper, woollen pants with suspenders, and a felt cap.

"Miss Eleanor, here, has informed me that Kalmia has broken her ankle and is lying at the foot of a steep precipice many hours away," he exclaimed. "To reach her will require the most able men. I want all men who think they can make an all-day trek to the rescue scene and return on foot."

Eleanor grimaced at how Mr. Sneeze had elaborated on the details of Kalmia's plight.

"It is too late to make a start tonight," said Sneeze. "I want all men ready for this challenge to be at the gate at dawn tomorrow." He then proceeded to list off the emergency supplies they would need: the stretcher to carry Kalmia out of the mountains, ropes to scale the precipice, and food and water to sustain them. He asked for volunteers to put up their hands if they were willing to take on the tasks.

By nightfall, the meeting came to a close, and the crowd dispersed, abuzz with the worry and excitement of it all. Eleanor was left standing at the community hall door, watching the crowd disperse, when she thought about Ozzie. *Where did he get to?* she wondered. *Where am I going to stay tonight?* She then realized she had her knapsack with the cape Kalmia had made. A small brook ran near the community hall where she found a quiet flat spot and curled up for the night. Moments later, Ozzie arrived to curl up beside her.

CHAPTER 19:

The Rescue

The dawn chorus of warblers, thrushes, and finches awoke Eleanor at the first hint of light. She rose, stretched, used the bushes as a loo, and lit the camp stove. She boiled enough water to make tea and to fill her flask for the hike ahead. A few scraps of food in her knapsack would have to do for her and Ozzie.

At the gate, two young men were shifting from foot to foot to keep warm and to limber up.

"Are you here for the search party?" asked Eleanor.

"Yes," said one of the young men. They were very fit and in high spirits. "My name is James Harty, and this is Anthony Harty. We run the fells to keep in shape."

"Well, I think you will be sorely needed today," Eleanor replied.

Soon others began to arrive. Many were middle-aged men who noses betrayed their patronage of the Fox and Chickens. There was one very lean man who towered over the others and several with moustaches, tweed caps, and coats that looked like more of a liability than an asset. Among them was Mr. Sneeze with an enormous backpack. He was explaining to a few of the men the first aid equipment he had brought along. By the time the sun was about to peak over the ridge, about thirty people had assembled. A few women were serving tea, and they plied Eleanor with freshly baked slices of bread, cheese, and a real treat: two apples. Mr. Sneeze got everyone's attention.

"Good morning, fine citizens of Brooksmere. We will set off in a minute, but I want everyone to know we have a long trek ahead of us. If you do not think you are up to it, now is the time to stay behind. We will be climbing the gate trail to its summit and then follow various ridges to the north. We are looking for a brightly coloured scarf that will indicate the site where Kalmia fell off the precipice. For the people who are staying behind, we should be back by nightfall, but do not worry if we do not return until the next day. Each of us is prepared to stay the night. Any questions? If not, let's get going."

Mr. Sneeze led the way with Eleanor at his side. She was travelling light with just the knapsack and a few clothes. Mr. Sneeze was carrying a mountain of a pack, and it wasn't long before he could no longer carry on a conversation. He pushed on while his face turned red and sweat beaded on his forehead. Eleanor could see he was labouring badly.

"Mr. Sneeze?" she asked. "Do you have many rescues each year?"

"It has been . . . quite a while . . . " he gasped.

"Do you get up in the hills often when there are no rescues?" she asked.

"My business . . . keeps me . . . pretty busy," he replied.

Eleanor knew that was a leading question. Mr. Sneeze did not look the mountain type. Unlike Kalmia, who was tanned, sinewy, and lithe, Mr. Sneeze looked like he rarely left the town. *How busy can a watch maker in a small town be?* she thought.

Before long, Mr. Sneeze called for a break. He slung his pack to the ground, puffing heavily. Eleanor turned around. Winding behind her was a line of struggling men looking like they were on the Klondike Trail. Some had already stopped to catch their breath. Only the Harty lads were marching on ahead. Eleanor realized the party was quickly spreading out. They could quickly become their own liability.

"Mr. Sneeze?" she asked. "I don't wish to interfere, but I don't know if the rescue party is up for this challenge."

Mr. Sneeze knew her comment included him.

"What do you suggest?" he asked.

"Why not let the Harty lads go ahead to get to Kalmia as quickly as possible. They run up here regularly and can probably get there before sunset," she suggested.

"Good idea, Miss," he said.

"Harty," he yelled, "I have a plan for you." He described to them what Eleanor had said. She reiterated to look for the scarf. She took six hours to get to the town. They would likely take less than that. She suggested they note the time. They suggested she come with them. That way, she could show them the exact location where Kalmia would be found. Mr. Sneeze agreed, so with Ozzie and the two young men, Eleanor set off and was soon out of sight. Behind them wound a trail of weary, huffing, and puffing men. Mr. Sneeze would never admit it, but underneath he was pleased. The young people could do the hard work, relieving his entourage to take their time. He wanted to be sure all the remaining team reached the top of the ridge so they were out of sight of the townspeople.

By nine o'clock, the motley party led by Mr. Sneeze had crested the first ridge, where they stopped for a break. He was relieved to finally be out of sight of Brooksmere. Eleanor and the Hartys, meanwhile, had made good progress along the ridge. Their hike was going to take many hours, but Eleanor was feeling more at home having traversed the route twice.

Late in the morning, one of the Hartys spotted something large along the ridge.

"Miss Hutchinson, what is that?" he said pointing anxiously ahead. Whatever it was, James Harty knew it was too large to be a bear. It appeared to be carrying something.

"Looks like a horse," said Anthony, squinting into the morning air.

"What's a horse doing up here?" James asked.

The three rescuers continued toward the horse, which dipped down into a gulley to emerge closer to them. The rider waved and Eleanor waved back. There was a second person walking alongside the horse. A sharp whistle caught Ozzie's attention, and he raced from Eleanor's side toward the horse and rider.

"It's Kalmia," shouted Eleanor. "Kalmia is riding a horse!"

Eleanor and the Hartys began to run toward the horse.

"Kalmia," shouted Eleanor. "We feared the worst, but look at you arriving like a princess on the back of a horse."

Eleanor then recognized the man walking beside the horse. It was the shepherd she had seen the previous afternoon.

"How do you do, Mr. . . . ?" Eleanor asked the shepherd.

"Jones," he said.

"This is something to celebrate," said Eleanor, and the others agreed. Mr. Jones helped Kalmia off the horse, and on one leg, she hopped over to a rock where she sat down. The others gathered around except for Mr. Jones, who tended the horse. Eleanor pulled a small flask of Scotch out of her knapsack.

"I got this from an undisclosed source in the village," she said as she winked.

They toasted each other on their roles in rescuing Kalmia. Then Kalmia explained what had happened.

"After you told Mr. Jones of my plight and my approximate position, he saddled up his horse, Big Ben, and in the few hours of daylight left, he rode part way to where I was sheltering. This morning, he rode the rest of the way, arriving in early morning. Mr. Jones realized that the rescue party on foot would take a few days, and they would struggle to carry me out of the mountains, whereas his horse could do it in a day. So, here I am thanks to Mr. Jones."

"Thank you, Mr. Jones," said Eleanor, hoisting her cup. "The rest of the rescue party is making their way along the ridge someplace down the trail."

"Rescue party?" questioned Kalmia.

"Yes. Mr. Sneeze and a dozen or more villagers are coming to find you," said Eleanor.

"Oh my," said Kalmia. "Perhaps we should get moving then."

Mr. Jones hoisted Kalmia back in the saddle and took Big Ben's reins.

"I didn't ask how the ankle is doing," said Eleanor.

"Much better after some rest," said Kalmia. "I can't put much weight on it yet."

The party of five, plus Ozzie and Big Ben, began to plod toward Brooksmere. About two hours later, they spotted the rescue party lumbering along the ridge about two kilometres away. Kalmia put her fingers to her lips and whistled. The rescue party came to a halt. She whistled again, and one of the rescuers whistled back. Within minutes Eleanor, the two Hartys, Mr. Jones, Ozzie, and Big Ben bearing Kalmia reached the first of the rescue party. From on top of the horse, Kalmia could see people with packs, some sporting bright clothing, all seemingly exhausted and slowly moving in a long line that strung out for a kilometre or more along the trail. At the front was Mr. Sneeze. He greeted Kalmia and turned to the rescuers within earshot.

"I am pleased to report that we have rescued Kalmia," he said. "The quick-thinking Mr. Jones has saved us all from a long night in the mountains."

Mr. Sneeze then turned to Kalmia. "May I look at your ankle?" he asked.

"It's fine, Mr. Sneeze," she returned.

"I am trained in rescue proceedings, Miss Rosenblum," he said, using her surname for emphasis, "and it is standard protocol to examine the injury and to assess if you have any other injuries. Falling off a precipice like you did could result in a brain concussion that you might not be aware of. Or you – "

Kalmia cut him off short. "I didn't fall off a precipice. I slipped on a steep slope where I twisted my ankle. Never did I hit my head."

"Maybe so, Miss Rosenblum, but I will need to fill out a mountain rescue form M889, in which I need to report any injuries you sustained," said Mr. Sneeze.

"Well, I am not going to get off this horse. I might injure myself," she said defiantly. "Maybe when we get back to town."

"Right," said Sneeze. "Okay, everyone. Let's turn around and return to town. Let the horse and rider through, please."

Mr. Sneeze got in front of the line where he tried to keep up to Kalmia on Big Ben, Eleanor, the young Harty boys, and the shepherd, Mr. Jones, but his large pack was making him breathe heavily. Mr. Jones saw his plight, took the pack, and tied it to the horse's saddle, allowing Mr. Sneeze to keep pace with them.

The crowd of rescuers made their way across the ridge and arrived by late afternoon, following the trail that descended down the valley to the town. Two kids playing along the road were the first to see the rescuers' entourage and ran to tell their parents. The church bell began to peal, and soon the entire town was assembling at the gate to welcome the arrival of the successful rescuers. Out in front of the procession was Mr. Sneeze, proudly leading the battleweary rescuers back to town. Behind him rode Kalmia on Big Ben with Mr. Jones walking beside them.

Next came Eleanor and the two Harty boys. Then there was a string of townsmen, including Mr. Green the grocer, Mr. Flanigan the butcher, a handyman named Joe, two men who no one seemed to know what they did for a living, the postman that the children called Mr. Stamp, three former Home Guard members, Mr. Archer who thought of himself as an artist, the land baron Mr. Henry Biggleton-Smith and his son Reginald, and a dozen or more misfits. The parade of would-be rescuers that stumbled into town that fateful day stretched up the hillside for several hundred yards. Waiting to greet the hometown heroes were their wives and girlfriends, the Reverend Brandon Rand that everyone called Rev. Rand, a gaggle of children, a few barking dogs, and the Brooksmere Brass Band.

When the procession was near the gate, the band began to play "See the Conquering Hero." Mr. Sneeze held his head high as he marched toward the gate. The band stopped playing when he arrived at the gate. Mr. Sneeze stood on the first rung of the gate so everyone could see him. Eleanor noticed he had ripped the bottom of his woollen pants and smiled to herself.

"My dear citizens of Brooksmere," Mr. Sneeze began. "Today is indeed a day to celebrate. Because of careful planning and the dogged determination of the Mountain Rescuers, we have brought safely home our dear Kalmia."

The crowd cheered, applauded, and smiled at each other.

"There were some of you who thought our mission folly, but with steadfastness, we scaled the mountain and return tonight with the prize."

Eleanor thought to herself, *The prize?* She turned to see Kalmia squirming in the saddle. She was trapped in the crowd and required help to dismount. There was nothing to do but endure the speeches.

"This day will go down in the annals of Brooksmere as one of our finest triumphs," Sneeze spewed. "I led these heroes on to victory to bring home one of our own."

The crowd erupted in whoops and applause.

"Young dear Kalmia, although accustomed to the mountains, was ill-prepared to face the dangers brought on by a fall from a high precipice. If not for the plucky Miss Hutchinson, we would have been none the better. She knew when she came to town to look up the Mountain Rescuers and not a moment too late."

Eleanor began to chuckle to herself. She wondered what Gerald would make of all this.

"When I called on all of you last night, many came forward, and to you, I hale you as the Heroes of Cumbria," announced Mr. Sneeze. The crowd was in his hands. He could see in their eyes they craved more. Brooksmere rarely experienced such a day, and Sneeze was going to make sure no one forgot it. Mr. Jones, the real hero, looked at the ground.

"Tonight, we will celebrate at the Fox and Chickens. Be sure to be there to witness history in the making."

He climbed off the gate to let the heroes pass and hug their loved ones. The band struck up again, and the dogs barked. A reporter from the Brooksmere Banner cornered Mr. Sneeze, where he told the story of the rescue, how he had sent the young men off to find Kalmia while he had prepared medical treatment and got his men ready to carry Kalmia if necessary. He told of how Kalmia had fallen from a precipice over one hundred feet tall and, when pressed by the reporter, said it might have been closer to fifty. He told of how his plan to get the horse for Kalmia worked with well-oiled precision. The reporter dutifully jotted down his every word. *This is indeed an epic story*, thought the junior reporter, *that just might make my career.*

Meanwhile, Mr. Jones quietly helped Kalmia dismount from Big Ben, bade her farewell, and led his horse away down the road. The crowd was dispersing, enjoying every minute of the charade. They were laughing and joking. A few of the women told Kalmia they were so relieved she was not more badly injured. Some men also acknowledged they were pleased that everything had turned out well. Rev Rand said his prayers were answered and offered to drive Kalmia, Eleanor, and Ozzie back to Lakeview Cottage. He said he would also take Eleanor to the station to catch her train the next day. They quickly accepted his offer and left the town to celebrate in the Fox and Chickens.

The following morning, Kalmia was hobbling about her cottage while Eleanor packed her things in anticipation of Rev. Rand's arrival.

"The past few days were a little more eventful than I had planned," said Kalmia.

"Yes," said Eleanor. "There was rarely a dull moment."

"You saved my life, and to you I will be eternally grateful," said Kalmia.

"I think Mr. Jones and Big Ben saved your life," returned Eleanor.

"Mr. Jones wouldn't have been any the wiser if it hadn't been for you, Eleanor," said Kalmia.

"Okay, I will take a piece of the credit, but the whole town came out to see you home. To know that an entire town is willing to stop what they are doing to see you safely home . . . Their care was on full display," said Eleanor. "You are something special to them."

"Thank you, Eleanor. I feel we have got to know each other, and I hope we meet again. You are now a mountain woman, and we have lots to share," said Kalmia. Then she turned her head. "I think I hear the Reverend's car coming for you."

Eleanor reached for her bag and thanked Kalmia. Kalmia gave Eleanor a hug.

Eleanor said, "Oh, I nearly forgot." She reached into her coat pocket and handed Kalmia a handful of lichen. "You left that on the ledge where you slipped."

A huge grin came over Kalmia's face. "I will cherish it forever."

The reverend's car horn tooted outside. Eleanor turned to leave. Kalmia waved goodbye with Ozzie by her side as Eleanor climbed into the car and sped off for the train.

CHAPTER 20:

Writing About Robins

leanor stretched out in her favourite garden chair, shut her eyes, and began to dream. She began to reminisce about her adventures. Several experiences with the library would assist her in attaining her dream at the museum, she realized, but she needed one more thing, and that piece was the most daunting. She needed to show she could publish scientific papers in scientific journals. She had received Gerald's advice. Now she had to start to write.

She opened her eyes to ponder how to proceed but was distracted when she heard Thales singing in her yard. *So much has happened in my life since I first noticed him*, she thought. Eleanor made a gin and tonic that accompanied her into the garden. Where she sat in the garden, she could see the elm trees, the lane, and the hedge along Mrs. Quimby's back garden. She wondered how Kalmia's ankle was healing and smiled at the thought of Mrs. Quimby being a mathematician. Who would have thought? She smiled broadly thinking about Mr. Sneeze and felt a warmth toward the quiet Mr. Jones. Eleanor imagined herself moving to Brooksmere to live a life trekking the hills – a mountain woman, as Kalmia had called her – but banished the thought when she realized she had no way to finance such a dream, and she thought she would grow bored with it before long.

Her mind returned to the task of writing a scientific paper. Her training as a librarian meant she had been able to read many works by ornithologists in the journals *Ibis* and *British Birds*. The authors seemed to write so breathlessly.

Eleanor rose from her garden chair to return to the cottage, where she opened her notebooks. She then opened an atlas to a map of the British Isles and held it against one of the windows so the light shone through. She placed a piece of paper over the opened page and drew an outline of the British Isles. She noted the location of major cities and geographical locations on her tracing, and then she returned to the desk. With her map before her, she began to note the locations where she had recorded the breast plumage colouration of robins. The points included Rabbit's Burrough; Wytham Woods in Oxford, which Christopher had shown her; Edinburgh, Inverness, and Mularchy from her visit with the Spratts; Minsmere, where she had visited the woodlots with Peter and Patrick; the Brecon Beacons in Wales where Gwyn lived; and several locations in the Lake District from her visit with Kalmia. She had also gleaned some sightings from around London during her daily commute to the library. Once all the points were on the map, she held it up and thought the number of locations was quite impressive. It represented a wide coverage of Great Britain. She also thought it represented much of her life in the past few years.

Eleanor then numbered each location on the map and a corresponding number on a piece of paper. Beside each number she added details of the locations, dates she visited them, and who accompanied her. She also added a column labelled "Robins," beneath which she listed each sighting at each of her locations with the colour swatch of breast plumage colour based on her watercolour code. Several hours went by before she had transferred the data in her notebooks to the sheet of paper, and when she was finished, she held it up and smiled at how many she had managed to record. She was now ready to compare the colour of robin's plumages across Great Britain. Would it align with what had already been reported or not? If not, how would she, an unknown in the ornithological circles, ever question the conclusion of well-established professional ornithologists?

She laid aside her map and data sheets, stood up, stretched, and walked into the kitchen where she made a cup of tea. She was feeling a little hungry and realized that she had been at work for quite some time. Eleanor opened the fridge and started to make dinner. While she cut up vegetables and warmed a frying pan for sausages, she could not shake her self-doubts. *Maybe this idea of me being a museum ornithologist is all a romantic fantasy*, she thought. *The tedium of writing scientific papers might not be how I want to spend my time.*

Eleanor fussed with the food, set the table, and pondered her future.

The data I have on the map is quite impressive, she said to herself. *What a shame it would be to not let the world see what I have found.*

Another voice in her head said, *How will you deal with rejection? What will you do if the editor or the reviewers of your scientific paper say it is not worthy of publication? All that hard work will have got you nowhere.*

There was only one thing to do: write to Gerald. She wondered what she could ask him that he had not already told her. Then she realized that what she needed to do was to send him the manuscript for comment. He might guide her on changes she needed to make before submitting it to the editor. He might also tell her what additional data she needed to collect and add before submitting it. Or he might tell her outright that the paper was not worthy of publication. *I have to be brave and write the damned thing*, she thought. She would never be able to face herself if she did not follow through.

Eleanor was washing up after dinner when there was a knock on the door. When she opened the door, she saw Peter standing on the doorstep with a big grin.

"Do you want to go bird-watching?" he said with a smile. "I was out for a stroll and thought you'd like to join me, to watch birds, of course."

Eleanor said, "Let me get my binoculars," as she turned back into the cottage. This was just the distraction she needed.

Peter led Eleanor up the lane past Mrs. Quimby's and into the church grounds.

"Swifts," called out Peter, pointing to the belfry. "Up there, going into the steeple." Sickleshaped wings and highspeed flights were all the clues that Peter needed to identify them.

"There is a tawny owl that roosts in a tree in the hedge along the road over there," he said, gesturing past the church.

Sure enough, huddled against the trunk of a sycamore was an owl looking grumpily at the two humans who were staring back. They proceeded along the hedgerows where Peter called out names of birds and had Eleanor listen to their songs.

"Did you call this evening to go bird-watching, Peter, or did you have something else on your mind?" asked Eleanor.

"Like what?" teased Peter.

"Oh, I don't know," said Eleanor. "I was just wondering."

"Well," Peter replied, "there is something more."

"I thought so," said Eleanor.

"The library has had a donation that needs to be brought to London," said Peter. "Miss Bradshaw thought you were the person to do it, but she wasn't sure if you were up to it after the debacle in Wales."

"Why are you asking me instead of Miss Bradshaw, Peter?" asked Eleanor.

"Because she wanted me to travel with you," he said.

"Now I am intrigued, Peter," said Eleanor. "You are saying that Miss Bradshaw has asked you, who does not work for the library, to ask me if I want to go on a mission with you. This sounds about as far-fetched as you can get. Look, Peter, if there is something you want to tell me, you don't need to make up stories."

"Let me ask you another way, Eleanor," said Peter. "Forget my participation in the donation. Would you accept another mission given what happened in Wales?"

"Yes, I would," said Eleanor, "but I might request someone accompany me for safety."

Peter smiled broadly.

Eleanor also smiled and, with a laugh, said, "You are going to accompany me for safety! Now I get it."

"Okay," said Peter. "Then it is settled. You and I are going to travel together to get the next donation back to London."

"Just a minute," said Eleanor. "You still haven't answered my question. Why you?"

"Because the donation is a bird book that Miss Bradshaw wants to authenticate," Peter replied. "I am the designated expert on its authenticity. The reason I brought you bird-watching was to discuss the plan away from any prying eyes. So, you are in then?"

"I would be delighted," she said.

"You haven't asked where we are going," Peter replied.

"Okay, where are we going?" Eleanor said.

"France," Peter said.

"France!" Eleanor exclaimed. "Why France?"

"Do you remember meeting Mademoiselle Dupont in Mularchy?" Peter asked.

"Yes. She was quite chic, as I recall," said Eleanor.

"That's her," said Peter.

"During the war, many of the valuable possessions were stolen by the Nazis," Peter said, "but some were safely hidden away. Mademoiselle Dupont saw how culturally important objects could so easily be lost and wanted to send any British items to this country for safe keeping. She also thinks they should go to where they originated for the use of the citizens. I will notify Miss Bradshaw of your acceptance of the mission, and she will inform you of the details."

They wandered back to Eleanor's cottage discussing birds, and Peter eventually bade her good evening. She entered the cottage and then saw the map and data sheet of her robin observations, which reminded her of the unfinished letter for Gerald.

Eleanor J. Hutchinson, Robinsong
Cottage, Deacon's Lane, Rabbit's
Burrough, Herts.

June 24, 1948

Dear Gerald,

I hope this letter finds you well wher-
ever you might be. The months have flown
by since I last wrote, and so much has
happened. I have had the opportunity
to travel to the Lake District where I
met Kalmia Rosenblum. Her family knows
the Ashfords, who you know through the
BMNH where Christopher Ashford volunteers as a visitor guide. I was able to
see more robins while I was in the Lake
District, which tonight I amassed into a
summary data sheet. I also made a map of
the locations.

This evening, I was about to begin
writing when a villager stopped by
wanting to go bird-watching. It turned
out he had more than bird-watching
on his mind. He asked if I would go
to France on another mission, as he
called it, to bring home a donation for
library. I have agreed to go.

In the meantime, I have to be honest,
I am struggling on how to start the
scientific paper on robins. My worry is
that it will not be seen as adequate
for publication. The editor could turn
me down because of the writing style,
the quality of the data, the analysis,

```
and my interpretation of the results. I
don't wish to burden you with my inad-
equacies but would be very appreciative
if you would consider reading the manu-
script before I submit it to the editor.
I hope I have not been too presumptuous
by enclosing a copy in this letter.

Sincerely,

Eleanor
```

Eleanor put aside the letter in the envelope to work on the manuscript. She imagined his response and thought he would encourage her to look at similar articles in the journal. Her confidence had grown over the months, and she was finding she needed Gerald's support less and less. Despite this, she enjoyed receiving his letters because they kept her imagination alive as she envisioned travelling abroad in search of exotic birds. She also had grown fond of his kind words and felt a certain kindred spirit with him. He seemed to know her mind uncannily well. The day had been a very full day of work, as she had spent it assembling her data, bird-watching with Peter, and writing to Gerald. Eleanor was ready for bed.

The following morning, Eleanor awoke to the song of a robin. She opened the window and bade good morning to Thales. She followed the same routine of getting to work where she spent the day with the laborious tasks of a librarian. She spent her break reading scientific papers that were similar to her robin manuscript to get an idea of how to compose her paper. In the evening at home, she was ready to get started.

The data showed a clear demarcation between breast plumage intensity of robins at Hertfordshire: robins to the south were not as intense as those to the north. Eleanor had shown widespread confirmation and used a novel method to do so – her watercolour colour chart. All she had to do was to learn to write like a scientist. She was a voracious reader but had written little more than correspondence.

She read several of the papers on the subject. Most British robins had a more intense reddish-orange plumage on the breast than those in eastern England and the continent. The line of separation was fuzzy but appeared near Hertfordshire, which was coincidentally where Eleanor lived. She looked at the map where she had plotted the breast colours, and there was a concordance with a gradient of colour from east to west as far as Hertfordshire. She began to write first by describing what others had concluded and then by proceeding to describe her novel method of using a colour chart to record plumage intensity. She would follow this explanation with a list of all the places she had been, the robins she had seen with their corresponding plumage colours, and the dates of each visit. To illustrate the distribution of plumage variation, she included the map of Great Britain.

She typed quickly, not worrying about typos or the flow of the words. She wanted to get the pertinent details on paper. It took Eleanor several tries to get a draft she was happy with, and then she went to bed.

Eleanor was still harbouring self-doubts about whether this final hurdle – the publication of a scientific paper – might allude her and prevent her from attaining a job as an ornithologist. The manuscript sat on her desk, and each evening she scribbled in the margins and on the manuscript itself, noting the changes she thought were needed. After several tries, she had a manuscript she thought was nearly complete. She had made a carbon copy, which she enclosed in the letter to Gerald. The following day, she posted the letter. She wasn't sure where Gerald might be in the world, but he had mentioned remaining in South America. Eleanor estimated how long before she heard from him and thought she might have time to go to France first.

CHAPTER 21:

France

Eleanor was feeling the anxiety of travelling overseas to France. Not only was she about to travel to a foreign country with a different language and customs but she couldn't shake Gwyn's words about the moral dilemma of war. She wondered how she would deal with a firsthand experience of our dark side when the beast had escaped with ferocity and viciousness. She too had been a victim of this ferocity when her parents had been killed in the night bombing of London. She was about to see the ferocity on a grand scale, and she was worried.

Despite the melancholy of the war, news that the Olympics were to be held in London brought an air of infectious enthusiasm to the city. Eleanor too was in good spirits. She had had several opportunities to test her mettle and succeeded in all of them. This had not gone unnoticed, and it was the reason Miss Bradshaw had called upon her once more for a mission, this time to France.

Miss Bradshaw invited Eleanor into her office in midJuly as a heat wave was about to descend on the city. There was great interest in the library from the citizens of London, and the library was looking for something to make headlines.

Eleanor sat down on a chair opposite Miss Bradshaw, who sat behind a large oak desk. Her office was panelled in dark oak, and a framed diploma declaring that Miss Lilian Bradshaw was a certified librarian hung on the wall. On either side of her diploma were two tall windows where bright summer sunlight streamed into the room, creating shadows behind Eleanor and her chair. Against the rear wall was a sofa and a coffee table on which two cups and a teapot stood. The day's issue of the London Times was folded neatly on the coffee table. Against the far wall was a large table on which a few recently acquired books lay opened.

"I understand Peter has spoken to you about a mission to France to bring back a donation?" asked Miss Bradshaw.

"Yes, he has," said Eleanor with a smile.

"And you have agreed to go?" queried Miss Bradshaw.

"Yes," said Eleanor.

Eleanor knew she had done a good job to bring home donations from the Spratts and Gwyn Llewelyn. She also knew that the latter donation had required some cunning on her part, which Miss Bradshaw thought of as quick thinking, although somewhat unorthodox.

"We will attempt to not repeat the danger you faced and, may I say, navigated brilliantly during the Wales excursion," said Miss Bradshaw. She knew how to flatter and be practical in her choice of words.

"I have decided that Peter will accompany you on this journey, which I suspect you already know," she said.

"Peter did tell me he was coming along, but is it true that the reason is because he will authenticate the donation?" asked Eleanor.

"Some of what you say is true, but here is the reason," started Miss Bradshaw. "The book that is being donated is about British birds, of which he is an expert. Moreover, Peter speaks French, which I presume you do not."

Eleanor nodded in agreement.

"The books are Thomas Bewick's *A History of British Birds*, published in the eighteenth century, and Arthur Butler's 1896 edition of *British Birds with their Nests and Eggs*. The latter is not terribly valuable but will be a nice asset for the library. It is Bewick's book that we are most interested in. Are you familiar with these titles?"

"No. I am not," said Eleanor.

"Bewick's book has some of the finest wood engravings ever made, and moreover, his book inspired giants of British literature, the likes of Tennyson, Brontë, and Wordsworth. The book is valuable but not like the pocket Gospel you brought from Wales. I don't expect any trouble, but just in case, I have enlisted Peter's help. Just his presence will be a deterrent to any ne'erdowells."

Miss Bradshaw was remarkably efficient, and she showed it in her demeanour. She wore a matching short navy-blue jacket and skirt hemmed below the knee. Her hair was pulled back in a bun, and she wore reading glasses that clung to the end of her nose. Never married, Miss Bradshaw was about forty years old and still had her youthful shape. If there was a man in her life, Eleanor knew nothing of him.

Eleanor quite liked Miss Bradshaw for her efficiency, intelligence, and attention to detail. She saw Miss Bradshaw as a model librarian, which Eleanor could easily become if it were not for the museum, but she was not about to tell Miss Bradshaw. At least not at this time.

Miss Bradshaw continued, "You and Peter will travel by ferry from Folkstone to Calais, where you will be met by Mademoiselle Dupont. She will drive you to her residence, where you will pick up the books. Peter will inspect them, so you don't need to worry about their authenticity. Mademoiselle Dupont will provide accommodations at her residence. She is an important patron for the library, so if you deem it worthwhile and Mademoiselle Dupont is in agreement, you have approval to stay an extra day."

Eleanor was secretly thrilled to have an all-expenses-paid travel to France with Peter. Who wouldn't? *In-between library business, we could bird-watch and sample French cuisine, or who knows what else*, she thought. Peter had travelled to France several times prior to the war and would be keen to visit old haunts, Eleanor imagined.

"When do we leave?" asked Eleanor.

"As always, we need to be discrete. I am not expecting any trouble like you faced in Wales, but you need to be cautious and not lose sight of the mission," said Miss Bradshaw. "The

Olympics coming to London is going to draw all the public's attention, and so this is a good time to slip over to France and pick up the books. You will leave tomorrow morning. Peter will meet you at your cottage at 6:30 a.m. You will take the bus to the train station and travel to Folkstone together. You will purchase a ferry ticket and walk aboard. You will need your passport for French customs onboard the vessel."

Miss Bradshaw opened her desk drawer. "We arranged for your passport."

She handed it to Eleanor, who thumbed it open briefly before putting it into her pocket.

"Once you get to Calais, you will find Mademoiselle Dupont waiting with her automobile at the ferry landing. She will drive you and Peter to her residence a few hours away. It will be up to you and Peter to decide the order of events, depending on what the Mademoiselle decides. All you need to do is to package up the books and reverse your steps," concluded Miss Bradshaw. "Any questions?"

Eleanor wondered how Miss Bradshaw managed to get her a passport, but wasn't about to ask. Instead, she asked, "How will we clear the books through English customs on our return?"

"In this envelope are the letters of agreement signed by Mademoiselle Dupont to donate the books the library, a letter from me agreeing to accept the donation, and a custom's declaration that has already been approved. English customs officials have already been notified," said Miss Bradshaw.

Eleanor smiled with admiration at Miss Bradshaw's efficiency and attention to detail. This was not the first time Miss Bradshaw had accepted overseas donations, but nevertheless, she was impressively efficient.

"Well, thank you, Miss Bradshaw," said Eleanor. "I will await Peter's call first thing tomorrow morning." And with that, she left the library for home.

The next morning brought with it warm weather. *Nothing could be finer than travelling to France on a warm summer day*, thought Eleanor. Peter arrived right on time, and they caught the bus and train to Folkstone, where he bought two tickets to France. They boarded the ferry looking like a married couple or lovers masquerading as a union. The French customs agent looked at the two passports, noticed that their surnames were not the same, and then glanced at Eleanor's hand. She was not wearing a wedding ring. He looked into Eleanor's eyes and then smiled slyly at Peter.

"Enjoy your time in France, Monsieur and Mademoiselle," he said with a coy smile.

"Merci," Peter replied and took Eleanor by her arm down the companionway. He had a big smile on his face.

"What's so funny?" asked Eleanor.

Peter whispered in her ear, "He thought we had eloped."

Eleanor yanked her arm free. "Of all the nerve," she said.

"We don't want to make a fuss and draw attention to us, remember, Eleanor," he said with a grin.

"Stop it," she replied.

"Take my arm. We can pretend," said Peter.

She reluctantly took his arm and walked on in silence. After a minute had passed, Peter said in jest, "We would make a good couple, you know."

"And when we get back to London," Eleanor said, "we can tell Miss Bradshaw we gave up on the donation and decided to get married instead."

They both laughed.

Just a few short minutes out of the Folkstone dock, the ferry began to heave, and so did Peter. Eleanor felt cold and clammy, perspiration arose on her forehead, and deep in her stomach, a churning feeling was taking hold. She burped a few times and felt stomach acid burn her throat. She looked at Peter, who was already curled into a fetal position. *He looks green*, Eleanor thought.

The ship rose on huge waves and slammed into their troughs. The entire ship convulsed, and so did most people onboard. A few passengers that seemed unaffected carried on a conversation as if on a summer cruise in the Lake District, but for most, Eleanor and Peter included, the journey couldn't end soon enough.

"I think I am going to be sick," said Peter.

"Go the doorway where you can feel the wind and watch the horizon," she suggested.

Peter rose and staggered like a drunkard as the ship tossed him about. He grabbed the backs of chairs and door handles for stability and eventually made it to the doorway. He gulped several breaths of air while standing and staring out to sea. Eleanor wasn't feeling all so well herself but found that watching the horizon seemed to help. *The crossing is only a few hours*, she said to herself. *A few hours! France had better be worth it!*

CHAPTER 22:
Mademoiselle Dupont

True to Miss Bradshaw's word, Mademoiselle Dupont was waiting for Eleanor and Peter at the ferry dock. She was sporting sun glasses, a tailored jacket, a blouse opened at the neck with a colourful scarf, and a kerchief wrapped around her head.

"Bonjour, Miss Hutchinson and Mr. Saunders. I trust your crossing was not too difficult."

Eleanor noticed the unusually silent Peter was not on form.

"To be honest, Mademoiselle Dupont, I found it a bit rough. This is the first time I have been on a ferry boat," said Eleanor.

"First time!" exclaimed Mademoiselle Dupont. "Then this must also be your first time to France. I will have to show you the best we have on offer then."

She turned to Peter to touch his arm.

"How is my dear Peter," she said.

"Not very well, I am afraid," he replied. "I never have got used to travel at sea."

"Let's find a small café where you can recover, shall we?" said Mademoiselle Dupont.

They picked up their bags to follow Mademoiselle Dupont out of the ferry terminal station to her waiting car, a burgundy Peugeot roadster. Eleanor and Mademoiselle sat in the front seats while Peter slumped in the rear.

"I've never seen Peter in such a state," said Mademoiselle Dupont.

"You've known each other for some time then?" enquired Eleanor, thinking that there might be more to their relationship than what she knew. Peter was an interesting character. He loved birds, but he also enjoyed the finer pleasures of life. He was not averse to stealing away for a weekend to Bristol or to enjoying a show in London. He had spoken of travelling in Europe, and France was a favourite destination. Although he worked for the RSPB, his life was not defined by it.

Mademoiselle Dupont steered the car along the cobblestone streets. Destruction from the war was evident everywhere. Shards of once multi-storey buildings refused to collapse into the rubble of bricks littering the roadside. Stumps stood where there had once been trees. Despite the pall, life had returned to France as the citizenry and government tried to put the past behind them.

"We have a little drive ahead of us," said Mademoiselle Dupont as she motored onto the highway and looked at Peter in her rearview mirror. "In your present condition, I think we should stop for a refreshment. There is a café not far from here."

She drove into a small town with narrow streets to park on the roadside alongside a small café called Lydia's. Once Peter had pulled himself out of the back seat and stretched, the threesome entered the café. The waitress brought three espressos and croissants to a small table with wicker chairs and an ashtray.

"What is your house like, Mademoiselle?" asked Eleanor.

"Oh, Miss Hutchinson," said Mademoiselle Dupont until she was stopped short by Eleanor.

"Please call me Eleanor. Everyone does."

"If you insist, Eleanor," said Mademoiselle, emphasizing Eleanor's name.

"Now, where was I?" asked Mademoiselle. "Oh, yes, I live in Chateau de Rivière near the town of Bayeux. The town has just had the tapestry returned after it was in hiding during the war. Unfortunately, the chateau was not in the best condition prior to the war, and after the Germans and then the Allies used it as a headquarters and hospital, the old family home is in a poor state. I have arranged for you to stay nearby in an abbey. We can meet at the chateau during the day but will have our meals elsewhere. I can then spoil you with some fine cuisine of this region."

Peter was beginning to regain his form. "Eleanor and I would also like to watch birds if there is an opportunity." Eleanor turned to look at Peter, who was a little dishevelled, gave him a little smile, and then looked back at Mademoiselle Dupont.

"I think we can do that," she said. "Are you ready for a drive through the countryside?"

They finished their coffees and climbed back into Mademoiselle's car. Eleanor and Peter were quite content to let Mademoiselle Dupont chauffeur them around France; the ferry trip had been quite draining, and the last thing they wanted was to have to make a long drive on their own.

Much of the countryside was arable farmland where, only a few years before, German and Allied forces fought and pursued each other. Many of the cities and towns bore the scars of the conflict, but as Eleanor and Peter puttered along the road with Mademoiselle at the wheel, the warmth of the evening made the war seem like a distant memory.

After a few hours of driving, Eleanor was feeling hungry. Mademoiselle Dupont looked at her watch and seemed to read Eleanor's mind.

"Let's find a restaurant where we can have dinner," she said as she wheeled off the main road into the town.

The night had descended by the time the dinner was finished, and they still had a few hours of driving ahead of them.

"I have arranged for accommodations for you at the St. Jude's Abbey not far from my chateau," said Mademoiselle Dupont. "They are aware you might be a little late arriving, so no worries."

Peter quipped, "Ah, St. Jude, the patron Saint of hopeless causes. That's us, Eleanor."

"Hopelessness is their specialty, Peter," fired back Eleanor with a smile. Mademoiselle stared straight ahead.

It was well into the evening when Mademoiselle reached the entrance of the abbey. A few lights were all that indicated someone was about. Eleanor and Peter climbed out of the car and slung their bags over their shoulders.

"Bon nuit," said Mademoiselle. "I will pray for you tonight Peter," she said with a smile.

"Bon nuit," Peter replied. "What time should we be ready tomorrow?"

"I will arrive at 8:30 for an early start."

"Good night," said Eleanor as Mademoiselle drove off.

"I will pray for you too, Peter, but what good it will do, only God knows," she said.

Eleanor was assigned a spartan room with a carving of Christ on a crucifix over the bed. The sheets were white and unadorned. The unheated room was very cool despite the warm summer weather. A small window was the only connection to the outdoors. The lavatory was down the hall and shared by other guests. She climbed into bed and went off to sleep in complete darkness.

The next morning, the sun pierced her room through the tiny window to light up the crucifix on the wall above Eleanor's head. She leapt out of bed and hastily got ready for breakfast. Down the hallway, she could hear faint noises of breakfast being prepared. She entered a great hall where nuns and a few guests were eating around large wooden tables. Peter was mingling with the nuns, who were smiling at him as he told stories. They were likely as interested in having a man share their table as they were amused by his stories. Peter saw Eleanor enter the room and gestured for her to join him. She waved him away and went to a vacant table where he joined her. "Not up for the company of nuns today?" he asked with a smile.

"Piety is not my strong suit," she returned. "With all the death and destruction in recent years, it must be difficult to maintain the faith."

She and Peter had some time before Mademoiselle was to arrive, so they went for a walk on the grounds. They saw a few robins, which Eleanor dutifully noted for their breast plumage intensity. Before long, they heard the Peugeot sputtering down the driveway toward the abbey with Mademoiselle Dupont at the wheel, her sunglasses on her nose and silk scarf in the wind.

"Sleep well?" she asked.

"Yes," said Eleanor. "It was unearthly quiet."

"Today, I want to show you the Bayeux tapestry, have lunch near the sea, and then take you to the chateau to look at the books I want to donate," said Mademoiselle. "I also want to give you a gift from France, Eleanor. We need to make a quick stop at the chateau."

They climbed into Mademoiselle Dupont's car to arrive a few minutes later at the chateau. Mademoiselle Dupont led them through the front door and into the foyer, where they were joined by a thin man in a black suit with a tape measure around his neck. The foyer was a gleaming white against which a black wrought-iron balustrade wound itself up to a second floor. Overhead hung a massive black chandelier. A door on the east side of the foyer was open where morning sunlight streamed into the foyer and where a silhouetted man stood.

"This is Henri, my tailor," she said. "He designs and creates all of my outfits. I have asked Henri to do the same for you, Eleanor."

Eleanor was quite taken aback by the offer. She had always bought her clothes off a rack or had her mother sew them on an old foot-powered machine.

"What do you think, Henri?" said Mademoiselle Dupont. Henri stepped forward out of the light and into the coolness of the foyer.

"She is very beautiful. This will be an easy task for me," he said.

Eleanor blushed and looked at Peter, who had an impish grin on his face. Henri pulled out his tape measure and began measuring Eleanor. She felt a little uneasy having him touch her, even if he did it so gently.

"I think a classic design is called for. Nothing too over-stated. Is that how you say it in English?" said Henri.

"Neutral colours, maybe navy blue with a white blouse and a scarf as an accent," he muttered. "Fine, that is all I need. Go enjoy your day."

"Come," ordered Mademoiselle, and Eleanor and Peter followed and climbed into her car to drive into the ancient city of Bayeux.

Eleanor had read about how Bayeux was the first city to be liberated by the Allied invasion of France on the day after DDay. She could see how the city had been spared the bombing and fighting of other coastal towns so that the cathedrals and old city were intact. Narrow roads in Bayeux wound between taupe two-storey stone buildings with slate roofs. Shuttered windows added to the austerity of the town, but its ancient past made up for its simplicity of design. The recent past was not something to celebrate, and Bayeux seemed to be quietly awaiting a new day. Mademoiselle Dupont parked the car, and together they went by foot to the museum to view the tapestry.

Eleanor was taken aback by the eleventh-century Bayeux tapestry illustrating the now-famous war between Harold and William, Duke of Normandy, that stretched over two-hundred feet long. She found the story equally vibrant as the embroidered colours. After they had absorbed the historical immensity of the story of William the Conqueror, Eleanor emerged with Peter and Mademoiselle into the sunshine of a warm summer day. It was time for lunch, and Mademoiselle had chosen a quaint restaurant near the cathedral.

Eleanor could feel the warmth of the afternoon building in the sunshine, and so she moved to stand in the shade where a young boy, not much more than nine years of age and in need of a bath and new clothes, was staring up at her. His blue eyes and sandy hair made him look innocent despite his outward appearance. He was saying something to her in French, which she did not understand, all the while gesturing for her to follow. She looked at Peter and

Mademoiselle, who said, "He is inviting you to come hear him sing. At their practice session. In the cathedral."

"Tell him we are about to have lunch. Maybe afterwards," said Eleanor. Mademoiselle spoke to the boy, who then departed toward the cathedral.

The restaurant served Normandy-country-style terrines and game at small tables overlooking the street. A large bar, behind which a thriving kitchen staff was preparing meals, served to separate patrons from workers. The floor of small black and white tiles squeaked as Eleanor adjusted her wrought-iron chair under the table. The conversation was friendly, in which Mademoiselle described the region and its highlights, what life had been like in the past few years during and after occupation, and what she saw for the future.

Feeling full and contented, the three friends – Eleanor and Peter had warmed to Mademoiselle Dupont very quickly, and the feeling was mutual – stepped into the sunshine. Eleanor reminded her two companions about the invitation from the young boy, and they decided to visit the cathedral. They followed where the young boy had disappeared up a cobblestone incline to the great wooden doors of the cathedral. Peter pushed open a smaller passageway door, through which Eleanor and Mademoiselle Dupont entered.

Rising from the apse was the sweet sounds of boys' voices. The repeated harmonies of "Miserere mei, Deus" bounced off the stone walls of the cathedral to echo down its full length. The cathedral was empty except for Eleanor, Peter, and Mademoiselle Dupont. Eleanor was moved by the transcendental quality of the voices of boys, who looked more like street urchins than the voices of the Holy Spirit. Singing to God to wash away sins where thousands had been recently killed and whole towns had been demolished seemed especially poignant, although Eleanor couldn't help wondering why it had happened in the first place. She sat in a pew and closed her eyes to allow her mind to immerse itself in the harmonies. When she opened her eyes again, the sunlight entering through the stained-glass windows had created a kaleidoscope of colour across the floor. A white marble effigy of Mary and Jesus stared coldly and unmoving at her.

Back in the warmth of the afternoon sun, Mademoiselle Dupont gave Eleanor and Peter a summary history of the regions.

"There have been many wars here over the centuries," she said. "You saw the tapestry of Guillaume le Conquérant, who departed from Port de Divessur-Mer not far away from here to kill Englishmen on your beaches. During the war a few years ago, many young soldiers from many countries lost their lives on our beaches. I would like you to see a cemetery. Many British died here."

She drove the car to a cemetery in Bayeux. Eleanor got out of the car where line upon line of thousands of white crosses awaited her in deathly silence. She was stunned and also stood in silence.

"One of our donors told me his son died on the beaches during the DDay surge," she said to Mademoiselle Dupont. "He might be buried here."

"There are over four thousand British soldiers buried here. Also, many Canadians. And Australians," she said.

"I think I need some time alone," said Eleanor.

She stood silent for several minutes and then began to walk among the crosses. She could hear Gwyn's words of his nightmare where his son took his last breath. The names of the fallen men were etched in each cross. Eleanor read them one by one as if in tribute to ears that could no longer hear and voices that could no longer speak.

After a while, she noticed a grounds-keeper working a garden nearby. She sauntered over to him, who stopped raking leaves to listen to her.

"Bonjour, Mademoiselle," he said.

"Parlez-vous anglais, monsieur? Do you speak English, sir?" she asked.

"A little," he said.

"Is there a list of names of the buried soldiers?" she asked.

"Oui. Dans le batiment. In the building," he said pointing to a building on the edge of the cemetery.

Eleanor thanked him and walked to the building where she found a directory. She turned to the section with surnames beginning with an L, ran her finger down the list to Llewelyn, and stopped. She stepped back with her mouth agape. She saw Rhys Llewelyn's name halfway down the page. Beside it was a coordinate for the location of his burial plot in the cemetery. She jotted down the location, walked back to the cemetery, paced to the correct row, and began to walk, counting crosses as she went. After a few minutes, she stopped to see Rhys Llewelyn's name engraved on a gleaming white cross. She began to weep.

"Hello, Rhys," she began. "We have never met, and this was not the way either of us had intended it to be, but so it is."

She told Rhys about meeting her father, where he lived, shared a few humorous moments, and talked about how his father missed him.

"I will tell him we meet and send him your love," she said. The cross, silent as always, tracked the shadow of the sun in lockstep military precision with all the other crosses. Rhys's was no different than the others.

Suddenly, Eleanor realized she had her sketch book and watercolours. She hastily took them from her bag and began to draw Rhys's cross. She let the white of the paper be the cross against a deep blue and purple shadow cast by the trees behind. Some green grass at the foot of the cross represented new life. When she was satisfied, she packed up her things and began to walk away. Then she stopped.

"Oh, I nearly forgot to say farewell," she said, and with tears streaming down her cheeks, she walked back to find Mademoiselle and Peter.

"Had enough, Eleanor?" asked Peter.

"For now," said Eleanor. "Mademoiselle Dupont, do you think I could see the beaches where these men died?"

"Why yes, of course. I am always keen to show anyone interested in the war," she said.

After a short drive, they arrived at the beach. Eleanor asked to be left alone for a while. She didn't know how long she stared out to sea, but eventually she took off her shoes, rolled up her pant legs, and walked to the water's edge. She turned around to look at the shore and imagined that fateful day that Rhys had come ashore. She closed her eyes to hear the screams and gunfire Gwyn had described. Like Rhys, she fell to her knees, and the sea cooled her legs. She reached into the sand and imagined him letting the grains slip away from his hand while his life slipped away from his body. With a start, she opened her eyes. There were no soldiers. No armed vehicles, no whizzing of bullets. Instead, it was Peter. He reached down with his hand to help Eleanor stand.

"It is very moving being here," he said. "The solemn sea and the loss of lives."

They turned away from the sea and moved toward the land.

"I lost my parents during the war, Peter," Eleanor said. "They died in the bombing. I was left an orphan at sixteen. I was the lucky one."

When they reached the car, the sea breeze was ruffling the leaves on the trees, and Mademoiselle's hair was blowing into her face.

"I think it is time for a glass of wine," she said, "back at the chateau."

CHAPTER 23:

Donated Books

Eleanor sat silently in the car speeding along the country lanes where cows in fields stood in sleepy farmyards. Mademoiselle Dupont turned the Peugeot into a treelined driveway that made its way to her derelict chateau.

"My dear family home has seen better days," she lamented. "The Germans used it as a command centre until the Allies chased them out to use it as a hospital. The army men were very understanding and helped where they could, but things just disappeared. Before the invasion, I took the precaution to hide most of the cherished art and objects, including the books I want to donate. I realized that the books were vulnerable here, and because they deal with British subjects, the library in London seemed the best and safest home for them."

Eleanor and Peter stepped from the car to follow Mademoiselle Dupont through the front door of the chateau. Mademoiselle Dupont led them up the stairs to a waiting room that had a few ornate couches and chairs, a table, and a foot-worn carpet on the floor. Eleanor could see that the chateau's glory days had passed. The walls were barren and the windows were curtain-less. One window was open, letting fresh air and birdsongs waft through the room. *At least life goes on outside*, she thought.

A few minutes later, Mademoiselle arrived with a bottle of wine, three tall-stemmed wine glasses, and two books.

"Before we look at the books, let me pay a toast," she said while uncorking the bottle of wine.

She handed a glass of wine to Eleanor and Peter before raising her own.

"To my newfound friends, Eleanor and Pierre, whose good graces are always welcome at Chateau de Rivière."

After a sip of wine, Peter raised his glass and said, "To Mademoiselle Dupont, who is a bridge between nations and a friend to all. May her graces spread around the world."

"Hear, hear," said Eleanor followed by a sip of wine.

"Now," said Mademoiselle Dupont, "the moment we have all been waiting for."

She placed both books on the table. Eleanor and Peter walked to the table where they peered at the old texts. He opened Bewick's book and carefully turned several pages.

"The book is in remarkably good shape," he said, "considering its age. I have admired Bewick's woodcuts for a long time, and so this is a special privilege to see a first edition with his illustrations." He continued to look through the book, peering every so often at fine details through a small magnifier.

"The British Library will be all the more enriched by having this lovely book in their collection," he said.

Then he turned to Butler's book of British birds. He followed the same procedure of turning several pages, checking the binding, and squinting at details through his magnifier.

"This too is in fine nick," he said. "Libraries don't usually have Butlers, but in this case, we will make an exception."

Eleanor smiled, and Mademoiselle said, "I will miss my Butler."

"Now, I know this has been an eventful trip for you," said Mademoiselle, "and we need to unwind, so I have arranged for dinner in Bayeux. After dinner, I will drop you off at the abbey for the night, and in the morning, I will bring the books and pick you up to make the drive to Calais."

Eleanor was more than happy to let Mademoiselle make all the decisions for the next twenty-four hours so she could think and wonder. *Peter will be good company for me*, she thought.

As promised, Mademoiselle Dupont treated Eleanor to French cuisine, the likes of which she had never tasted. Peter had travelled to France often enough to know what to expect, but both enjoyed the hospitality. The conversation was lively and fun, the food was novel and delicious, and the wine flowed. By 10 p.m., Eleanor and Peter were ready to settle in for the night. Mademoiselle drove them to the abbey where she bade them bon nuit.

The following morning, Mademoiselle Dupont arrived as planned with the books in tow. She handed them to Eleanor, who wrapped the books in paper and placed them in a box and then into a bag marked "British Library." She offered the front seat of Mademoiselle's car to Peter so she could have time to herself in the rear.

"And here is my gift for you, Eleanor, care of Henri," said Mademoiselle Dupont, handing Eleanor a simple box tied with a ribbon and stamped with Henri's logo on the upper left corner.

"I am speechless at your generosity, Mademoiselle Dupont," said Eleanor.

"I rarely get to meet lovely young people, and so this is my opportunity to treat you like a good friend," said Mademoiselle.

The car wheeled out of the abbey, along a country road, and to a highway to Calais. The uneventful journey was several hours long, which gave Eleanor plenty of time to think about what had happened in France and ponder the world she inhabited.

Eleanor and Peter bid adieu to Mademoiselle, thanking her for her donation and hospitality before boarding the evening ferry to Folkstone. Peter said he was going to use the time onboard to catch up on his sleep, leaving Eleanor on her own to roam the ferry. She left Peter resting on a seat to step on to the outer deck. The air was still and the ocean was calm. The sun was setting as the ferry pulled out of the dock, its huge diesel engines throbbing as it took a heading for Folkstone. The sea parted, leaving a wake as the bow pushed forward through the reflective water surface.

Eleanor was alone in her thoughts. She began to ponder the immensity of what she had just witnessed in the past few days. The deaths of thousands of young men laid out row upon row, each with a name and a cross. The sombre sight brought flashbacks of the birds in the museum laid in rows with name tags affixed to each of them. Like the birds in the museum, the soldiers in the Bayeux Cemetery were international, hailing from Britain, Germany, Canada, Poland, Australia, New Zealand, Russia, France, and Czechoslovakia. Both the young men and the birds had died but for different causes. She wondered about the grief surrounding all this death. She wondered where God was in all of this. She wondered about the young choirboy singing ever so righteously and how he reflected the unwavering love of God. She wondered about all the young men that died while young women were spared. So much despair was swirling around in Eleanor's head as the ferry glided on across a sea of tranquillity.

By the time Eleanor and Peter arrived in London, the library had closed for the day. There was a festive air to the city from the Olympics, and crowds of people were milling about. Peter drove his car to a rear door that Miss Bradshaw opened to let them in.

"How did it go?" she asked.

"Swimmingly," Peter replied. "Eleanor was an exemplary representative of the British Library. I was in charge of choosing the wine."

Unmoved by Peter's nonsense, Miss Bradshaw said, "Let's see what you have got."

She led Eleanor and Peter into the main library where her office door was open. Inside Eleanor immediately recognized Patrick and Mrs. Quimby among the invited guests. She acknowledged them with a partial smile.

"You can put the books on the table, Eleanor," said Miss Bradshaw.

Eleanor stepped forward to place the bag marked "British Library" on the large oak table. The crowd gathered around.

Miss Bradshaw spoke to the small crowd. "The two books you are about to see are a donation, a generous donation, from one of our finest patrons, Mademoiselle Dupont of Bayeux, Normandy. As many of you know, Bayeux has been in the middle of the atrocities of the war, and Mademoiselle Dupont's home there was occupied by both German and Allied forces. She expected such a turn of events, so she took the commonsense approach to hide away her precious things, including these two books. Her concern, rightly so, was that her home would be looted, which did occur, and without hiding them, all her precious things would have been lost forever. The two books you are about to see are part of the history of our two great nations. The books are written by British writers for a British audience, but their survival is due to the care and attention of our dear Mademoiselle Dupont. She decided that the books, being British and due to the recent events in her home country of France, should find a home in the British Library. Miss Hutchinson here, under the watchful eye of Mr. Saunders, has come straight to the library this evening with the books in tow."

With that, Miss Bradshaw opened the flap of the bag and pulled out the books wrapped in paper. She placed them on the table for all to see and gently opened the paper. The two books gave off a faint pungent aroma as the paper was removed from around them. The crowd moved near as Miss Bradshaw opened Arthur Butler's 1896 edition of *British Birds with their Nests and Eggs*. She carefully flipped open a few pages for the crowd to see.

"This will be a lovely addition to the library, Eleanor," Miss Bradshaw whispered to Eleanor. "Well done."

Then she turned to the crowd and said, "This book, Butler's 1896 edition of *British Birds with their Nests and Eggs*, will be available to view by permission in our Reading Room later this month. Now, for the pièce de résistance, here is the book we are especially pleased to have received. This, ladies and gentlemen, is Thomas Bewick's *A History of British Birds* published in the eighteenth century. For some of you, the name Thomas Bewick might not mean anything, but in his day, Bewick was considered one of the finest engravers in the country. If you look closely, you will see that his engravings often show tiny human figures in the composition. His ability to illustrate such fine details brought him accolades."

She carefully opened the pages to one of the tail pieces, whereupon the crowd moved in closely. The crowd was in awe at the works, and several people surrounded Eleanor and Peter to hear about their time in France. Peter was regaling and gently embellishing the story of their time in France, much to the delight of the crowd.

She noticed that Patrick and Mrs. Quimby were at the table looking intently at the Bewick book.

"Just look at the fine lines he accomplished. It is a remarkable work of art," he said.

"Indeed," replied Eleanor. "Mrs. Quimby, I wasn't aware of your interest in birds and art."

Eleanor's questioning was penetrating, but like Patrick, Mrs. Quimby was unmoved.

"Patrick said he was coming to drive you and Peter home after the event and asked if I would like to come along," said Mrs. Quimby. "A night out with a handsome young man. How could I say no?"

"I see," said Eleanor. "Well, I hope it was worth it."

"Indeed, it was," said Mrs. Quimby.

Eleanor returned to the crowd, puzzled by Patrick and Mrs. Quimby's responses. She could see no reason why that particular book was so important, and she also wondered why Mrs. Quimby would say that Patrick was going to pick them up when Eleanor had come with Peter in his car. Something wasn't quite right.

The wine was loosening up the crowd, and after an hour or so, Miss Bradshaw announced that Eleanor and Peter had had a long day and that they should be relieved of their duties to go home. It was a polite way to have the crowd leave.

Eleanor and Peter said goodbye to Miss Bradshaw, Patrick, and Mrs. Quimby.

Patrick replied, "I forgot that Peter had his own car. I will see Mrs. Quimby home then. Goodnight." He waved farewell.

Eleanor glanced back and saw Patrick, Mrs. Quimby, and Miss Bradshaw leaning over the book once more. Something didn't add up, but they weren't about to tell her. Neither was Peter going to divulge any secrets on the drive back to Rabbit's Burrough.

It was midsummer, which should have been a halcyon time for Eleanor, but she could not rest. She had too much on her mind. Fortunately, she had the weekend to herself. She had made a cup of tea to take into the garden where she had found solitude in the past. A large wicker chair awaited.

Eleanor leaned back so her legs were straight out in front of her and rested her head on the back of the chair so she could stare up into the clouds. In the blue sky between the clouds, she could see the sickle-shaped outline of migrating swifts coursing overhead in pursuit of flying insects, en route to their winter destination in Africa. Behind her, in one of the tall elms that towered over the cottage's property, a wood pigeon cooed a gentle soothing call. Down by the garden patch where her late crop of courgettes awaited harvesting, she heard Thales singing his robin song. The songs of birds and the smells of the late summer normally made Eleanor feel very rested, but she had Gerald on her mind. She wondered if he might have gone to Panama as he had mentioned previously, so she loaned out some books on the subject. She read about its history and what little was known about its birds. *Panama seems like a good destination for Gerald to explore*, she thought.

When Monday arrived, Eleanor went off to work at the library, and like most days, her only stop was to post her correspondence. A few days later, she arrived home at the end of the day, where she met Jack MacLaughlin, the postman, doing his rounds.

"Letter for you, Miss Hutchinson."

"There is no return address on it, so it might be something secret," he joked.

"I get plenty of mail in my job, as you know, Mr. MacLaughlin."

She closed the door behind her and went to the drawing room where letters from Gerald were piling up on a desk. She sat down, opened the letter, and began to read.

```
Gerald Benson, c/o British
Museum (Natural History), South
Kensington, London.

July 15, 1948

Panama City, Republic of Panama

Dear Eleanor:

I received your letter here in Panama.
I decided, after a trip to Ecuador, to
```

stop in Panama. I am interested in this
isthmus of land because of the mix of
Nearctic and Neotropical birds whose
ranges overlap here.

I spent the first few days getting
settled into Panama City and visiting
the seashore. The old part of the city
called Viejo was the first European
settlement on the Pacific, which overlooks an extensive beach with a large
number of waders, both the Scolopacidae
and the Ardeidae. In the next few weeks,
I plan to venture into the Darien region
in search of land birds.

I see my advice on writing a scientific
paper was useful, and thank you for
enclosing your manuscript. On the face
of it, I think you have a good story
worthy of publication. The reviewers
might think that you are not offer-
ing much more, so you might wish to be
prepared for a rebuttal. What you have
that is new is the colour swatch used
to compare plumages, which is worthy
of publication in my opinion. In all, I
think you have a good chance of having
your paper published and recommend

```
you submit it. Don't be deterred by
the process.

Sincerely,

Gerald Benson
```

Gerald's last words, "don't be deterred," resonated with Eleanor. She garnered up the courage to read her draft manuscript once more and to make corrections. She thought it was ready for submission to the editor. Eleanor drafted a letter to accompany the manuscript, which was ready for posting to the journal, but set it aside. She held the same concern as when she had first decided to write to the museum. *What would I do if the paper was outright rejected?* she thought. *Maybe I am not suited to a job there.* Eleanor's visit to France had also left her unsettled about the ethical dilemma of killing birds to add to the specimen collection at the museum. She wasn't sure if or how to approach Gerald with her dilemma, but after a while, she decided she would confront him.

```
Eleanor J. Hutchinson, Robinsong
Cottage, Deacon's Lane, Rabbit's
Burrough, Herts.

August 2, 1948

Dear Gerald,
```

Thank you for your letter from Panama
and for your advice on submitting a
paper for publication in a journal. You
have been very generous with your time
and advice.

I am pleased that you have an opportunity to explore Panama. The country is
not one that I know much about, but from
what I read, the birdlife is impressive.
I wish you luck in your endeavours.

Once again, I apologize if I am asking
for too much advice, but I have found
myself in a dilemma following a trip
to France. I travelled there to get two
books that were donated to the library
by a Mademoiselle Dupont of Bayeux.
While there, I visited the Bayeux
Cemetery where thousands of soldiers lay
buried. Ever since, I have been haunted
by the similarity between the tragedy of
their deaths with the killing of birds
for the museum. I hope you do not take
this as an affront to your profession.
My intentions are to find justification
for the practice. The soldiers died for
a cause. Can a similar justifiable cause
be found for the killing of birds?

While travelling across northern France,
I saw the destruction of the towns and
the countryside where war raged a few
years ago. Many soldiers died, but so
did the countryside. Few birds sang in
the most heavily shelled areas. I saw
what the world would be like without
birds. Rather than collecting specimens, I wonder if we should shift our
focus to protecting the places where
they live. To do that would require a
fundamental change in people's views
of nature from one of exploitation to
one of protection. That might be a tall
order in postwar Britain where rationing
has just ended and people are struggling
to survive, but maybe one day soon, the
discussion will begin.

I would appreciate hearing your views on
the subject.

Sincerely,

Eleanor

The following morning, Eleanor posted the letters on
her way to the library. She expected Gerald's letter from
Panama would take about ten days to arrive in her letter
box, and once again she was right.

Gerald Benson, c/o British
Museum (Natural History), South
Kensington, London.

September 15, 1948

Panama City, Republic of Panama

Dear Eleanor:

I received your letter of August 2. I
am pleased you are proceeding with the
manuscript for publication but was left
troubled by your ethical dilemmas. Killing
birds does not delight me. To the contrary, I find it a necessary task of my
profession. Many of the bird specimens
held by the BMNH were collected years
ago by prominent naturalists of the day.
Rather than toss them away, we are fortunate the museum has found room for the
millions of specimens. I know that does
not justify current actions, which you
are correct, might need to be modernized.
The museum regularly discusses its role
and function. They might be interested to
hear your views. One point I want to make
is that no one can predict the future with
much accuracy, and the specimens held by
the museum could become a gold mine of

life on Earth in the past. New techniques
are being developed that might unlock new
secrets. You drew a parallel between the
loss of life of soldiers with that of the
birds. Unlike the soldiers, whose lives
are now memories, the birds offer opportunities to learn more about our natural
world. As you have seen firsthand, you
can explore ideas of plumage variation in
robins from the museum's collection.

I agree with you that protection is an
important activity if we want to help
birds, but that takes a new breed of
person willing to garner the support.
Once again, the museum could assist
in showing British people the immense
diversity of birds and some exhibits on
the need for their conservation.

I can't say I have all the answers you
are seeking, Eleanor, and your thought-
ful questions have made me consider my
role more closely. I am hopeful we can
continue pondering these philosophical
and ethical questions.

Sincerely,

Gerald Benson

Eleanor had found a patient and understanding soul-mate in Gerald, although they had only corresponded by mail. Nevertheless, whenever she had a dilemma, she knew she could turn to him for advice.

CHAPTER 24:

Operation Magpie

Early September was a busy time at the library, leaving Eleanor little time to think about Gerald or the ethical dilemma she was in. Each day was full of regular librarian duties, and she longed to find some time to read about Panama. On Tuesday, Eleanor was assigned to the Reading Room where visitors could request to see books that were too important to go on loan. Eleanor was working her shift when an outgoing middle-aged man approached her desk.

"How can I help you?" she said.

The man said, "I understand that you have just acquired Thomas Bewick's book on British birds."

"Yes, we have, but we haven't catalogued it yet," said Eleanor.

"I have come all the way to London in hopes of seeing it. I have an interest in birds but am most excited to see the woodcut illustrations," said the man. "Do you like birds, Miss?"

"Yes, and the book is as special as you claim," said Eleanor.

"Is it possible to see it?" enquired the man.

"We don't normally allow views of uncatalogued books, but I can show you the book as long as you promise not to touch it. Once it is catalogued, you can come back and spend as long as you like perusing its pages," said Eleanor.

She rose from her desk and disappeared into a back room, returning moments later with the book. She was wearing white cotton gloves and placed the book on a table.

"I have been waiting a long time to see the original," said the man. "Thank you so much."

"You can't touch the book, sir," said Eleanor, "but I can show you some pages."

She opened the book, and the man stared intently at the images while Eleanor watched over his shoulder. He spent nearly a minute without uttering a word, and then said, "Thank you. I will take up your offer for a longer look later." With that, he walked out of the Reading Room. Eleanor was puzzled that he did not want to look at other pages but shrugged, closed the book, and returned it to the back room.

Tuesday was often the quietest day of the week at the library. Despite the lower turnout, Eleanor was still very busy all day and had no time to catch up on her research of Panama. She wanted to sound knowledgeable in her correspondence with Gerald but was finding little time to do so. The only solution was to stay late. She was in her office at closing time when Miss Bradshaw knocked on the door.

"Working late, Eleanor?" she said.

"Yes. I am researching birds in Panama, of all things, but won't be long. I will lock up after the cleaning staff leave."

"That is fine, but don't stay longer than that. You need your rest, and I worry about you travelling home at night. It is imperative you leave before nine," said Miss Bradshaw. Eleanor thought it odd that Miss Bradshaw used the word *imperative*.

The cleaners came and went by 8:30 p.m. and locked the doors behind them. Eleanor was quite enjoying the uninterrupted time alone in the library and missed the nine o'clock deadline. The long hours got the better of her, and Eleanor dozed off on a couch. Sometime after 1 a.m., she was awoken by a distant thud. She wasn't sure if it came from the library or outside, but it woke her up. She switched off the small reading lamp as a precaution.

Soft footsteps. She could hear footsteps ascending the stairs to the Reading Room. Eleanor moved silently to her door just in time to see the shadows of two people climbing the stairs. She thought she should call the police, but the intruders would hear her. Instead, she slipped like a cat to the base of the stairs to see if the intruders were armed. They were now on the second floor and out of sight. Ever so slowly, she crept up the stairs to the door of the Reading Room. Eleanor could see a faint light at the end of the Reading Room. Two men were fumbling to open the door to the precious books. They muttered something to one another, and then one man managed to open the door. Eleanor wondered how that was possible; the precious books were always kept in storage behind lock and key. Once the precious-book storage-room door was opened, the two men went inside, and Eleanor made her move. She slipped into the Reading Room and hid behind a bookcase. From there she could see and hear what the men were up to.

After a few minutes, the men emerged with an armload of books. They slipped the books into a bag and carefully closed it tight. Eleanor could see that the men had opened the precious-book storage area and were helping themselves to books worth tens or hundreds of thousands of pounds. One of them was the pocket Gospel she had just got from Gwyn. She was outraged.

One of the men then slung the bag over his shoulder and turned on his torch to find his way through the darkness. As he shone the light across the room, he thought he caught sight of someone behind a bookcase. He turned away and whispered in the ear of the other man, who promptly walked toward the opposite end of the bookcase where Eleanor lurked in the shadows.

Before Eleanor realized it, he had grabbed her from behind. The man with the books made a dash for the door while his accomplice attempted to subdue Eleanor. She stomped on his foot and dropped with all her weight, forcing her assailant to let go. She ran out the door and down the stairs where three constables were detaining the man with the books.

"Are you okay, Miss?" called out one of the constables.

"Yes," she said, gasping for air and pointing up the stairs. "There is another man upstairs in the Reading Room."

Two constables dashed past her and into the Reading Room. Muffled noises emanated from the room as the constables apprehended the second man.

Eleanor collapsed on the stairs. Suddenly, Miss Bradshaw appeared with Patrick and Mrs. Quimby.

"Eleanor," shrieked Miss Bradshaw. "What are you doing here? Are you hurt?"

"No. I am fine," she said. "What is going on? Why won't you tell me what is going on?" She was on the verge of tears.

"I will explain later," said Miss Bradshaw. "Right now, we need to get you taken care of. Come along to my office. Patrick, can you see that everything is alright with the constables and that the library is secure? We will need to see what damage was done later."

Eleanor was feeling very confused when she reached Miss Bradshaw's office.

"I can make you some tea, or I can get you something stronger if you wish," she said.

"Tea is fine," said Eleanor.

Patrick appeared at the door. "With a quick look, seems all is fine, except for one of the robbers. He appears to have a broken toe."

"What did you say?" said Miss Bradshaw.

"It looks like the robber was on the losing end of a confrontation," he said.

Miss Bradshaw looked at Eleanor and, seeing she was in stress, said, "Patrick, I think you need to take Eleanor home. We can discuss all this in the morning."

Patrick dropped Eleanor at her cottage after 4 a.m., and despite her tiredness, she did not sleep well. At 8 a.m., she decided that she wasn't going to fall back to sleep. Patrick arrived in his car around 10 a.m. to drive Eleanor to the library.

"You will need to make a statement to the police about last night," he said. "Miss Bradshaw wants to convene a meeting with you and with Mrs. Quimby and me as well. After that, you should be allowed to go home for some rest. Would you like to have lunch before I drive you home?" he asked.

"That is very kind, Patrick, but let's see how the morning unfolds," said Eleanor.

Eleanor and Patrick arrived at the library near noon. The police were patrolling inside and outside the library, and the press was busy taking notes. Cameras flashed, and a small crowd of onlookers were milling about, wondering what the fuss was all about. Patrick took Eleanor's arm and quickly escorted her through the press lines and the front door of the library. They made their way to Miss Bradshaw's room where she and Mrs. Quimby were speaking to a constable and what Eleanor suspected was a plainclothes policeman.

"Ah, here is Eleanor now," Miss Bradshaw said, rising from behind her desk. "She can give you a statement in the adjoining office if you like." The two men rose from their chairs and followed Eleanor into the room next door. She gave a statement of what she remembered from the previous night. They thanked her and departed.

Eleanor then returned to Miss Bradshaw's office where she, Patrick, and Mrs. Quimby were in a serious conversation.

"Ah, Eleanor," said Miss Bradshaw. "I can imagine you are wondering about last night's events?"

"Well, yes," said Eleanor, feeling somewhat puzzled. So much had transpired in the last few hours. She was feeling very tired, and thinking straight was not easy.

"Sit down and I will explain," said Miss Bradshaw. "Can you get the door please, Patrick?"

Once he returned, Miss Bradshaw continued. "Patrick, would you like to begin?"

"Sure," he said while he sat back in his chair and crossed his legs. "For some time now, we have been aware of an international smuggling ring that targets valuable objects for wealthy clients. I am not at liberty to tell you anything more than that except to say we got wind that the library might be one of the targets. The way the ring works is through well-coordinated actions of many individuals who only know the details of a small part of the grand plan. For example, there are people who do the breaking and entering, others who carry the loot across the country, and still others who transport the goods by sea or air. Then there are other individuals who work with the clients. Any one project involves a lot of people. The genius of the scheme is that if any one member is caught, he or she is unable to identify other members."

"So, if I have this right," said Eleanor, "what transpired last night was step one of an elaborate plan to take stolen books from the library to overseas collectors."

"That is correct, although sometimes the collectors are homegrown," said Patrick.

"So how did you know that the robbery would take place last night?" asked Eleanor.

"I am not at liberty to explain how we knew. Do you recall a young man who came to you in the Reading Room asking to see the new acquisition of Bewick's book on British birds?" asked Patrick.

"Yes, he was quite charming. Was he part of the ring?" Eleanor said with astonishment.

"We think so, although we have not identified him yet," returned Patrick.

"What did he have to do with the heist?" asked Eleanor.

"We think he was scouting the Reading Room," said Patrick.

"I thought I saw the men open the door to the precious books without the key," said Eleanor. "It is always locked. I make a point of it."

"It was someone inside the library," said Patrick.

"How do you know that?" she asked.

"We have suspected that a ring was operating for a long time. That is why we had Captain Furlough accompany you from Scotland."

"I am confused. Are you saying Captain Furlough was not who he said he was?" she asked.

Patrick smiled. "We were not aware of how the ring was operating. We wanted them to know the library had obtained more precious books but not to get their hands on them. Furlough was there to ensure that never happened."

"So how did you figure out that there was someone inside the library behind the scheme?" asked Eleanor.

"We've known ever since your near encounter at Gwyn's cottage in Wales," said Patrick. "Do you recall that Mrs. Quimby alerted us to a message in the newspaper that indicated you were a possible target?"

Eleanor nodded.

"No one knew you were going on that excursion except library staff. We just didn't know who alerted the thieves, but by those actions soon after you left, we were certain it was an inside source. We used you to increase the prize by collecting more precious books from donors in Scotland, Wales, and France to flush the would-be thief out from cover. And it worked," he said with a grin.

"But how did you know that last night would be the night of the robbery?" asked Eleanor.

"We weren't certain, but when the young man came looking for the copy of Bewick's that only the library staff would have known about, we thought the raid was imminent. The library has been under surveillance."

"I am sorry that I got in your way," said Eleanor.

"Well, it all turned out well," said Patrick.

"Who was the staff person on the inside behind all of this? You don't suspect me, do you?" asked Eleanor.

Patrick laughed. "Part of an elaborate international smuggling ring? I don't think so. You were already working for us."

"What do you mean?" she demanded.

"You were part of an elaborate plan to collect the donated books in the first place," he said. "With Miss Bradshaw's approval, of course. We just couldn't let you know until the culprits were caught."

Eleanor was stunned by all she had just heard. Patrick had been using her to break up a ring, and Mrs. Quimby was far more than a landlady. Mrs. Quimby obviously knew Patrick, although she hadn't let on until now. What did Miss Bradshaw know, and what about Peter or Mademoiselle Dupont? Did everyone but her know what was taking place? How was it that Mrs. Quimby became a codebreaker? There were plenty of unanswered questions.

Miss Bradshaw, who was listening intently from behind her desk, turned to Eleanor and said, "Now you know that everyone in this room agreed to collaborate to break up the book smuggling ring. I should have insisted that you leave the library last night rather than get you mixed up in all of this, but I didn't want you to know what was about to transpire. You had said you would lock up at nine after the cleaners left, but that didn't happen."

"I am sorry, Miss Bradshaw," said Eleanor. "I became so engrossed in my reading that I dozed off."

"Well," said Miss Bradshaw, "You managed to subdue one of the suspected robbers. Where did you learn to do that?"

"My father taught me how to defend myself against an attacker," she said. "I never thought I would need to use it in the library."

Patrick squirmed and thought to himself how formidable Eleanor had become. The woman he had thought to be mildmannered and docile harboured far more than met the eye.

"Well, Eleanor," said Miss Bradshaw. "Take the rest of the day off. Patrick will give you a lift home."

Eleanor, Patrick, and Mrs. Quimby left Miss Bradshaw to deal with the police and press. Mrs. Quimby said she had some shopping to do and would find her way home, leaving Eleanor with Patrick.

"Can I entice you to some lunch?" he asked.

"I am famished," she said. "I would be pleased to take you up on your offer."

Patrick had in mind a small intimate Indian café not far from the library. They arrived after the rush and found a table where they ordered their food.

"Patrick," began Eleanor.

"Hmm," he said, eyeing the wine list.

"I learned a lot about you today," she said.

"Uhhuh," he said.

"I presume you are not going to answer many of my questions," she said.

"Probably not," Patrick replied while still staring at the wine list. "Cabernet be good?"

Eleanor knew he was not going to divulge any more than he had to. That was his job.

"How long have you known about this robbery attempt?" she asked.

"Can't answer that," he replied.

"You aren't going to answer my questions, are you?"

Patrick put down the wine list and glanced around.

"Have you considered my question at Minsmere?" he asked.

"What question?" she asked.

"Have you considered a job with the Foreign Service?" he asked.

"I told you before," she said. "My interest is in birds and being a librarian."

"Maybe so, but that doesn't mean you couldn't come work for us," Patrick returned.

"What do you mean?" she asked. "Since when has the Foreign Service been interested in birdwatchers?"

"Ever since you agreed to pick up the books in Scotland," he replied.

Eleanor was stunned by his comment. She realized that her interest in birds was a perfect front. She had unwittingly been working to bring a gang of robbers to justice.

Patrick picked up the wine list again. "Cabernet it is," he said. "Suitable for a toast."

Following a relaxed lunch, Patrick drove Eleanor home to her cottage. He stopped the engine and said, "Thank you for being a good sport, Eleanor. You can be proud of what you did at the library. I wish you the best of luck in finding the perfect bird job, and if I can assist, don't hesitate to ask."

"Thank you for your kind words and lunch today. And thank you for giving me a lift home," she said.

"By the way," Patrick said. "Do you know James Bond, the ornithologist? Wrote *Birds of the West Indies*."

"No. Why should I?" returned Eleanor.

"Just wondered," said Patrick.

Patrick backed his car out of the driveway while Eleanor opened her cottage door. A robin sang in the back garden. She stopped to listen and said, "Good evening, Thales. How was your day?"

CHAPTER 25:

The Scientific Paper

With Gerald's encouragement, Eleanor felt it was time to submit her paper to a scientific journal.

She wrote a letter to the editor using the abbreviated name of E. Hutchinson so as not to draw attention to her being a woman; she didn't need an added complication. She had used India ink to draw and letter a map that showed the locations of robins she had recorded in Great Britain. She made three copies of the manuscript, as described in the journal. Eleanor bundled the copies into a large envelope and dropped it into the post the following morning.

A week passed before she got a letter from the editor saying he had received the manuscript and sent it out for review by two peers. He expected a response in about a month. Eleanor went about her work at the library, quite content that they had put no extra demands on her. She needed some rest after the heist.

About one month had passed when Eleanor arrived at her cottage in Rabbit's Burrough to find a letter addressed to "E. Hutchinson, Esq." She looked at the return address, which read it was from the editor of the journal. Taking a deep breath, she placed the letter on her desk and went into the kitchen to make tea. She shuffled back and forth between her right and left foot, waiting for the kettle to boil, until finally she could wait no longer. She returned to the drawing room, opened the envelope, and began to read.

"Dear Sir," it began.

Dear Sir! She thought and then frowned. *Of course, the editor would assume E. Hutchinson is a man. That is why I abbreviated my Christian name in the first place.* She read on.

```
re: Plumage variation of Robins
"Erithacus rubecula" in Great Britain.


I have received the reviews of two
experts of your paper submitted to our
journal for publication. I am pleased
to inform you that the paper was deemed
acceptable for publication following a
few changes.
```

Eleanor shrieked with excitement. She was a published author. Even with little education, she had succeeded in being accepted as a scientist by experts, many of which held university degrees. She held the letter over her head and danced around the room.

"Thales. I need to tell Thales," she shouted. She ran to the front door, flung it open, and yelled, "Thales! Where are you, Thales?"

The garden was silent. Many of the birds had migrated or were on migration and none were singing. Except for the robin. Thales held a year-round territory down by her vegetable garden, but she could not find him.

"Thales? Thales, where are you?" she called.

Down where the bean stalks from last summer were wilted into a brown stringy jumble, she spotted his red breast. He was on the ground searching for food.

"Thales," she said, quite relieved, her voice coming down in pitch and carrying less urgency. "I have some good news. We are now published authors. Well, not you exactly, but you are one of the data points. Look." She opened the map of Great Britain with robin sightings marked as black dots and pointed to a dot in Hertfordshire. "That one is you! And look, I acknowledged you in the acknowledgement section. 'I wish to thank Thales for allowing me to use his data of a sighting in Hertfordshire.' " She waved to the robin, which paid no attention and continued to search for food. As she got close to her front door, she heard a distant robin singing. She smiled and looked back over her shoulder. There was Thales on a tree limb in full song. She smiled and said, "The pleasure is all mine."

Back inside, Eleanor began to read the editor's letter more closely. He said that, although differences in plumage variation had already been described, her confirmation added greatly to this conclusion. However, what mostly impressed the reviewers was her novel use of a colour swatch to compare plumage variation. There were a few grammatical errors and sentences that needed reworking, but overall, the changes were minor. In her excitement, she had forgotten about the kettle, which was now whistling loudly on the stove. Eleanor promptly moved to the kitchen to take the kettle off the flame and pour the water into her teapot. With her cup of tea, she returned to the drawing room and read the letter again. She could feel butterflies of excitement well up inside her as she reread, "I am pleased to inform you that the paper was deemed acceptable for publication." It was time to make dinner.

Eleanor prepared her meal and ate it feeling quite giddy. Her mind started to go over all the places she had been and the events she had witnessed in the past few years. She thought about Gerald and his encouraging words that had helped her through all the ups and downs of recent times. She realized how much she had come to rely on his advice despite never having met or spoken with him. She pondered how she had been so hesitant to write to the museum in the first place and how the letters he had sent had bolstered her confidence. Now she was a published author and was ready to join the ranks of the ornithologists. All she needed was a job opening to arise and for her to be considered a candidate. With no education beyond secondary school, Eleanor would have to rely on her experience and publication record.

The following day, Eleanor arose still feeling the thrill of being accepted as an author by her science peers. She read the letter once more to make sure she had not missed anything. Once she was satisfied, she made notes on what she needed to correct to make the paper acceptable. In the evening, when she got home from work, Eleanor went to work revising the manuscript and, by bedtime, had made all the changes. She wrote a covering letter to the editor explaining the changes she had made and packaged the manuscript in an envelope to post the following morning. She was about to go to bed when she thought a letter of thanks was due for Gerald. She got a sheet of paper and began to type.

Eleanor J. Hutchinson, Robinsong Cottage, Deacon's Lane, Rabbit's Burrough, Herts.

October 24, 1948

Dear Gerald,

I hope this letter finds you healthy and happy. My wish is that you could be here to celebrate the publication of my first scientific paper on plumage colour variation in robins with me. Today I received a letter of acceptance from

```
the editor. As you said in your previ-
ous letter, the reviewers pointed out
that previous studies had shown the same
variation, but the editor explained that
my additional data was deemed worthy of
publishing because it corroborated the
earlier view based on far less data.
Also, as you pointed out, they were
impressed with my use of a colour swatch
to compare plumage variation. You can
probably tell from my letter that this
news is very exciting for me. I owe you
for your encouragement and suggestions.

Sincerely,

Eleanor
```

With the letter and manuscript ready to post, Eleanor crawled into bed where she fell into a deep sleep. The following morning on her way to work, she dropped the letter and manuscript into the Royal Mail letter box. She smiled and set off to the library with a spring in her step.

CHAPTER 26:

The Job Application

Miss Bradshaw had been the first to recognize that Eleanor had an unusually high level of resilience. Despite being put into potentially dangerous situations, Eleanor seemed to thrive and find solutions. It was this trait that gave Miss Bradshaw confidence in Eleanor. Patrick had also seen her ability at an early stage. That was why he wanted to recruit her to the Foreign Service. But try as they might, Eleanor's passion was the study of birds, where she had also shown promise. She had attended the British Ornithologists' Union meeting, where she had engaged in scientific debate. She had travelled to Oxford, despite no formal education, to hear a lecture and tour the field station at Wytham Wood. Miss Bradshaw secretly wished she knew how Eleanor excelled in her position all while remaining modest and bringing prestige to the library. Miss Bradshaw outwardly displayed the confidence and skills expected in her role, ones that would have been noticed more if she had been a man, but underneath, she knew her limits and was quite happy to let Eleanor engage in travel and dealing with patrons. *Together, we make a great team*, she thought.

In Eleanor's mind, things were quite different. She admired Miss Bradshaw for her efficiency, abilities, and personal side. However, Eleanor was wondering about the future. Unlike Miss Bradshaw, Eleanor was still very young, and she had many years ahead of her. For Eleanor, the notion of spending the next decade or more shelving books was not what she wanted to do. She was looking to contribute to ornithology. That was why she had gone on bird-watching trips with Peter, attended the ornithology meetings and lectures, travelled to look for robins, and wrote a scientific paper about it. Miss Bradshaw could see the writing on the wall. Despite all the perks of travel and adventure, Eleanor's focus was on something other than library service.

Many weeks passed after Eleanor's paper had been accepted for publication in a bird journal, which reminded her that she had not yet heard from Gerald. His last letter was from Panama, to which she had written a previous reply. It was now well into the autumn, and she thought a letter should be forthcoming. That was, if Gerald was still in Panama.

Eleanor spent the evening writing correspondence to library patrons and couldn't stop thinking about what

Gerald might say. She imagined him in a warm tropical room overlooking a jungle or perhaps on the Pacific Ocean typing his letter to her. A few days later, and to Eleanor's ongoing delight, a letter arrived.

```
Gerald Benson, c/o British
Museum (Natural History), South
Kensington, London.

November 8, 1948

Panama City, Republic of Panama

Dear Eleanor:

The news in your letter arrived today,
and I wanted to congratulate you right
away at becoming a published author.
From my limited experience, that was
very a courageous move to put yourself
through. You should be justifiably
proud. The publication will bode well
for any future endeavours in ornitholog-
ical circles. If it is of interest, you
might watch to see if a posting comes
up at the British Museum of Natural
History. Your experience and publica-
tion might be enough for the museum to
consider an interview. I am not sure
where I will be going next, but you
```

```
can continue to write to me through the
BMNH. If I don't reply promptly, it will
be because of the difficulty of the mail
service locating my whereabouts.

Sincerely,

Gerald Benson
```

Eleanor had been gaining confidence and didn't feel she needed Gerald's support as much as in the early days, but she also did not want to lose him. She thought that her motives were perhaps too selfish, and she should have considered him more. Nevertheless, he was perhaps signalling to her that he was moving on too.

Eleanor put down the letter and smiled slightly while reminiscing about how well things had turned out after that first letter to Gerald. *It couldn't have gone much better*, she thought. Gerald was there with encouraging words when she needed them most. It was as if he could read her mind. *What a remarkable friend to have*, she thought.

Gerald's suggestion to watch for postings at the museum was also on Eleanor's mind. What she wasn't expecting was the notice in the newspaper the following morning. The notice read:

"British Museum (Natural History) is seeking a candidate for the position of Assistant Curator (Birds). Candidates should post a letter and CV to the Chair of the Search Committee at the museum."

Eleanor had to read the notice twice. This was her dream job. She felt very excited and, throughout the day at the library, began composing her letter in her head. It was time to notify Miss Bradshaw of her plans.

Eleanor sat on a chair on the opposite side of Miss Bradshaw's desk.

"Miss Bradshaw," she began, "I wanted to tell you how much I enjoyed working here at the library and how appreciative I am of your support. Without the job here, I don't know where I would have ended up. You know how interested I am in birds. A position has come up at the Natural History Museum that I intend to apply for. Would you consider writing a letter of reference for me?"

Miss Bradshaw was well aware of Eleanor's interest in birds.

"I learned early on how exceptional you are, Eleanor. Your mettle was tested on the various trips you made on behalf of the library. I didn't think we would be able to hold on to you for long and knew this day would come. So yes, I will write you a letter of reference."

"Thank you, Miss Bradshaw," said Eleanor. "I hope we can continue to find a way to work together in some capacity. If I am successful, that is."

When she got home that evening, Eleanor pulled out the typewriter and began to type.

```
Attention: Chair of the Search Committee

The British Museum (Natural
History), London.
```

E. J. Hutchinson, Robinsong Cottage,
Deacon's Lane, Rabbit's Burrough, Herts.

November 24, 1948

Dear Sirs:

I am writing to apply for the position
of Assistant Curator of Birds as posted
in the London Times newspaper. Enclosed
is my résumé.

Your notice said that the preferred candidate would hold a university degree,
which I do not have simply because of
my circumstances. My intentions were
to attend university until the bombings brought that to an end. Both my
parents were killed during the raids,
leaving me an orphan. To support myself,
I found a job at the British Library,
where I am currently holding a position
as an assistant librarian. While there,
I have endeavoured to enhance my education through reading on the subject of
ornithology. You will also notice in my
resume that I have embarked on several
excursions around Great Britain and once
to France on library business. It was
those opportunities that allowed me to

```
collect the data for my recent paper
on robin plumage variation accepted for
publication in a scientific journal.
I have also attended a meeting of the
British Ornithologists' Union and a
lecture by Professor Brown at Oxford.
To be considered for a position at the
British Museum (Natural History) would
be a great honour.

Sincerely,

E. J. Hutchinson
```

Eleanor folded the letter and put it in an envelope along with her résumé. She stood it on her desk and said to herself, *Well, this is the moment I have longed for. Why am I feeling such trepidation?*

Many people suffer from various forms of social anxiety, and although Eleanor had learned to mask it well, she still felt the uneasiness. She tried to not let the negative aspects of her anxiety overtake her emotions. She sat in her drawing-room chair, running the scenarios over in her head. *I could just stop all of this*, she thought, *and be content at the library for the rest of my days. The job there has plenty of perks, and I really enjoy immersing myself in a book. But then again, I might get the job of my dreams, although it is a long shot. If I don't try, I will never know. If I am unsuccessful, I still have my librarian position.*

R. W. Butler

She was rising to walk into the kitchen when Mrs. Quimby arrived at her door. "I hadn't spoken to you since our meeting at the library and thought I should see how you are faring," she said, holding a plate of cookies.

"I was just about to make a cuppa," said Eleanor. "I will put the kettle on."

The two women sat in the drawing room to await the kettle.

"How are you doing after our little escapade the other night?" Mrs. Quimby asked.

"I am fine now," said Eleanor, "but the event was unnerving. I had no idea you were a decoding expert, Mrs. Quimby," Eleanor said quizzically.

"Oh, that. I was good at maths in university where I met Patrick," she said. "He thought I might be able to decode the message from the book thieves. I got lucky." She reached out to touch Eleanor's arm and smiled in a way that made Eleanor think she was holding back a secret.

"You sure impressed me," Eleanor replied. "Mrs. Quimby, I am thinking of applying for a job at the British Museum in their bird section. I think the odds are slim that I will get it, but if I do, I wanted you to know I had hoped to continue to live here. The pay will be better than the library, and I would be willing to increase my rental payment to you in accordance with my pay raise."

"I hope the other night's escapade didn't frighten you off library work," said Mrs. Quimby.

"No, not at all," Eleanor replied. "I have wanted to work at the museum for over a year, and a position has just come up. I trust you will keep this in confidence, since I will not likely succeed in beating the competition."

"It is our secret, Eleanor," said Mrs. Quimby. "If you succeed, I want to be at your party."

"You will, Mrs. Quimby. I hear the kettle," said Eleanor, rising from her chair to go into the kitchen where she poured the water on the tea and returned with the teapot and two cups into the drawing room.

Eleanor and Mrs. Quimby finished their tea.

"I must be going," said Mrs. Quimby, and she stepped out the door. "Nice to see you are doing well," she said as she walked down the driveway.

CHAPTER 27:

The Interview

A week became ten days and then two weeks without a word from the museum. Then, when Eleanor was giving up hope, a letter with the museum letterhead arrived at her cottage. Eleanor opened the letter, which read:

British Museum (Natural History), South Kensington Street, London.

Dear Mr. Hutchinson, Esq.

The search committee for the position of Assistant Curator of Birds at the British Museum (Natural History) invites

you to attend an interview at 10 a.m. on
Wednesday December 7. Please introduce
yourself to Miss Anderson at the front
desk, who will show you to the interview room.

Sincerely,

W. J. Swanson, DPhil

Curator of Birds

Eleanor was overwhelmed with excitement, although
the assumption she was Mr. Hutchinson was a little
galling. *How would they know when I addressed it "E.
Hutchinson" for that very reason? I didn't want to give them
any more ammunition to dismiss me*, she thought. There
were enough weaknesses in her CV as it was.

She went to work reading up on the latest reports,
donations, acquisitions, and policies of the museum. She
pored over books of avian taxonomy and tried to memo-
rize the scientific names of some of the more common
birds in Great Britain. She tried to think of questions
they might ask and rehearsed her answers in front of a
mirror. She needed to look confident but not overly so.
Her answers had to reflect her knowledge in a subtle but
impressive way. On the weekend, she visited the museum
to look at the bird exhibits and the overall layout of the
museum. Eleanor had hoped she might see Christopher
so she could peruse the specimen collection to refresh her

memory. She thought about the kinds of questions that men might ask a woman and how to respond respectfully and not be condescending. As much as she despised it, Eleanor knew how important it was for women to not upstage their male colleagues while also not appearing meek. She decided to wear the stunning classically designed jacket and skirt that Mademoiselle Dupont had gifted her.

Wednesday the 7th of December was clear and cool when Eleanor arrived at the museum for her interview. She entered the big front doors where a young woman was waiting.

"Good morning, Miss Anderson?" asked Eleanor.

"Good morning," Miss Anderson replied. "How may I help you?"

"I am here for an interview," said Eleanor.

"An interview?" said Miss Anderson with a quizzical look.

"Yes," replied Eleanor, "for the Assistant Curator position."

"And what is your name, Miss . . . ?" returned Miss Anderson.

"Eleanor Hutchinson," she said.

"We have no one by that name on our list, Miss," replied Miss Anderson.

Eleanor was puzzled. Did she get the date wrong? She pulled out the letter to show Miss Anderson, who leaned over the counter to read it.

"Oh. You are E. Hutchinson, I suppose. We have an E. Hutchinson on our list. I apologize. I thought E.

Hutchinson was a man," said Miss Anderson. "Please take a seat."

A young man was sitting on a wooden chair looking very nervous. He smiled briefly at Eleanor as she sat down. She noticed he took a quick look and then turned away. He was likely there for the same job interview.

At 9:58, another middle-aged man in a tweed jacket and tie arrived at the front desk, looked at the names of the interview candidates on Miss Anderson's list, and walked over to the young man fidgeting on the chair next to Eleanor.

"How do you do, Mr. Hutchinson?" he said reaching out with one arm to shake the young man's hand.

"My name is Billingsley, sir," said the nervous young man next to Eleanor.

"Oh, I am so sorry," said the middle-aged man. "Miss Anderson," he called out, "has Hutchinson arrived yet?"

"Yes," said Miss Anderson. "*She* is sitting in front of you."

The middle-aged man turned to catch Eleanor's gaze.

"Oh, how embarrassing," he said. "I thought – "

But before he could complete his sentence, Eleanor rose and said, "So nice to meet you Mister . . . ?"

"Maxwell," he blurted out. "James Maxwell. Are you ready for your interview, Miss, or is it Doctor?" he asked meekly.

"Miss will be just fine," said Eleanor.

James Maxwell led Eleanor down a corridor to a small room with a closed door. He showed Eleanor the door and said, "You can go in. The committee is waiting for you."

Eleanor had been in far worse situations and was feeling quite confident when she opened the door. Three older men in well-worn jackets and ties sat behind a table. She stepped into the room dressed in her French-designed jacket and skirt.

"I am sorry," said one of the men. "We are holding interviews in here. Who are you looking for, Miss?"

"I am E. Hutchinson, Eleanor Hutchinson, here for the interview," she said.

The three men went silent momentarily. Like James Maxwell, they had been expecting only men to apply and especially not a young woman in a tailored French outfit.

Then one of the men jumped out of his seat and pointed at a chair.

"So sorry, we thought – " He was stopped short by Eleanor.

"A man. That happens all the time," she said. "No need to apologize."

The men had already noted her East London accent when she first spoke and couldn't miss her stunning French clothing. She was an enigma, for certain, in the stereotypical view of men in the profession. More importantly, they were intrigued. They looked at her CV and back at Eleanor. They didn't seem to match up. The CV told of her travelling; visiting Oxford, attending lectures by a preeminent ornithologist of the time, Professor Brown; and publishing in a scientific journal. In front of them sat a young woman not much more than twenty years of age, they thought, dressed with style and speaking like an East Ender.

One of the men began the questioning.

"Miss Hutchinson," he said. "This posting usually attracts university-trained ornithologists. I don't see any university training on your CV. Could you explain how you think you might be more qualified than a candidate with a Bachelor or Doctoral degree?"

Eleanor was expecting this question.

"You are correct that I lack the formal university training usually found among your colleagues, sir," she said making sure to add "sir" to her sentence as a sign of respect. "However, unlike your university-trained staff, I have spent the past few years as a librarian immersed in the great books of the world. Not only have I read Darwin's *Origin of Species*, but I also read his *Voyage of the Beagle*. Alexander Humboldt's great masterpiece on geography I have also read. I found Marian Sibylla Merian's masterly art illuminating and her descriptions of insects engrossing. I have read about Linnaeus, the father of taxonomy, and just finished Mayr's recent book, *Systematics and the Origin of Species*. Have you read it?"

The three men shuffled, and one of them said, "No, I have been awfully busy, but I understand it is thought-provoking."

Eleanor continued, "I doubt any of your candidates will have read it either. Students are very busy these days, I find. Few spend much time in the library."

It was a decisive jab at the interviewer, who was feeling quite uncomfortable.

"There are many other great books in ornithology and the humanities that interest me, but that can wait,"

Eleanor said. "The library also has several ornithological journals, which I follow closely, especially the papers on taxonomy. I have much to learn."

The interviewers shuffled and sighed. After a moment of silence, one of the men said, "I would like to ask you a few questions about the taxonomy of birds. How many species of birds reside Great Britain?"

Eleanor responded, "That depends on your definition of 'resides.' If you mean the number of wild native species ever recorded, the number is over five hundred."

The interviewer then asked, "Do you know how many families of birds there are in the world?"

Eleanor replied, "Depending which authority you follow, there are about two hundred families."

The interviewers were scribbling notes while Eleanor sat patiently. She was wondering what was going on in their heads. Then one of the interviewers said, "Miss Hutchinson. I see that you have done some domestic travel to places like Scotland and Wales. Oh, and also to France. These are all civilized places with easy travel, accommodations, and importantly for you, safety. Do you really think you, as a young woman, are ready to travel to remote, dangerous places, where the conditions are a far cry from what we have here in Britain, to collect specimens?"

Eleanor flinched at the condescending question but maintained her composure. She looked down and paused for effect and then began.

"Sir, with all due respect, just because I am a woman does not mean I cannot carry out the duties you describe. I want to remind you that Evelyn Cheeseman, who has volunteered here for years, has been travelling on her own to the South Pacific for decades where, because she was a woman, she was able to access places off limits to men. In her case, being a woman is an asset. I hope I would be a similar asset to the museum. She deserves an OBE, in my opinion."

The interviewers were scribbling once more, and Eleanor thought she might be being too harsh on them. As a man, such behaviour would be expected, but for a woman, such brashness was frowned upon. She thought she needed to tone down her responses.

The third interviewer looked up. "I would like to return to your lack of education, Miss Hutchinson. Why did you not attend university? Was it your grades?"

It was biting question, and the interviewer knew it.

Eleanor went silent. "Miss Hutchinson," he said. "Please answer the question."

Eleanor looked up, took a deep breath, and began.

"Sir," she said. "As you can tell from my accent, I was not born into privilege. I attended an East London school where I learned the basics. I excelled in my class and was hoping to attend university. My father was an artist and my mother a grocery clerk. Neither had the funds for me to attend, but my plan was to earn my way, even if it took several years to accumulate the money. Then the war came." Eleanor paused. She looked down to get her composure. The three interviewers had stopped writing. They came from privileged backgrounds and could not fully appreciate the difficulties Eleanor had endured as a child. They were about to get a lesson.

Eleanor looked up and sat up straight.

"On the night of December 7th, 1941, eight years ago today, London was under attack from bombers in the night sky. My family had got used to the routine of running for shelter in the underground, but the terror of those few minutes haunted my mother and me every day. We heard the sirens, and my father yelled for us to run quickly as possible to the shelter. My parents pushed me ahead of them and yelled 'Run. Run as fast as you can. We will catch up to you in the shelter.' I started off down the road. I could see lights flashing as bombs hit electrical wires, setting buildings on fire. Sirens were blaring. Then I saw a bomb hit in front of me, sending bricks and glass hurtling through the air. A shard of grass glanced off my head, leaving this scar."

She pointed to a small scar hidden beneath her hair. "Then another bomb hit closer. There were screams from children. I saw a mother hurled through the air from one of the explosions, her body falling to earth with a thud like a sack of potatoes. A small child – her daughter – stood still, frozen with fear, screaming uncontrollably. I grabbed her hand and swept her into my arms. We raced for the shelter as more bombs riddled the road. At the shelter's entrance were scores of people trying to get in through the narrow doorway. I turned to let my parents in the passageway. They were not there. I looked down the street where we had run. The flames leapt up the walls of shattered buildings. A huge explosion lit up the road, and I saw two bodies hurled into the air. I froze, uncertain of where to turn and what to do. I was trembling. I imagined my mother's voice. She was calling out to me to find shelter. My parents never made it to the shelter.

"When the bombing ended, I went back to our home. My parents were not there, and neither was our home. I asked the fire brigade, but they hadn't seen my parents. I realized I was alone; I was an orphan. I had to find my own way in this world. That was when I applied for a job as an assistant librarian at the library. A very generous woman offered me a cottage at nominal rent, which has become my home. And so, my dreams of university came to an end, and I decided I would educate myself by reading at the library."

Eleanor stopped talking. The three men were silent. They had stopped writing. None of the men had ever experienced anything even close to what Eleanor had just described. Finally, one of the men spoke.

"There has been so much devastation from this damned war. I too am devastated by your story, Miss Hutchinson," he said.

Eleanor was the first to speak. "I apologize for unleashing this story on you. It has nothing to do with the job, and I would be happy if you could continue with your questioning."

After a pause, one of the men said, "I want to return to your comment about taking care of yourself in dangerous situations. Clearly you had to do that during the bombings, but do you think you could take care of yourself if you were, say, attacked by a man?"

What an odd question, thought Eleanor. *They are trying to say that women cannot do this job.* "Sir, do you recall the attempted heist at the library a few months ago, when a couple of men, under the cover of darkness, attempted to steal precious books?"

"Yes, I do," he said. "I recall they were caught in the library by some quick-acting staff." He then realized that Eleanor might have been there. "Was it you?" he asked with wonderment.

"I was there," said Eleanor, "but what wasn't reported was that one of the men attacked me from behind in an attempt to subdue me. I left him with a broken foot that slowed his exit sufficiently for the constables to apprehend him in the library."

"You were attacked and survived?" said the astonished interviewer. "Tell me more!"

"One thing my father taught me before he died was how to react to an attack by a man from behind. He had been in Army Service where he learned self-defence, which he passed on to me."

The three men were quite astonished at how the interview was going. The young woman had a lifetime of harrowing experiences that surpassed any formal education.

One of the interviewers changed the subject. "I want to ask you about scientific publications," he said. "Not many candidates your age will have published anything, let alone carried out the research. I see from your résumé that you developed a technique to match plumage colours to a colour swatch, thereby reducing the subjectivity in making comparisons. Can you tell me more about your method and results?"

Eleanor began. "I have had a long interest in robins, and when I heard Professor Brown was to present a paper on the subject at the British Ornithologists' Union meeting, I decide to attend. There I learned of a boundary between pale continental robins and our robins in Great Britain. My travels on library business allowed me to collect data on that very subject, which corroborated what he had found."

"Yes, but what about the colour swatch?" asked the interviewer.

"Oh, that," said Eleanor. "I was painting birds in the museum cabinets downstairs when a volunteer offered to show me the robin specimens in your collection. I was able to use my watercolours to match the colouration of the breast plumages that I could then take into the field. I then assigned the colour swatches to my sightings map to show there was indeed a boundary in Hertfordshire as previously proposed."

"I am pleased to hear the museum could be of assistance. I also heard from my colleagues that your colour swatch method is unofficially being referred to as the Hutchinson Method.

"Oh my," said Eleanor. "I did not know that. How nice."

"I have one final question for you, Miss Hutchinson," said one of the interviewers. "The museum is constantly changing to keep up with current scientific discoveries and interest by the public. Our dinosaur exhibit has been hugely popular with the British public. If you were to succeed in getting the job as Assistant Curator, what changes would you envision?"

"That is a broad question, sir," said Eleanor, "and one I have given considerable thought. During my travels to France, I became acutely aware of the thousands of young men our country lost to war. I think there are some parallels with the bird specimens housed at the museum. Both represent killing of living beings, and in both cases, we need to keep their sacrifices relevant. For the soldiers whose lives were abruptly ended, there are crosses and a lovely cemetery to their sacrifice. For the birds, we have them locked away in cabinets out of sight of the public. I know some are mounted in living positions in the exhibit space, and those are very helpful for the public. What I fear is that the scientific collection might fall out of favour and be seen as anachronistic. This view, in my opinion, is short-sighted. A day will come when the destruction of the natural world will be of worldwide concern. The birds in our collection will then become a snapshot of what we lost and what we might be able, and with new thinking, restore. The RSPB is at the forefront of this new movement to preserve places where birds reside. I can foresee growth in that segment, and with it will come a new vision of the world. I wouldn't be so bold as to claim to have all the answers or that my prognostications will be proven correct, but there are indications that I am on the right track. I would like to see the museum draw more people to the exhibits with things they can do for birds in their gardens or with lessons on the basics of bird-watching, and perhaps they could hear some stimulating talks by our staff on some of the latest bird discoveries."

The interviewers scribbled their notes. They finally stopped and smiled at Eleanor.

"Well, Miss Hutchinson. It has been a pleasure to meet you. Whatever the outcome, I am sure you will have an interesting life. We have a few more candidates to interview, after which we will contact you about our deliberations."

He rose and held out his hand, and Eleanor shook each man's hand in turn.

"Thank you for the opportunity to meet you."

As Eleanor stepped out through the door, she overheard a sigh from inside and some muttering. *I made an impression, but was it sufficient and the right one to land the job?* she wondered.

Days turned to weeks before Eleanor received a reply. It came in the form of a letter in an envelope marked "British Museum." Her heart began to race when she saw the address on the envelope. It felt thin, like there was only a letter enclosed. For the past few years, she had anticipated this moment; the possibility of a job at the museum was why she had concocted her plan to write to Gerald. His replies had encouraged her to travel, visit Oxford, attend the British Ornithologists Union meeting, visit an RSPB reserve, and learn to write and submit a scientific paper. She had got to know parts of the world she had only dreamed about while researching for the letters to Gerald. She had had brushes with thieves, stayed with aristocratic families, heard stories of the loss of young men during the war, sampled French cuisine, and been given a tailored outfit. She had met fascinating people, such as Christopher Ashford and his family, David Brown and students at Oxford University, Peter Saunders from the RSPB, Patrick from the Foreign Service, and Mrs. Quimby – who knew she was a mathematical genius, and what exactly had she done during the war? There was Gwyn in Wales and his country cottage, the Spratts and their outrageously fun masquerade party with amusing guests. There was Captain Furlough, who she had come to learn had been on a real mission, and Bernard – poor Bernard – the socially shy young man with a passion for birds and music far exceeding his years. She had travelled to France to meet Mademoiselle Dupont, who had opened Eleanor's eyes to French taste, cuisine, music, and culture.

She had also witnessed the ongoing struggles of women and social distinctions, despite changes in Britain. Eleanor realized, in the few short years she had been at the library, many exciting events had unfolded of which she got to partake. She said to herself that if the letter was a rejection to her application for the position of Assistant Curator and the British Museum, she could always continue at the library. Miss Bradshaw had been very good to her, and it wasn't as if Eleanor wanted to leave all that behind. She had just seen the position at the museum as a closer fit with her life ambitions.

The thin envelope stood upright against the back of her desk for some time while Eleanor prepared a pot of tea. She thought that the letter might be a big turning point in her life and that, regardless, she had managed to get to an interview on her own initiative. The interview was something she could be proud of, especially considering her humble upbringing.

She sat in her favourite chair, took a sip of tea, and stared at the envelope in her hand. This was the moment she had been waiting for, and her rumbling stomach was telling her so. She opened the envelope and pulled out the letter.

```
British Museum (Natural
History), London.

Miss Eleanor Hutchinson, Robinsong
Cottage, Deacon's Lane, Rabbit's
Burrough, Herts.

December 20, 1948

Dear Miss Hutchinson:

The search committee for the position of
Assistant Curator of Birds has made its
deliberations. I would like to meet with
you in person in my office in the New
Year on Monday January 3, 1949 at 9:30
to discuss the decision.

Yours sincerely,

W. J. Swanson

Curator of Birds
```

Eleanor read the letter again. It was noncommittal on whether she had successfully won the position or not. *Why would the curator want to see me in person?* she thought. *I must have lost out, and he wants to console me.* Eleanor was feeling frustrated that the letter wasn't more decisive. She would have to wait weeks to find out, and top of that, Christmas was nearing.

CHAPTER 28:

The Waiting

Eleanor knew how Christmas across Great Britain was an opportunity for communities and individuals to give back to each other. Rationing had meant hardship for many, and the sharing of food and goods had become commonplace. However, the Christmas of 1948 would go down in the memory of many, including Eleanor.

Eleanor was mulling over the indecisive letter from the museum when Mrs. Quimby arrived at her door. She was dressed in a long woollen coat with the collar pulled up around her neck. On her feet were shoes in which woollen socks spilled over the tops.

"Come in, Mrs. Quimby," she said, folding the letter and slipping it into her pocket.

A cold wind swept in through the door.

"Why, thank you, Eleanor," she said.

"Let me take your coat," said Eleanor.

Eleanor helped Mrs. Quimby slip her arms out of her coat and proceeded to hang it in a closet.

"Sit by the fire where it's warm," Eleanor said, directing Mrs. Quimby with her outstretched arm.

"Are you warm in the cottage, Eleanor?" asked Mrs. Quimby. "Because you can always stay with me if it gets unbearable."

"No need," said Eleanor. "The burner keeps the cottage toasty warm. Would you like some tea?"

"No thank you, dear," said Mrs. Quimby, getting settled in a large chair by the open fire. She stretched out her legs so that her feet were closer to the flame. On her feet were socks she had knitted for occasions like this.

Mrs. Quimby began. "The reason I came over, Eleanor, was to see if you were planning to attend the village Christmas. Rabbit's Burrough has been holding these events every Christmas."

"My mind is not made up yet," said Eleanor. "I generally have a quiet Christmas. After the death of my parents, I have little reason to celebrate. I find it quite difficult, actually."

"Well, I can understand how you must feel, Eleanor, but I hope you change your mind. The Village Hall Christmas might be a good tonic."

Mrs. Quimby rose from her chair and, with a smile, said to Eleanor, "It will be fun, and I will take care of you."

Eleanor felt annoyed as she closed the door behind Mrs. Quimby. She was trying to deal with the uncertainty of the letter from the museum, and at the same time Mrs. Quimby was telling her she was going to have a good time. Without a definitive answer, Eleanor just wished Christmas was over so she could resolve her dilemma. After some thought, Eleanor decided to go along to the Village Hall as Mrs. Quimby had suggested rather than spend a night alone in the darkness. She pulled on her long coat and wrapped a scarf around her neck to step into the night air that was cold enough to snow. She trudged through the town, which was eerily quiet. A few glowing lights were the only signs of habitation.

Despite the war having been over for a few years, Eleanor and the citizens of Rabbit's Burrough, like most Britons, were still feeling the effects of rationing. Some food and soap, in particular, were hard to come by. The austerity of the war years, however, had brought the community closer together in support of one another, and that spirit was in evidence when Eleanor entered the Village Hall in Rabbit's Burrough.

The Village Hall was a brick building with arched windows framed by sashes painted black. Inside, the hall was a simple rectangular space with a kitchen at the far end. Wainscotting ran a few feet up the walls, the rest of which were painted white and followed the vaulted ceiling to its peak. From exposed jousts and rafters, which were painted black to contrast with the white walls, were Union Jacks and strings of coloured paper chains that created a festive atmosphere. There were tables covered in white cloths that stretched from one end of the hall to the other, on which stood jars as centre-pieces overflowing with English ivy, sprigs of spruce, and red-berried holly.

The wooden floorboards creaked as Eleanor entered the hall, where she was met with a din of people milling about, laughing, and chatting. Down at the far end and in the kitchen, a team of women were busily cooking the Christmas meal. Geysers of steaming water erupted from pots, accompanied by the clanging of lids and utensils. Bill Bigglethwaite and his Hog Band, this time dressed in red and wearing artificial beards, were setting up their instruments at one end of the hall. A large crowd had assembled, and the din from children scampering about the room in anticipation and the adults catching up on the latest news conveyed how the community worked. When times were difficult, the people of Rabbit's Burrough had taken up allotments where they grew most of their own vegetables. Mr. Allenby, the hog farmer whose claim to fame was the escape of pigs and the subsequent All Hogs Day party, agreed to supply a roast pig. When people needed help repairing their homes, their clothes, or their relationships, the community banded together to bring them through the dark times. This evening was a time to celebrate Christmas, but it was also a celebration of the community's survival through another year.

Standing in the corner of the hall was a wire Christmas tree. Mr. Parson's chicken coop had provided a section of chicken wire that would serve as a support for fir boughs to create a reasonable facsimile of a live Christmas tree. The children were inserting boughs into the wire under adult supervision when Eleanor arrived. She watched the joy on the faces of the youngsters, who knew this was the night of Father Christmas. Once the tree had been completed, the adults and children stood back to admire their creation.

"Not a bad tree, if I do say so myself," one of the fathers said.

Then followed the decorating, which again involved the children. There were paper chains to hang between the limbs, glass baubles for the boughs along with sprigs of holly, and a star for the top of the tree.

A ruckus outside the Village Hall diverted the attention from the children and the Christmas tree to four men with a roast pig on a giant board hoisted onto their shoulders marching in the front door. A cheer went up, and the Hog Band launched into a rendition of "The Derby Ram Song." People started singing along and clapping to the beat as the steaming pig was carried into the kitchen to be sliced into portions. It was as if a rendition of an ancient tradition from the dawn of time was playing out before Eleanor.

Everyone began to sit at the tables. Eleanor found a seat beside Mrs. Quimby. Out of the kitchen came steaming plates of pork, potatoes, carrots, and Brussel sprouts. Once the platters were on the tables, the crowd stood, sang "God Save the King," and then sat down. All went silent when the reverend got up to say grace for the dinner while everyone dutifully bowed their heads. Once the prayer was over, the din rose again as the food was passed around. Women from the kitchen scurried in with full platters and out with empty ones. There was immense laughter and smiles. Eleanor felt a certain warmth among the community that had been lacking in her world. She wondered how Gerald would spend Christmas. Her smile dissipated when her mind went back to the museum letter. She considered writing Gerald for his advice, but there was too little time between now and her meeting with the museum curator on January 3. For once, she would have to navigate the emotional storm on her own.

"You look a bit troubled," came Mrs. Quimby's voice from beside Eleanor. It startled Eleanor back to the present.

"I was just thinking about how lonely Christmas can be for some people," she replied. "Thank you for inviting me. It seems nearly everyone in the village is here."

Mrs. Quimby replied, "There is a good turnout, but a few chose not to come. Alan Westerly, for example, is having a tough time after his war service."

"That is so sad," said Eleanor. "Did he see action?"

"He doesn't speak much about it," said Mrs. Quimby, "but his mother says he is reluctant to come out of his room and is haunted with nightmares."

"Do you think a visit would be helpful?" said Eleanor.

"I am not sure. Perhaps you could ask his mother. They live on the other side of the village, not far from Peter," said Mrs. Quimby.

Once the meal was finished and dishes were being washed in the kitchen, the Hog Band began to play Christmas carols, which many people joined in. Some of the younger children were growing tired and rested their heads on their mothers' laps or were held in their father's arms. The older children, some in their teens, clustered at the back of the hall pretending they were somewhere else, but deep down, they longed for the time when they had believed in Father Christmas. The lights were turned down in the hall for the grand finale. A mountain of a Christmas pudding on a huge platter was brought into the hall where it was set ablaze. Someone overestimated the amount of alcohol for the cake, and with the sudden whoosh of air, flames leapt from the table, igniting the paper chains suspended from the rafters. The men jumped from their seats, swatting at the blazing chains. They hauled down the decorations and began to stomp them out while wisps of smoke fizzled under foot. Mothers took their children and headed for the door, their faces showing their uncertainty about whether they should stay with their husbands or leave with the children.

"All is okay," shouted the reverend as the smell of charred paper filled the room. "No need to panic. Everything is under control."

The crowd calmed and stared at each other.

"The Good Lord has spared us," he shouted.

Before he could hold a prayer, the Hog Band started to play again, and the festive mood returned. Briefly.

Eleanor heard it first. A distant ringing bell approaching fast, a scurrying of feet and muffled yells, and in burst the local volunteer firefighters dressed in helmets, boots, and fire coats. One man had a hose in his hand at the ready. Another two held axes. They quickly looked about the hall.

"Where's the fire?" one of the firefighters yelled.

"The fire is out," said the reverend. "With God's help, the brave men of Rabbit's Burrough were able to contain the fire and extinguish it. Would you like to stay for tea?"

The firefighters realized that there was no more danger and agreed to have tea. The women in the kitchen were more than happy to serve them.

As the evening progressed, the families with younger children began to leave first, followed gradually by more families. The young people stayed the longest and were enlisted to help with the cleanup. Eleanor jumped in to assist, and after washing dishes, she left the Village Hall pleased that she had attended. She walked along the main road through the village. Snow began to fall. Mrs. Quimby had departed earlier, so Eleanor was left in her thoughts. She arrived back at her cottage in the dark where she opened the door, turned on a light, and sat in her chair. The letter stared back at her. She took it from her desk and reread it. There was nothing new to be learned, so she put it back on the desk. She could hear the faint voices of carollers along the main road. Otherwise, the cottage was still, and the quietness seemed a welcome antidote to the boisterous evening. She smiled at the thought of the evening dinner, the families, and the arrival of the fire-fighters. Then she thought about her parents and began to weep.

CHAPTER 29:

The Lost Soldier

Eleanor, like most everyone, had a desire to be wanted by her community, which was something the war had brought into clear focus for thousands of young men and women. She was fully aware that many men had died as heroes and many thousands now suffered from mental breakdowns. Tragedies of war seeped far beyond the battlefields, leaving its lasting stain in cities, towns, and villages, including Eleanor's beloved Rabbit's Burrough.

The morning following the village Christmas party, Eleanor arose to the song of Thales singing down near the garden as he usually did. She climbed out of bed, slipped on a jumper over her night clothes, and lit the space heater. She could see her breath as she entered the kitchen to light the stove. She had the day off and she wondered how to spend her time. *Perhaps I will pay a visit to Alan Westerly*, she thought.

After breakfast, Eleanor got dressed, pulled on a warm woollen coat, wrapped a scarf around her neck, and donned a tweed cap. Around her neck she hung binoculars. The air was crisp on her exposed face as she trudged through a dusting of snow from the previous night. Her mind was still occupied with the previous night's events when she reached the main road and began to think about what she would say to Alan. She knew precious little about him or his condition but felt an urge to see if she could be of assistance. It was Christmas time, after all.

By the time she reached the Westerlys' cottage, the sun was well above the horizon. The shadows from the leafless trees cast silhouetted fingers across the road as if they were the last desperate hands of drowning sailors or injured soldiers.

She stopped often along the hedgerow leading along the main road to watch birds. A blackbird probed for worms and insects under the shrubs where the snow had not accumulated. A small flock of blue tits moved nervously along the hedgerow toward the safety of a woodlot; their yellow breasts and blue caps were like beacons against the snow on the top of the hedgerow, making them easy targets for a hungry sparrow hawk. Eleanor noticed a gold-crest among the blue-tit flock and then heard the distinctive calls of a flock of bramblings in flight over one of the fields. She had discovered the therapeutic effect of bird-watching when she had felt overwhelmed. The birds distracted her from thinking about her problems and rewarded her with their lovely colours, delightful songs, and antics. Everyday bird-watching was a new adventure for Eleanor in more ways than one. She hoped to introduce Alan to bird-watching.

It was midmorning by the time Eleanor got to the Westerlys' cottage. She could see Mrs. Westerly through the window busily tidying the kitchen. Eleanor had not told the Westerlys she was coming, so she hoped she was not intruding. She knocked on the door, and Mr. Westerly opened it with a look of surprise. He was wearing woollen pants held up by suspenders over a blue-striped shirt. His grey hair was tousled, and he sported a bushy moustache. His pipe gave off a sweet smoky smell. He had a welcoming face.

"Hello, Miss. May I help you?" he asked.

"Hello, Mr. Westerly. My name is Eleanor Hutchinson. I live on the other side of the village on Deacon's Lane."

"Are you Quimby's tenant?" asked Mr. Westerly.

"Yes," said Eleanor.

"So, what can I do for you?" he asked.

From inside the house, Mrs. Westerly called out. "Invite her in, Richard."

He smiled and said, "Yes, of course, do come in. May I take your coat?"

"Thank you," said Eleanor as she removed her hat, coat, and binoculars.

"Are you a birdwatcher, Miss Hutchinson?" said Richard, eyeing her binoculars.

"Yes," replied Eleanor. She coyly said, "I hope to be an ornithologist someday."

"An ornithologist!" replied Richard. "I wouldn't even know where to begin."

Joyce Westerly appeared from the kitchen. "Hello, Miss Hutchinson. My name is Joyce Westerly, and this is Richard."

Mr. Westerly apologized for not doing the introductions and then said, "Would you like some Christmas cheer?" as he moved to open a liquor cabinet.

"It is a bit early for that, Richard. Can I offer you some tea?" said Joyce.

"That would be lovely," said Eleanor.

"Take a seat then," said Richard as he directed her to a large sofa in the drawing room.

The room was snug with a log burner burning red at one end. Sprigs of holly, English ivy, and spruce bows adorned the mantle-piece where a few Christmas cards stood. A large carpet of dark reds with black and yellow highlights adorned the floor. She noticed a picture of a man in uniform on one wall.

"Is that your son, Alan?" Eleanor asked.

Richard sighed and said, "Yes. Alan has had a difficult time adjusting after his war service. He seldom leaves his room."

"Does anyone come to see him?" asked Eleanor.

"He doesn't seem to want to see anyone," said Richard.

"Oh dear," said Eleanor. "Do you think he might like to see me, being quite close in age?"

Joyce arrived with a tray of tea and biscuits.

"What do you think Joyce?" asked Richard.

Before she could answer, Eleanor said, "I hoped he would. That is why I came to pay a visit."

"I will ask him," said Joyce as she put down the tray.

"It might be better if I do that," said Eleanor.

Joyce looked at Richard and then turned to Eleanor.

"Alright, dear, but be prepared to not get much response from him," said Joyce.

"Does he get angry?" asked Eleanor.

"No," said Joyce. "He just sits in his room. He will come out for meals and use the loo, but otherwise, he just stays in his room. He's shell-shocked, I think the medical people called it."

"Let's have tea, and then I will poke my head in his room to see if he might like a visit," said Eleanor.

After they had finished tea, Eleanor said she would like to see Alan. Joyce showed her to his room and then returned to the drawing room.

Eleanor felt anxious, not knowing to expect. She raised her hand to knock and then touched her lip in thought. *I'd better knock very gently*, she thought.

She tapped lightly while calling Alan's name. "May I come in?" she asked.

There was no reply. She gently opened the door so she could peer inside.

"Alan. My name is Eleanor. May I come in?" she said.

As she pushed the door open wide, she saw Alan sitting in a wheelchair staring out the window. No one had prepared her for that.

"Alan?" she asked.

He slowly turned the wheelchair and said, "Hello, Eleanor."

He was young man in his early twenties, not much older than Eleanor. He had straight dark hair that fell over his right forehead and was quite handsome. He wore a white shirt and cotton trousers. He had a troubled face. His spartan room was meticulously clean and orderly. The bed was made with carefully tucked-in blankets. He had a picture of his parents on the wall, and there were a few books on a small bedside table with a reading lamp.

"Would you like to go bird-watching, Alan?" asked Eleanor.

He looked surprised. His eyes shifted left and then right before staring at her. Then his brow furrowed, and Alan said, "How can I do that? Can't you see I am in a wheelchair?"

"We don't need to go far to see birds, Alan," said Eleanor. "They come right to your door. I saw half a dozen species outside your cottage on my way over."

Alan was briefly lost for words. The silence was disturbing, and Eleanor decided to break it.

"Well, if you change your mind, let me know. I live here in the village." With that, she got up to leave.

When she got the door, Alan said, "Yes."

She stopped and turned to look at him. "Yes, what?" she asked.

"I would like to go bird-watching. With you. Now," he said.

"Very well. Where's your coat?" she asked.

He gestured and she handed it to him. She watched as he struggled to put it on but didn't help. She thought he would ask if he needed help. Alan turned the wheelchair and headed out the door ahead of Eleanor.

When they reached the drawing room, Richard and Joyce were standing up.

"Hello, you two. Seems you have hit it off well," said Joyce with a wide smile.

"Alan and I are going bird-watching – just around here," said Eleanor, gesturing with her hand. "I will take care of him."

She opened the front door with Joyce and Richard hovering behind. Alan gingerly lowered the chair down the single step and started to move along the path to the road.

"We won't be long," Eleanor shouted to Joyce and Richard.

The path slightly inclined up to the road, and in normal weather, Alan could have manoeuvred the wheelchair up the slope, but on this day, the wheels slipped in a cluster of snow. Eleanor took the handles and pushed him up to the road.

"Okay," she said as they stopped for a breath. "Let's see what is about. Look under the hedgerow. Can you see the blackbird?" Eleanor pointed ahead.

"Yes," said Alan.

She handed him her binoculars. "Look for the yellow beak," she said.

"I see it," he replied.

They continued along the road a short way, spotting starlings, bull finches, gold finches, bramblings, and a long-tailed tit. With each bird, Eleanor described the field marks and something about its natural history.

"You are well versed in birds, Eleanor," said Alan. "You should be an ornithologist." He chuckled. Eleanor thought that might be the first time Alan had laughed in a long time. She wasn't going to ask him what living on the front had been like and what he might have seen. Gwyn had already described the horrors to her on her visit to Wales. Alan needed to get his mind off the demons, and bird-watching might be his salvation.

Eleanor pushed Alan's wheelchair whenever it slipped in the snow, and where the snow had melted from the road's surface, Alan kept pace with her.

On a quiet side road, Eleanor told Alan to stop and close his eyes.

"Listen to the bird calls," she said. The twittering and chirping brought a smile to Alan's face. Eleanor was enjoying seeing Alan smile. *This might be the first time he has smiled in weeks*, she thought. Then a robin sang.

Alan's smile suddenly froze. He covered his ears and shouted, "No, no, no!"

"What is it, Alan?" asked Eleanor.

He had already turned his wheelchair around and was heading for home.

"What did I do, Alan?" Eleanor asked.

Alan looked frantic, and Eleanor thought it best to just get him home as soon as she could.

Whatever it was, this was not the time to ask questions. He needed to get home. She pushed his chair to speed up the return, both saying nothing.

Alan was puffing and sweating by the time they got back to the cottage. Eleanor helped him manoeuvre down the slope to the front door, where he swung the door open wide and went straight to his room.

Joyce and Richard, sitting in the drawing room, jumped up.

"Alan. How was it?" Richard asked as Alan sped past without a word.

Joyce asked frantically, "What happened, Miss Hutchinson?"

"I don't know," she said. "We were enjoying watching birds, and I don't know if I said something or if something reminded him of the war, but Alan suddenly insisted on getting home. I am so sorry."

"Give him a few minutes and then go to see him," said Richard. "He might explain the problem. He is haunted by many war atrocities. I doubt it was anything you said or did."

Eleanor waited a few minutes before going to Alan's door. She knocked gently and asked if she could come in. Alan was on the bed, ringing his hands.

"Alan," she said quietly. "Will you tell me what happened to upset you? That was the last thing I wanted."

Alan sat up in silence with his eyes closed. "It's not you, Eleanor," he said. She breathed a sigh of relief.

"Are you willing to tell me what happened, or should we leave it for another time?" she asked. Alan was in torment, but Eleanor's words to "leave it for another time" meant she wanted to continue to see him. He felt a surge of emotions.

"Please sit," he said, motioning to the bed. She sat beside him. Alan took a deep breath and began.

"When I was on the front, our positions were often under fire from mortars and snipers. Every day there were new casualties. During the day, hours would go by in silence while we trembled in terror. I still hear the guns in my head, and I see men dying in my sleep. On many days, a robin sang nearby. The soldiers said it was the devil trying to lure us into the open to be killed. Whenever I hear a robin singing, the memories flood back. That's what happened this afternoon."

Eleanor hugged him, and he began to cry.

"Oh, Alan. It can't get much sadder when even a bird-song triggers such memories," she said. There was silence in the room for a long time. Alan sat up and stared out the window like he had when Eleanor had first come into the room.

"Alan," began Eleanor. "I want to tell you how different my reaction is to robins in hopes that you will see them in a different light. I don't expect it to make you change how you react, but I want you to know that there are good things in this world.

"I became interested in birds as a child," said Eleanor, "but it is recently that I have really become focused on learning about them. One of the reasons I like birds is that I have the opposite reaction to you when I hear a robin sing. You see, in my garden lives a robin I have named Thales for the Greek philosopher of science who coined the term 'know thyself.' Each morning, I am greeted by Thales singing in my back garden. I got so interested in him that I have been to lectures by ornithologists to learn more and recently published a scientific paper on the colouration of their plumage. So, the same bird with the same song that triggers such frightening memories for you does the opposite for me."

Alan was silent and continued to stare out the window. Eleanor was hoping he might reply. She rose and stood behind him with her hand on his shoulder. After a few minutes, she said, "Alan. I need to go now. You know I wish you all the best, and I hope we can go bird-watching again. Just call when that time comes."

Alan remained silent. Eleanor let her hand slip from his shoulder and left the room. In the drawing room, she explained to Richard and Joyce how the robin's song triggered his memories and apologized for how it had turned out. They were both understanding and pleased that she would take time to help their son even though things had not turned out as well as hoped. They told Eleanor she was welcome anytime. She left by the front door, climbed the incline to the main road, and set off across the village for her cottage in the cool winter afternoon air. As she approached the front door, she heard Thales singing in the garden.

CHAPTER 30:

Meeting with the Curator

10 a.m. January 3, 1949. Eleanor had marked the time and date on her calendar that hung in her kitchen, although that seemed unnecessary considering she couldn't get it out of her mind. When the day finally arrived, she awoke feeling listless and ready to hear whatever the curator had to say to her. In her mind, a voice was preparing her for the worst. Dwelling on those thoughts got her down, so she busied herself with anything to keep her mind at ease. She was nervous, and her appetite was gone. She forced a cup of tea and a piece of toast down her throat and then got dressed. She decided to wear the same French-designed outfit from Mademoiselle Dupont that she had worn to the interview. She looked at herself in the mirror, glancing from side to side to check all was

in order. When all was ready, she stepped out the door where she heard Thales singing. His pure voice brought a smile to her face before she turned to briskly walk down Deacon's Lane to catch the bus.

Eleanor arrived in London at 9 o'clock and had made her way to the Natural History Museum by 9:15. The museum was a Victorian Gothic Revival edifice with high windows and alcoves resembling a cathedral. Gargoyles with frozen grimaces overhung the eaves. She paced about outside the front entrance, checking her watch from time to time, and eventually walked in through the huge doors where she was met by Miss Anderson.

"Welcome to the Natural History Museum, Miss Hutchinson," she said with a friendly smile. "You've come for a meeting with Dr. Swanson, is that correct?"

"Yes, thank you," said Eleanor. "I am a few minutes early."

"Come with me. I will take you to Dr. Swanson. He's in the bird gallery," said Miss Anderson. She led Eleanor into the west wing past galleries labelled fish, insects, reptiles, and shells until they reached the bird wing.

Along the corridor, an older man stood with a wide drawer of stuffed birds opened before him.

"Dr. Swanson," said Miss Anderson. "Miss Hutchinson is here to meet with you."

"How do you do?" he said as he reached out his hand.

Eleanor thought he looked familiar but couldn't recall from where.

"Very well, thank you, sir," she replied.

"Thank you, Miss Anderson," he said, turning to walk down the corridor.

"I am so pleased you have come, Miss Hutchinson," he said. "Let's go into my office."

He opened the door to let her inside. The office had a large dark wooden desk, on which lay papers and books, and it backed onto an even larger window. An arching lamp lit the desk. Along the outer walls were floor-to-ceiling bookcases full of scientific journals and boxes labelled alphabetically by author. In the boxes were scientific papers from journals that their authors had shared with peers.

"Have a seat," said Dr. Swanson, gesturing to a wooden banker's chair. "Let me take your coat."

While he hung her coat on a rack, Eleanor got comfortable in the chair. She was trying to recall where she recognized him from. Dr. Swanson then took his seat behind the large oak desk.

"We have met before, Miss Hutchinson," he said. "Do you remember?"

She didn't remember where, but he was familiar.

"I do recall meeting you, but I am trying to recollect where that was," she said.

"We met at the British Ornithologists' Union meeting last January, or was it two Januarys ago?" Eleanor finally recalled the meeting.

"Yes. You were the kind gentleman who took me into the meeting as your guest!" she exclaimed.

"The very one," Dr. Swanson said with a big smile. "I remember you giving a brilliant question to Professor Brown that was right on the money, too," he said with a smirk. "All those young upstarts were taken aback. It was a sight to behold."

"My intentions were not to put Dr. Brown on the spot," Eleanor said.

Dr. Swanson replied, "Oh, I knew that, and so did Professor Brown. I suspect he liked getting a good question. It was the look on the young university students' faces that amused me. They get a little above their station sometimes, and having a . . . " He paused. "How do I say it?"

"A woman?" interjected Eleanor.

"Yes, a woman," replied Dr. Swanson. "Having a woman who no one in the audience knew ask such an insightful question was worth the price of admission."

Eleanor smiled and wanted to move the conversation on to why he had invited her to the museum in the first place. She thought he might be warming her up for some bad news. Dr. Swanson went on for several minutes about what it was like for students, how they tried to oneup each other by asking clever questions without humiliating the speaker who might be their future employer and had the power to make or break a career like the young Tom what's-his-name who had the crowd in stitches with his questions that made him sound more like a barrister than an ornithologist. Eleanor could feel the hard back of her wooden chair against her spine and shuffled. Eventually, Dr. Swanson stopped with his good-old-days stories.

"Oh, you don't want to hear all these stories," he finally said. "You want to know why I invited you to meet at the museum."

Eleanor smiled at him.

"Well, you got the job," he finally said.

Eleanor's eyes lit up. *Did I hear him correctly?* she thought. She was stunned and said nothing.

"Did you hear me, Miss Hutchinson?" Dr. Swanson asked.

"Wh-, wh-, why yes," she stammered and then smiled broadly. "Thank you, I never thought that . . . " She paused.

"You never thought you would be offered the position?" asked Dr. Swanson. "Why would you think that?"

"Well," Eleanor began. "I lack the education, the training, and the connections."

Dr. Swanson began to speak. "When the committee was deliberating their assessment with me after all the candidates had been interviewed, they were concerned about hiring a woman for a job that could entail travel to foreign countries, but as you had pointed out, Mrs. Cheeseman had been doing just that for years, and being a female actually allowed her access denied to men. The museum needs to modernize. I told them that you might lack the university education, but your knowledge of the world and its birds far exceeded any of the others. Moreover, you had travelled farther than many of them, and in particular, you used the travel to document an important scientific paper on robins, something that none of the others had achieved. You are also young, anxious to travel, and are unattached without family, as I understand."

"I am delighted," she said. "I will do my utmost to uphold the standards of the museum."

"To be honest, Miss Hutchinson," said Dr. Swanson, "when I saw you at the British Ornithologists' Union meeting, I thought you had promise. It is your fortitude and resilience that has allowed you to succeed. What's your secret?"

Suddenly, Eleanor remembered Gerald. She was about to mention his name, but withheld her breath. She would let Dr. Swanson believe that she had done it all on her own. Gerald was only a friend when she needed him, after all.

"There is no secret, Dr. Swanson," she replied. "Just a desire to pursue a dream."

"Hmm," he replied. "I wanted to ask you a little more about what you envisioned for the museum. What you mentioned in the interview."

"Do you mean the part about the parallels with the bird specimens housed at the museum and lost lives of soldiers?" she asked.

"Go on," said Dr. Swanson.

"Have you seen the graves of the soldiers in France?" she asked.

"No, I have not," he replied.

"Well, I was quite taken aback by the graves lined up across the fields and realized that both the graves and the museum collections represented the killing of living beings. As tragic as that might be, we need to keep the deaths relevant. We have birds collected by Victorians when killing living things was all the rage. Most of them are locked away in cabinets out of sight of the public. We need to find a way to keep the collections relevant in the new scientific era so that the killing was not all in vain.

My visit to Minsmere with the RSPB made me aware that nature is being destroyed along with the birds. The birds in the museum could become valuable in future conservation, which I believe will grow in popularity, and with it will come a new vision of the world. I would like the museum try to engage the public to help save birds."

"The museum is always open to new ideas," said Dr. Swanson, "and I suspect they will be very keen to hear your ideas, Miss Hutchinson. You are going to be a valuable asset. Now, when do you think you can start?"

"I will have to give notice at the library. Is there any time best suited for you?" she said.

"When you are ready," Dr. Swanson said. "You came well recommended by the library. A Miss Bradshaw, I believe was her name. When you decide to start, I will get one of the staff to familiarize you with the collections and meet the other staff. Would you like to see where your office will be?"

"Yes, please, if you can spare the time," Eleanor said.

He rose to get her coat and escort her out of his office. Eleanor was about to jump up and down with excitement but maintained her composure. Dr. Swanson led her down a corridor to a small office with a large window. An empty desk with a chair and empty bookshelves were the only furniture. Behind her office was large room for preparing specimens.

"This will be your home, I hope for some time," he said. "Now, I have things to do, so I will leave you to look around. Take your time and enjoy your day."

"Thank you again, Dr. Swanson. I will not let you down," said Eleanor.

She watched as Dr. Swanson turned to walk back down the corridor. She started to look at the cabinets full of birds but couldn't concentrate. She was giddy inside. After a few minutes of wandering about the collections, Eleanor left by the front door where she met Miss Anderson. "I heard the good news, Miss Hutchinson," she said. "It will be lovely to have another woman on staff."

"Thank you, Miss Anderson. I look forward to working with you," she said before turning out the front door.

Eleanor walked back to the train station filled with delight. She held a Mona Lisa smile on her face the whole way back to the library. Once she was in front of the library doors, she stopped and took a deep breath of air. This had been her home for the past few years, and she had had such wonderful experiences. It was now late in the morning and time to prepare for the afternoon shift. She hung up her coat and was about to go the Reading Room when Miss Bradshaw saw her.

"My, are you looking nice today," she said.

"Thank you, Miss Bradshaw. Do you have a few minutes?" asked Eleanor.

"Yes, of course," she said. "Come into my office."

Eleanor sat opposite Miss Bradshaw, who said, "How did the interview go?"

"Very well, thank you," she said. "I have been offered the job."

"Ah," said Miss Bradshaw. "Well, I expected no less. I will sorely miss you, Eleanor, and you will be hard to replace."

"Thank you, Miss Bradshaw. You have been very kind to me. I won't forget that," said Eleanor. "I suppose you need some time to find a replacement, and the museum has been kind to let me decide when I wanted to start. I was thinking of starting in about a month. Is that sufficient time?"

"That is fine, Eleanor," said Miss Bradshaw. "Until then, you can continue in your usual capacity. You might as well take the rest of the day off to get your rest. It has already been a long day for you"

"Thank you, Miss Bradshaw," said Eleanor as she rose and left the office.

By the time Eleanor boarded the train to take her home, doubts were creeping in that she might have gone over her head in the new position. A woman with few official credentials. She would have many detractors and many expectations. *A letter to Gerald might help*, she thought.

CHAPTER 31:

By Return Post

Eleanor arrived early in the afternoon with plenty of time to compose a letter to Gerald. She prepared a cup of tea while composing the letter in her head. Then she sat down, pulled out the typewriter, and was about to begin typing when a knock came at the door. It was Mrs. Quimby.

"I saw you come home early, Eleanor," she said, "and thought I would bring you some biscuits."

"Thank you, Mrs. Quimby. I was about to have some tea. Would you care to join me?" Eleanor asked.

"Why yes, dear," said Mrs. Quimby as she walked into the drawing room where she saw the paper in the typewriter.

"Oh, I see you were about to write a letter. Did I interrupt something?" she asked.

"No. No," said Eleanor. "It is only correspondence."

When Eleanor went into the kitchen to make tea, Mrs. Quimby started to walk around the drawing room. She noticed a pile of identical opened envelopes and Gerald's letters on the desk addressed to Eleanor.

When Eleanor returned to the drawing room with the tea, Mrs. Quimby pointed to the letters from Gerald. "I see you have quite a pile of letters there. Secret admirer?" Eleanor was clearly distraught. She quickly bundled up the letters and stuffed them into a drawer.

"He's just a friend," Eleanor said.

"What's his name? Do I know him?" asked Mrs. Quimby.

"His name is Gerald. Gerald Benson. No, you don't know him," she said testily.

Mrs. Quimby was no pushover. She sensed something unusual in Eleanor's demeanour.

"Maybe it is none of my business, Eleanor, but may I ask what he does for a living?" asked Mrs. Quimby.

Eleanor was getting very nervous. "He travels a lot," she said. "I keep in touch by correspondence. He has been very kind to me – a good friend – during the past few years."

Mrs. Quimby was smiling ever so slightly, wondering what Eleanor was trying to hide. She thought it better to not push too much.

"It is always good to have friends when you need them," said Mrs. Quimby. She sipped her tea.

A knock came at the door. Eleanor rose and opened the door to see Jack MacLaughlin, the postman, standing outside.

" 'ello there, Miss Hutchinson. Let's see what I have for you today. There are a few letters." He handed them to Eleanor. "Oh, yes. I also have a package of letters that you sent to the British Museum of Natural History. They said they were piling up at the museum and had no return address on them. They opened one of the letters where they found your address, so they sent them to me to return to you. They said to tell you that there is no one named Gerald Benson at the museum, so you can stop sending him letters." Jack peered into the drawing room where he saw Mrs. Quimby. "Oh, hi there, Marjorie. I didn't see you there. It looks like I am interrupting something, so I will be on my way. Good day to you, Miss." He nodded as he pulled his mailbag onto his shoulder and strode down Deacon's Lane.

Eleanor walked back into the drawing room with the handful of unopened letters. There was a momentary silence.

"Mrs. Quimby," she said demurely.

"Yes, dear," Mrs. Quimby replied in a tone of expectancy.

"I have to let you in on a secret," Eleanor said. "When I was a little girl, I became fascinated in birds. My father was an artist, and he encouraged me to draw them, so I got to know their names and became fascinated in their behaviour. My mother saw my interest grow into a passion, and she used to take me out in search of birds. There weren't as many birds in East London as here, but there was enough for a young girl. As time went by, I worked on my schooling and read books about birds. I thought I was going to become an ornithologist at a young age. I did well in school but soon learned that girls in East London are unlikely to attend university to get the academic training required to become an ornithologist. It bothered me that, because of my social position, I was not eligible for a job I had dreamed about for my entire life. I was also a woman in mostly a man's world. I thought that if I could speak to a curator at the museum, he might advise me on how to overcome these obstacles.

"For days, I stewed over how to write the letter and fretted about how I would respond if my letter was ignored. I lacked confidence and didn't know how to proceed. I especially could not face failure and rejection. So, I decided to make up a person at the museum who I could write to for advice. His name was going to be Gerald Benson. Over the past few years, whenever I needed advice, I would write a letter to the enigmatic Gerald, and a few weeks later when I expected a response, I posted a letter purportedly from Gerald but written by me. That way, I would always get the response I wished for. Lo and behold, a few days later, Gerald's letter would arrive. Those are the letters you saw on my desk. These letters in my hand are the ones I wrote to the nonexistent Gerald at the museum."

Eleanor eyes were welling with tears. She continued. "I chose the locations where I imagined my fictious Gerald had been sent to collect birds by reading the newspaper. Stories about Hawaii, the Galapagos, the Andes, the

Amazon, and Panama became the imaginary destinations for the imaginary Gerald. I spent hours researching the geography, politics, weather, birds, and anything I could find in books about each location to make his letters come to life. Most importantly, though, was that my dear fictitious Gerald gave me advice to carry on, write a scientific paper, and attend meetings of the British Ornithologists' Union and RSPB. They gave me the courage to carry on, which led to meeting new people who then helped me on my career path. I have just been accepted as the new Assistant Curator of Birds at the British Museum of Natural History as a result. This is my dream job, but if anyone was to find out about Gerald and my clandestine letter writing, I might be let go." She began to sob.

"Now, now, Eleanor," said Mrs. Quimby. "I will tell no one. You can trust me."

Eleanor looked up, red-eyed from crying. Mrs. Quimby took her hand.

"You are not the first person to have self-doubts and hear little voices speaking to them," said Mrs. Quimby. "You just made yours tangible. Gerald will always be our secret."

"Thank you, Mrs. Quimby, but I am terrified that the museum might find out," said Eleanor.

"Then destroy the letters," said Mrs. Quimby. "There will be no evidence."

Eleanor looked up. "You know, it is quite odd, but I have become quite attached to those letters, almost as if Gerald really does exist. I know this is silly, but I think I have come to believe my own delusion."

Eleanor continued, "You seem to have a knack for finding out little secrets."

"We all have our little secrets, Eleanor," said Mrs. Quimby.

"Did you have any hints about Gerald before today?" asked Eleanor.

"I was suspicious long ago," said Mrs. Quimby, "when you were taking letters off to the letter box. You seemed especially nervous. I also learned you were getting letters with no return address, which seemed odd. Then today, when you said Gerald was abroad, I thought something was not adding up. The envelopes on your desk that were purportedly from Gerald while he was overseas all had postage stamps from England, and they were postmarked in London."

"Oh my. What a fool I have been," said Eleanor.

"Nonsense, girl. You did nothing wrong. You broke no laws. You hurt no one. What you did is what most people write in diaries. They just don't post them," Mrs. Quimby said with a smile.

Eleanor smiled too. Mrs. Quimby was a great friend. She noticed how much Mrs. Quimby was like her deceased mother. Eleanor reached over and hugged Mrs. Quimby, who was not ready for the outburst.

"Oh dear, oh dear," said Mrs. Quimby. "Now, listen. I am going to make a nice dinner for the two of us at my house. I won't take no for an answer. You can tell me about your new job, and if you like, I will become your new Gerald." Mrs. Quimby rose and asked, "7 p.m., then?"

"Yes," said Eleanor. "7 p.m."

CHAPTER 32:

Celebration

More than a month passed before Eleanor had taken up her new post as Assistant Curator of Birds at the British Museum of Natural History. Her routine did not change much. Each morning, she rose to the song of Thales in her back garden, made breakfast, and set off for the bus and train to London. She needed a few days to adjust to walking to the museum rather than the library, which also gave her time to wonder how the library and Miss Bradshaw were faring. *Those were good years*, she said to herself.

She didn't feel quite at home at the museum because of all the new routines and procedures as well as the freedom to work on her own interests. Eleanor was orderly and efficient, which meant that she had started with getting her office set up so she could work seamlessly. After a week, she had met many of the staff and learned from Dr. Swanson the basics of how the museum operated and what its mission was. Many of the days ahead would likely be quite routine, but not this day. In the afternoon, the museum was sponsoring a welcome party for Eleanor in the large preparatory room located behind her office. She wasn't quite sure how many people would attend or what to expect, but she could hear quite a commotion. Dr. Swanson had prepared Eleanor for the celebration, telling her that it was a museum tradition to welcome new staff members so they could get to know each other better. He said that some of her friends would likely be there too.

Following lunch, Eleanor made her way back to her office. She hung up her coat and began to put books on her bookshelf. *You can't take the librarian out of me*, she thought to herself. There was a knock on the door to the large meeting room behind her office, and Dr. Swanson was peering through the opened door.

"Come along, Eleanor," he said. "It is time to celebrate your arrival at the museum." Dr. Swanson ushered Eleanor through the door to a large crowd. The room was adorned with balloons and paper chains. A large cake stood on a table, and the crowd, when they saw her, began to cheer. Eleanor was a little embarrassed by all the attention when Dr. Swanson began to speak.

"By now, all of you know Miss Eleanor Hutchinson as our new Assistant Curator of Birds, but many of you do not know much about her. I can attest that Miss Hutchinson is an exceptional woman who will be a strong asset for the museum. Eleanor is not the conventional ornithologist, like many of you, but that is only because of opportunity rather than ability. You see, Miss Hutchinson lost her parents during the war and became an orphan. For many of us, that experience would have been enough to quench any passion we might have had, but not for Eleanor. It was as if she was under divine direction."

Eleanor caught the eye of Mrs. Quimby in the crowd, who gave her an acknowledging smile.

Dr. Swanson continued: "Eleanor became well versed in the taxonomy and behaviour of birds. So much so that she has published her own research in a scientific journal. She is only twenty-two years old. Eleanor has also travelled the country, where she developed a technique I call 'the Hutchinson Method' to record the plumage colouration of robins. I first encountered Eleanor at a British Ornithologists' Club meeting a few years ago where she asked the most insightful question of Professor Brown. I could see then that she was head-and-shoulders above many of the young men from the university. When you have a chance, engage Miss Hutchinson in a conversation about the direction we might take the museum. You will find her refreshing and clever. Please welcome Miss Eleanor Hutchinson to the Natural History Museum."

After three cheers and applause, Eleanor began to look around the crowd. Among those she knew were Mr. MacLaughlin, the postman, in a corner with another man she didn't know. Peter and Patrick were in the opposite corner in high spirits. Anthony Ashford, the father of Christopher, and his wife Elizabeth were chatting with

Dougal and Marjorie Spratt. *What a big surprise*, she thought. *I wonder if Bernard and Christopher are here?*

"Hello, Miss Hutchinson," came a quiet voice. It was Bernard standing beside her.

"Hello, Bernard," she said in a voice of pleasant surprise. "I was wondering if you might make the party."

"Ever since you visited us," he began, "I have been watching robins more closely. You are correct about their plumage being a rich orange red." Bernard went into the finest detail on how the colour varied with light and how it contrasted against the grey of the bird's head.

"Well, look who is here?" came a voice from behind Eleanor. She turned to see Christopher Ashford standing behind her wearing a big grin.

"A belated Happy Christmas, Christopher," she said.

"Happy Christmas to you too," he said. "I was hoping there would be some mistletoe nearby." He smiled, searching around.

Eleanor, wishing to change the subject, said, "Christopher, I would like you to meet Bernard."

She turned around to see Bernard disappearing into the crowd.

"Not to mind," said Christopher. "My spies have been telling me all about you. It sounds like you are having far more fun than me in university."

"The year has had its events," she said.

"That's an understatement," Christopher replied. "I am so glad that you could make the party. I hope we can do this more often."

"That would be – " Eleanor was cut off short.

"Good evening, Miss Hutchinson," said a handsome man in a suit that she thought she recognized.

"Furlough," he said. "Captain Furlough. In Scotland."

"Oh, yes. I didn't recognize you without your uniform," said Eleanor. "How have you been doing?"

"Very well, thank you. I heard about your incident at the library," he said.

"The one with the two robbers?" she replied.

"Yes. I was relieved you came out unscathed and that the two scoundrels were apprehended. From what I heard, you are well versed in self-defence."

"Well, I do what I have to," she replied.

"I will keep that in mind around the mistletoe," he said.

Eleanor was getting a little weary with the flirting. She needed some relief, and it came with gusto.

"Eleanor!" came a shriek that she recognized. It was Kalmia Rosenblum with arms outstretched, ready to hug her. Kalmia wrapped her arm around Eleanor, who was a little bewildered by the public show of affection.

"Look who I brought?" said Kalmia.

Arnold Sneeze was standing beside them with a grin.

"Congratulations, Miss Hutchinson," he said. "You and Kalmia gave us a big scare, I have to confess, but it all turned out fine, didn't it?"

"Yes, it did," said Eleanor.

"Indeed," he said. "If it wasn't for the Brooksmere Mountain Rescue Team, who knows what might have happened to you young women."

Eleanor thought, *Oh no, here he goes again.* She smiled, and before he could go on, she asked, "Did Mr. Jones come along as well?"

"Mr. Jones?" asked Mr. Sneeze.

"Yes," said Eleanor. "If it hadn't been for him and his horse . . . " she paused. "What was his name?"

Kalmia jumped in. "Big Ben."

"Yes," said Eleanor. "Big Ben brought you home safely under Mr. Jones guidance."

Mr. Sneeze was shuffling about.

"Yes, Mr. Jones and his horse did play a role. We have commemorated the event. The community is going to celebrate the rescue every year."

"How nice," said Eleanor, turning to Kalmia. "How is your foot, and how is your weaving coming along?"

"My foot is fine," she said. Mr. Sneeze pardoned himself and moved away. "And the weaving is coming along. I have a few more new clients interested in my work."

"I am so happy," said Eleanor. "We must get together before long."

"May I congratulate you, Eleanor?" came a familiar voice.

"Miss Bradshaw!" exclaimed Eleanor. "Thank you for coming to my party."

"Well, Eleanor, I am delighted for you but sad to have you leave the library. I hope you will not forget us and drop by for tea sometime."

"Miss Bradshaw," said Eleanor. "I learned so much from you, for which I will be eternally grateful."

"Eleanor! Eleanor, ma cherie," came a loud voice from Mademoiselle Dupont. "My dear, how are you? That outfit you are wearing is stunning. Henri is a superb tailor, isn't he?"

"Did you come all the way here for this party?" asked Eleanor.

"Mais non. I am visiting friends," she said. "You are always welcome at my simple home."

Peter and Patrick were standing by, waiting their turn along with Mrs. Quimby.

"We, too, want to congratulate you," they said, "and wish you all the best."

"You will stay in the village, won't you?" asked Peter.

"Yes. Only the job is changing," said Eleanor.

"We did have some fun adventures," said Patrick.

"Without you, I might not be alive. I owe you a huge gratitude."

"Tut, tut," said Patrick. "You would have found your way through."

They turned to walk away when Peter said over his shoulder, "Let's go bird-watching soon."

Patrick whispered in her ear, "Don't forget the offer to join the Foreign Service, should you change your mind."

Eleanor looked across the crowd once more and saw Gwyn Llewelyn sipping tea alone.

"Hello, Gwyn," she said. "I am so pleased to see you here."

"I had to come to give you my best wishes," he said.

"Oh, that reminds me," said Eleanor. "Stay right here. I will be right back." She left to return to her office. She rummaged through her notebooks and came out with a piece of paper. She returned to the large reception room and walked up to Gwyn.

"While I was in France, I visited the Bayeux Cemetery," she said.

"That's where Rhys is buried," said Gwyn.

"That's right," said Eleanor. "I found his grave."

Gwyn went pale as the colour left his face. "Rhys's grave?" he asked.

"Yes," said Eleanor. "And I did a sketch of it for you."

She handed the watercolour sketch she had made at the grave-site to Gwyn, who began to weep.

"After you told me Rhys's story, I was determined to find his grave for you," she said.

"How can I ever repay you?" said Gwyn.

"Be kind to others, Gwyn. Be kind to others," said Eleanor.

Eleanor heard a distant knock. Moments later, she heard the knock again. It was someone at her office door. She stepped out of the preparation room, away from the crowd, and into the quietness of her office where she could see a silhouette standing at her office door. She opened the door to see a young man smiling back at her.

"Miss Hutchinson?" he asked. "Miss Eleanor Hutchinson?"

"Yes, that's me," she replied.

"I am so glad to meet you," he said.

"Thank you, but we are having a party back here," Eleanor said gesturing over her shoulder.

"Oh, I won't keep you then," said the young man. "I just wanted to say that I got your old job at the library where I heard all about you. You are a legend there with your travelling, dodging bad guys, bringing home treasured books, and the lot. I have heard so much about you, it seems that we have known each other for a long time, but of course we have never met."

"Thank you for your kind words, Mr . . . " She left the sentence hanging for him to complete.

"My name is Gerald."

Eleanor was shocked. A voice from the party called out her name, and she looked behind her.

"I will be right there," she called back. When she turned back to the door, there was no one there. She stepped forward to look up and down the long corridor. Gerald had vanished.

Acknowledgements

First, I wish to thank my wife Sharon, who joyfully assisted in developing and reading each chapter as the story unfolded. I want convey my thanks to all the ornithologists whose professional lives I shared and who gifted me the experiences that this story emerged from. To the late Peter Newbery, I offer my thanks for introducing me to the world of the Royal Society for the Protection of Birds, for introducing me to British ways and manners, and for accompanying Sharon and me to France. Several friends and family provided important feedback that improved the story: Sharon Butler, Sherri Lazaruk, Robert Elner, Rudi Kovanic, Linda McKinlay, Barb Anderson, Lorelei Driver, Joanne Swanston, Les Redford, Geneviève Raîche-Savoie, and Janet Kreda. To the staff at Friesen Press, I offer my thanks for their professionalism that made publishing a pleasant experience.

Author's Notes
and References

One morning as I awoke, I said to my wife Sharon, "I have a story. Would you like to hear it?"

"Yes," she said, and the story of Eleanor Hutchinson began. Each morning, I would awaken with a new chapter in the story for Sharon. Sometimes I would offer two plot lines, and we would discuss which was best.

The source of the story of *Letters from Gerald* is not entirely clear, but I recall being inspired by Monty Python's skit about the accountant who wanted to become a lion tamer and by Mr. Bean's Christmas skit in which he mailed Christmas cards to himself. Most of us dream of being something else in our lives, making the Python sketch especially funny, and many lack the confidence to take the plunge. The Mr. Bean sketch provided the modus operandi for Gerald's letters, which of course was a way to make Eleanor's alter ego tangible. The letters served to unite Eleanor's psychological and real worlds together. According to Andrew J. Liptak on his blog *Postal History*

Corner,[1] airmail service commenced to South America by 1946, allowing Gerald and Eleanor to correspond regularly. That meant the story could span two years, from November 1946 to November 1948, rather than being stretched out over many years.

If you haven't guessed by now, the village of Rabbit's Burrough is a play on words for the rabbit's habit of burrowing burrows. Eleanor lived on the lane leading to the church, hence Deacon's Lane, and she had a robin that regularly sang in her garden each morning, so Robinsong became the name for her cottage. In the opening chapter, the reader is introduced to a robin singing in Eleanor's garden, and that robin plays a repeated role throughout the entire book to connect the chapters and provide a focus for Eleanor's interest in birds. I required a species that was a resident and common around Hertfordshire, where she resided. The robin is as British a bird as any and conveniently sings year-round. I chose Thales for its name, which according to Wikipedia, was the name of a Greek philosopher who broke convention of following mythology in favour of scientific evidence.[2] That seemed a perfect fit for the robin and the theme of the book. Conveniently, Thales is purportedly the person who coined the phrase, "Know thyself" – the subtheme of the story.

---

1   "International Air Mail Letter Rates Part 1: 1920s-1953," Andrew J. Liptak, Postal History Corner: Canadian Postal and Philatelic History, accessed December 21, 2023, www.postalhistorycorner.blogspot.com.

2   Wikipedia. 2023. "Thales of Miletus". Wikimedia Foundation. Last updated January 18, 2024, https://en.wikipedia.org/wiki/Thales_of_Miletus

The description of Robinsong Cottage was loosely taken from my late friend Peter Newbery and the cottage he let in Abbotsley, as was the Fox and Crow Pub and the Westerlys' cottage location. So, too, was the character Peter Saunders very loosely based on Peter Newbery, who showed me many of the places in the book and worked for the RSPB reserves. We visited Minsmere together in the 1980s to look for avocets. One of the earliest field guides to birds in Britain was *The Handbook of British Birds* by H. F. Witherby, F. C. B. Jourdain, N. F. Ticehurst, and B. W. Tucker, published by H. F. & G. Witherby, London. It was popularly known as "The Handbook," and I thought this book would be the most likely field guide that Eleanor would have with her on her visit to Minsmere.

Peter Saunder's sidekick, Patrick, was entirely fictional. I decided he would work for the Foreign Office to add a little intrigue. For a while, I thought the plot might take Eleanor into the world of espionage but abandoned the idea to instead leave the reader wondering what Patrick's real motives were. He conveniently came to the rescue when Eleanor ended up in Wales with two thugs bearing down on her with intentions of robbing her of a precious book, and he appeared again later to foil the heist.

Mrs. Marjorie Quimby came onto the scene as a bit of busybody, but as the story unfolded, I decided to make her more than that. I had decided that Eleanor would travel the country in search of robins because of her interest in birds. Peter and Patrick provided the means of travel. I needed Eleanor to have some experience in a foreign country so that she could add it to her CV. That is when I decided on the trip to France, and out of that excursion, I needed something to liven up the overall story. A heist at the library came to mind, one that required a code between thieves. To break the code, I needed someone who had mathematical skills. That is when I decided it would be Marjorie Quimby. During the war, a select group of mathematically inclined women worked at Bletchley Park in Hertfordshire, near to where I had Eleanor living. In the 1940s, the code-breaking actions of these women was a national secret known to very few, all of whom were sworn to secrecy until the 1970s.

According to Wikipedia: "The [British Museum of Natural History] is recognized as the preeminent centre of natural history and research of related fields in the world. Although commonly referred to as the Natural History Museum, it was officially known as British Museum (Natural History) until 1992, despite legal separation from the British Museum itself in 1963."[3] I retained the original name of the British Museum (Natural History) for this reason.

The British Library was part of the British Museum until 1973 when an act of Parliament separated the two functions. The library contains millions of books and ancient texts referred to as the foundation collections. Major damage occurred to the library during the bombings, which I wove into the conversation with the Ashfords and Spratts. Charles Darwin's former home on

---

3 Wikipedia. 2024. "Natural History Museum, London". Wikipedia Foundation. Last updated January 13, 2024. https://en.wikipedia.org/wiki/Natural_History_Museum,_London

Upper Gower Street in London was destroyed in air raids on the night of April 16, 1941, and fires ravaged the city. Moreover, library staff were enlisted to the war effort, but libraries were kept open, which I used to create an opening for Eleanor. During the war, reading boomed in the UK, which led to the government-sponsored event, Homes for the Holidays, held in libraries. The British government realized the importance of reading as an escape for its people in times of trouble. Following the war, Lionel McColvin became a giant in the field of librarian-ship and was taken on to modernize the British library profession. He proposed a two-tier category for library staff, namely professional and nonprofessional. Professional staff would preferably be university graduates but would at least bear the Higher School Certificate. This was the level of education Eleanor obtained.

In Chapter 1, Eleanor refers to a story in *Nature* of new acquisitions by the British Museum (Natural History). *Nature* is a scientific journal that regularly reported acquisitions to the British Museum (Natural History).[4]

During my research I came upon a story about Ernest Bevin, who as Foreign Secretary in 1945, encouraged the maintenance of the British colonial empire despite economic hardship. That lent purpose to my story of Gerald collecting specimens for the British Museum of Natural History.

Eleanor meets the affable Christopher Ashford at the British Museum of Natural History in Chapter 2.

4 "Acquisitions at the British Museum (Natural History)". *Nature* 142, 786–787 (1938). https://doi.org/10.1038/142786c0

I introduced him so that Eleanor could go behind the scenes to see the specimen collection. I have not been into the collections at the British Museum of Natural History, but all museums share similar peculiarities. The smell of moth balls was prevalent in the early years, and the way birds were stuffed to make museum specimens was standard protocol. I wanted to give the reader a behind-the-scenes look at how these specimens were prepared. I have skinned several birds, which I admit, is a little macabre. Some people would feel queasy about it, which was all the more reason to write about it.

In Chapter 3, Eleanor visits Oxford by invitation from Christopher Ashford. I decided to introduce the class system in Britain that, although diminishing in its influence on the society, still held sway on people's ability to advance in their careers. Postwar England was a time of innovation and modernization. One of the symbols of this change was the motor car, which allowed me to write about the Triumph in Chapter 3, the Wolseley in Chapter 7, and the Peugeot in Chapter 22. Because of Christopher's pedigree, I needed a sporty car for him to drive. The Triumph introduced a few years earlier seemed the perfect choice. I also chose Oxford to be the Ashford family home so that I could show how families of privilege avoided the nightly bombings and I could describe life at the university.

In Chapter 3, with Christophers beckoning, Eleanor attends a lecture by Professor David Brown, who is a fictional character that was loosely shaped after a real person and a giant among ornithologists at the time. David Lack's books and papers influenced ornithology for many decades. David Lack's paper on robin taxonomy to the British Ornithological Club was published in 1946.[5] I was delighted at the coincidence that I had located Robinsong Cottage in Hertfordshire where Lack proposed a gradient in plumage variation in robins ended.

He also promoted field studies at Wytham Wood that actually exists near Oxford. The Wytham Woods website describes the site as follows:[6]

"Wytham Woods form an iconic location that has been the subject of continuous ecological research programmes, many dating back to the 1940s. The estate has been owned and maintained by the University of Oxford since 1942. The Woods are often quoted as being one of the most researched pieces of woodland in the world, and their 1000 acres are designated as a Site of Special Scientific Interest.

The wooded parts of the Wytham Estate comprise ancient semi-natural woodland (dating to the last Ice Age), secondary woodland (dating to the seventeenth century), and modern plantations (1950s and 60s). The fourth key habitat is the limestone grassland found at the top of the hill. Other smaller habitats include a valley-side mire and a series of ponds.

---

5   David Lack, "The taxonomy of the Robin Erithacus rubecla (Linnaeus)." *Bulletin of the British Ornithological Club* Vol. 66: pp. 55-64, (1946).

6   "Wytham Woods" web site. Accessed February 1. 2024. https://www.wythamwoods.ox.ac.uk/history

The site is exceptionally rich in flora and fauna, with over 500 species of plants, a wealth of woodland habitats, and 800 species of butterflies and moths".

I visited Oxford in the 1980s where I visited the Alexander Library in the Edward Grey Institute. Founded in 1938, its library became one of the best ornithological libraries in the world. The library collected published papers from ornithologists around the world. My graduate student adviser, Nicolaas Verbeek, attended Oxford where he routinely submitted his publications to the library. I recall that, on my visit, photographs of famous ornithologists hung on the walls of a stairway between floors and boxes held the publications submitted by ornithologists.

The village pub's name, Fox and Crow, arose from Aesop's fable *The Fox and the Crow* to fit with the discussion between the sly Mrs. Quimby and the postman, Jack MacLaughlin. I chose the name of the parish church in Rabbit's Burrough to be St. Jerome's, who according to Wikipedia, was known for teaching a moral Christian life and his attention to women's lives.[7] That seemed about right.

In Chapter 6, I decided that Gerald would travel to Hawaii. The island archipelago is remarkable for its endemic birds. Having Gerald visit Hawaii allowed me to introduce the plight of many of the birds endemic to islands in the South Pacific. I visited the Bishop Museum where I saw the magnificent feathered cape. The museum

---

7   Wikipedia. 2024. "Jerome." Wikimedia Foundation. Last edited, January 26, 2024, https://en.wikipedia.org/wiki/Jerome

would be a natural place for Gerald to gravitate to and provided an opportunity to describe the cape that visitors can see today. A description of the tsunami that hit the Hawaiian Islands on April 1, 1946 can be found in a report by F. P. Shepard and his colleagues.[8] Greater tsunamis have hit the islands in the distant past, including an immense surge estimated to have hit between 1425 and 1665 according to R. Butler (no relation) and his colleagues in the 2014 edition of Geophysical Research Letters.[9]

Peter and Patrick make their debut in Chapter 7. I decided to introduce the work of the Royal Society for the Protection of Birds by having Eleanor visit their flagship reserve in Minsmere. The story is true in many regards. Minsmere was purchased by the RSPB as part of a campaign to bring the avocet back to Britain as a breeding species. The drive to Minsmere allowed the story to reveal that Patrick worked for the Foreign Service and for Eleanor to begin to gather data on robin plumages necessary for her later scientific writing.

Once I decided Gerald would leave Hawaii, I chose South America for his next expedition. Chapter 8 covers his high seas travels. He could have either flown or sailed, so I chose the latter: crossing the Pacific via a ship would be the more romantic of the two options. Tramp steamers,

---

8   F. P. Shepard, G. A. MacDonald and D. C. Cox. "The tsunami of April 1, 1946." *Bulletin of the Scripps Institute of Oceanography* 5, (1949): 391-528.

9   Rhett Butler, David Burney and David Walsh. "Paleotsunami evidence on Kaua'i and numerical modeling of a great Aleutian tsunami" *Geophysical Research Letters* 19 (2014): 6795-6802.

as they were called, sailed the Pacific delivering goods by contract. Recall that none of this actually happened. Eleanor was imagining what it might have been like if Gerald existed and was actually onboard a steamer. That meant that the story began to unfold as seen through a librarian's access to books. The voyage became a romanticized adventure influenced by Josef Conrad's *Heart of Darkness*. The characters described by Gerald are a nod to Conrad. *Oceanic Birds of South America* by Robert Cushman Murphy[10] would have been available to Eleanor in the British Library.

I have had a career as an ornithologist and attended many international conferences. This life experience allowed me to imagine Eleanor attending one of the meetings for the first time. A big difference was that by the time I entered the ornithologist ranks, many women were entering the profession, although prejudices remained. This gave me the opportunity in Chapter 9 to describe how the male-dominated world was exclusionary. The chapter also showed the intellectual prowess of Eleanor who was held back by both her gender and her social class. The decision to introduce an anonymous elderly man who took Eleanor to the meeting as a guest was intentional because I wanted him to return at the end as her new boss. Dr. Swanson could see her exceptional abilities and was willing to dismiss convention to hire her at the museum. The British Ornithologists' Club was founded at a meeting

10 Robert Cushman Murphy. "Oceanic birds of South America." (New York: American Museum of Natural History, 1936). Pp. 1245.

of the British Ornithologists' Union (BOU) in London on October 5, 1892.[11] The aim of the club was to enable members of the BOU to meet regularly for discussion and provide opportunities to present papers and exhibit specimens. The presence of the club became Eleanor's opportunity to attend.

The Galapagos are like a shrine to many evolutionary biologists because it was there that the birds inspired Darwin's theory of evolution through natural selection. My visits allowed me to describe in Chapter 9 what Gerald saw. During my research, I discovered the story of the Norwegian teacher Borghild Kristine Rorund, who was a student and lived in a tent near Puerto Ayora, Santa Cruz. She mostly collected botanical specimens, two of which were new to science, but the story allowed me to introduce other women who were making their marks. Dorothy Garrod had become the first female chair at Cambridge in 1939, and Dorothea Bate led expeditions to the Mediterranean and collected fossils for the museum. Percy Roycroft Lowe, who became President of the British Ornithological Union at the time that Eleanor attended their meeting, had worked with Dorothea Bate, who would be appointed officer in charge at the British Trust for Ornithology. These real people provided a source to enter into the story of women in science. David Lack wrote a seminal paper on the Galapagos finches in 1945.[12]

11 "History of the BOC". British Ornithologists' Club. 2024. Accessed January 28, 2024, https://boc-online.org

12 David Lack, "Galapagos Finches (Geospininae): study in variation." (San Francisco: California Academy of Sciences, 1945). Pp. 336.

In Chapter 10, I took Eleanor far away to northern Scotland to bring back a donation to the library. The story had become quite serious, and I wanted to liven it up a bit. The garden party at Peter's with the story of All Hogs Day was a start, but I wanted to go whole hog. So, I thought that a town named Mularchy – a play on malarky – would be just the place. One morning I began to tell Sharon about the characters who would appear at the party put on by the Spratts. I hoped the reader might have caught on to the silliness by the choice of their names and Eleanor's quip about their interest in schooling. (Sprats are a small schooling fish.) The rest of the characters – such as Mr. Webb dressed as a spider, Captain Furlough on leave from the army, and conservative Eileen Wright (I lean right) – were pure malarky. The scene of Reginald courting Eleanor was taken with poetic licence from Shakespeare's Romeo and Juliet, but I kept to the malarky theme by him mistaking Bernard's room for Eleanor's. Mr. Spratt's comment about not eating any fat is nod to the nursery rhyme Jack Spratt[13] (and why Anthony Spratt was small in stature). The arrival of Mademoiselle Dupont and her inviting Eleanor to France is a nod to the book the Spratts donated: Fanny Burney's *Evelina, or the History of a Young Lady's Entrance into the World*, in which Madame Duval tries to lure Evelina away to France.[14] Mademoiselle

---

13 Wikipedia. 2024. "Jack Sprat" Wikimedia Foundation. Last updated August 12, 2023. https://en.wikipedia.org/wiki/Jack_Sprat

14 Fanny Burney, "Evelina, or the History of a Young Lady's Entrance into the World". (London: Thomas Lowndes, 1778).

Dupont would emerge later in the story in Chapter 21. Captain Furlough's offer to escort Eleanor with expensive books under her arm was a necessary part of the story where Patrick schemes to break up a theft ring.

When Gerald gets around to writing Eleanor from South America, I had him visit the Amazon, the Andean Cloud Forest, and the Andes to describe their birds and the life of Alexander Humboldt. Several years ago, I saw the rude hut Humboldt used as a base to explore the high Andes. I had also read Andrea Wulf's *The Invention of Nature* about Humboldt's fame and immense impact on how we view nature, and I spent a few days in the Amazon and the Cloud Forest.[15]

A defining moment for the British in the mid-1940s was the Second World War. My father had been to Normandy during the DDay invasion by the Allies, and I became interested in accounts of the few days during their arrival. I was fortunate that my father was not killed or injured, but thousands of others were not so lucky; their bodies lie in graves along the French, Belgian, and Netherlands coasts. I wanted to take the book deep into the impact of the loss of sons, and created Gwyn Llewelyn as the father of one of the fallen sons. I researched the way people responded to the losses and imagined the effect of the losses on their lives. Gwyn's story became that story in Chapter 13 and 14. The emotion was intended to gain the attention of the reader. The bad guys in Chapter 15 who

---

15 Andrea Wulf. "The Invention of the World. Alexander Von Humboldt's New World". (New York: Alfred A. Knopf, 2015). Pp. 473.

wanted to steal the pocket Gospel donated by Gwyn was a way to bring Patrick back into the story. He is up to something through his Foreign Office job, but that would have to wait. Gwyn's reference to the return of birds of prey was documented by A. W. Colling and E. B. Brown in 1946.[16]

By the time Kalmia writes to Eleanor in Chapter 16, Eleanor has had several successful excursions on behalf of the library. I decided to send her off to the Lake District where I had hiked some of the mountain paths with Peter Newbery. My intention was to introduce a young Jewish woman to the audience so I could write about the many young orphaned Jews who moved to the UK. After the war, many Jewish children were transported to the Lake District to start a new life.[17] The name Kalmia originates from *Kalmia latifolia*, an alpine laurel. Beatrix Potter made the Lake District famous with her tales of farmland animals and was where she raised endangered native Herdwick sheep. My wife Sharon is a fabric artist who provided the inspiration and insight to develop Kalmia's character as a weaver.[18] Our home is adorned with natural dyed fibres and the sound of the loom.

---

16 A. W. Colling and E. B. Brown, "The breeding of Marsh and Montagu's harriers in north Wales". *British Birds* 39: (1945): 233–251.

17 "Legacy of War: Windermere Boys." Lake District National Park, Accessed January 28, 2024. https://www.lakedistrict. gov.uk/learning/forteachers/archaeologyeducationww2/ archaeologyww2legacy#:~:text=In%201945%2C%20300% 20traumatised%20Jewish,the%20recovery%20of%20 the%20children.

18 "Sharon Butler: Fibre Artist". 2023. Accessed February 1, 2024. https://www.sharon-butler.com

I wanted to test Eleanor's resolve in an emergency and in the absence of Gerald. Kalmia's injury and subsequent rescue in Chapter 17, 18, and 19 allowed me to introduce the insecure personality of Arnold Sneeze. His surname came to me while thinking about Charles Dickens's choice of names. The tale also allowed me to show how modest individuals who deserve credit are sometimes pushed aside by people like Arnold Sneeze. Hence, I gave the shepherd, Mr. Jones, a very common name.

For most people, the world of science is an unfathomable profession, and the role of publications is even more distant. Chapter 20 allowed me to describe the process and the daunting task of getting a scientific paper in print. Publication is the ultimate indicator that a scientist has joined the ranks of the profession. Therefore, the chapter was a critical piece in Eleanor's bid to become an assistant curator among ornithologists at the end of the book.

France was a way to take Eleanor out her element and introduce some action and adventure. Sharon and I, along with Peter Newbery, toured northern France years ago where we became familiar with its towns and country-side. We visited Bayeux and ate in small cafés. The scene in Chapter 22 of the young street urchins singing in the cathedral actually happened. After a dinner in Divers, a young boy on his way to the cathedral invited us to listen to them practice. Peter sang in a choir in Cambridge and so was intrigued. What I describe is very close to what we heard that evening. We also discovered that William the Conqueror departed from the nearby river to defeat Harold at the Battle of Hastings. That historical event and location allowed Eleanor to ponder the tragedy of the DDay invasion and compare it with the rows of bird specimens in the museum. Mademoiselle Dupont's surname is a play on words, as she said in Chapter 10 that she was a bridge between nations, and "du pont" means "of the bridge." I introduced her as a seemingly flamboyant individual of uncertain integrity. Her donated book by Arthur Butler (no relation of mine)[19] and Bewick's lovely illustrations are actual tomes.

Chapter 23 saw Gerald in Panama, which was a country I visited on several occasions during my ornithological research. I chose Panama for this reason, but to be honest, I needed Gerald to stay away from England to allow Eleanor to complete her story.

There are hints in the book of Marjorie Quimby's role being more than a nosy neighbour, which is revealed when her code-breaking prowess came to the rescue at the library to foil the heist of precious books in Chapter 24. I called this chapter "Operation Magpie" from the widespread but false belief at the time that magpies have a penchant for bright shiny things. T. V. Shephard and others experimentally showed this myth to be unfounded.[20] The relationship between Mrs. Quimby and Patrick becomes a little more revealing, and Miss Bradshaw is

---

19 Arthur G. Butler, "British birds with their nests and eggs". (London: Brumby and Clarke, 1896). Six vols.

20 T. V. Shepard, S. E. G Lea, N. Hempel de Ibarra. "The thieving magpie? No evidence for attraction to shiny things." *Animal Cognition* 18: 393-397 (2015).

not innocent either. They all seem to know of Eleanor's whereabouts and appear when needed to keep her safe.

Chapter 25 completed the description of writing a paper for a scientific journal so that Eleanor could go to the interview in Chapter 27. I used this chapter to reintroduce Eleanor's self-doubts but growing self-esteem, and to provide another hint that Gerald might be something other than what his letters seemed. (There are plenty of hints throughout!) The interview in Chapter 27 is the most important scene: it was the make-or-break opportunity for Eleanor. I decided to withhold the decision on her job interview result to build the suspense and allow me to revisit the village and community in Chapter 28. The Historic UK web site describes a war time Christmas.[21]

The Christmas party allowed me to introduce a little humour when the firefighters arrived. That scene arose form Dylan Thomas's *A Child Christmas in Wales* when Mrs. Prothero asks the fireman, amidst the smoke and water, if they would like something to read.[22] I thought having the firemen arrive rough and ready only to find the fire out added comic relief. That was an intentional attempt to contrast the lightheartedness of the Christmas celebrations with the next chapter in which Alan Westerly is confined to his room and trying to forget the war. The idea of a robin song eliciting very different reactions for

21 "A World War II Christmas. Historic UK. Accessed February 1,2024.https://www.historic-uk.com/CultureUK/Christmas-in-World-War-Two/

22 Dylan Thomas. "A Child's Christmas in Wales". (London, J. M. Dent & Sons, 1968).

Eleanor and Alan was a way to show how different people perceive the same thing. During World War II, a German named Ludwig Koch aired his unique bird-song recordings with the BBC to soothe anxieties.[23] In recent years, there have been many studies that show how bird-song affects moods.

Chapter 30 is where Eleanor meets the curator who I had introduced as an anonymous man and who had taken her as his guest to the British Ornithological Union meeting. The curator of birds in the 1940s was a W. E. Swinton, which I changed to Swanson. I wanted the fictitious Dr. Swanson to represent an older but open-minded individual who valued merit without pretence and vision for the future. He represented fairness, understanding, patience, and willingness to take a risk despite his privileged past.

Chapter 31 is where the culmination of all of Eleanor's dreams and imaginings are revealed to no other than Mrs. Quimby. From the outset, Gerald was an inner voice reflecting Eleanor's lack of self-esteem. Many people are held back from achieving their potential because of inner doubts. I wanted to show that Eleanor had those same doubts, which she was able to process by masquerading as Gerald, but she also had to overcome her lack of education and social position to get the job she yearned for. Chapter 31 was a way to say she no longer needs Gerald

---

23 Robert Budd, Paul Greenhalgh, Frank James and Morag Shiach. 2018. "Being Modern". (London: University College London). Pp. 438.

now that she has conquered the obstacles. At least, that is what I wanted you to believe.

In the final chapter, Eleanor has come to realize that she has many new friends and supporters that helped her advance her career. Gerald is no longer needed. The previous chapter was the eureka moment when Gerald is revealed, but I wanted the reader to not be so certain. So, I had Gerald appear to her office during the celebration. Whether the Gerald at her door was real or fanciful, I will never tell!

Printed in the USA
CPSIA information can be obtained
at www.ICGtesting.com
JSHW021909250424
61865JS00001B/3